CW00792579

Never Murder a Birder

by Edie Claire

Book Eleven of the
Leigh Koslow Mystery Series

Copyright © 2017 by Edie Claire

Cover design by pbj creative studios

This book is a work of fiction. The names, characters, places, and incidents are products of the writer's imagination or have been used fictitiously and are not to be construed as real. Any resemblance to persons, living or dead, actual events, locales or organizations is entirely coincidental.

All Rights Are Reserved. No part of this book may be used or reproduced in any manner whatsoever without written permission from the author.

Dedication

To all the bird watchers who walk around with binoculars hanging around their necks not caring whether other people think they look dorky or not. I am with you. As for those of you who laugh at us… My life list is longer than yours.

So there.

Prologue

The giant heron gave a slow but powerful flap to his wings, his head hunched back over his shoulders as he cruised through the night sky over Mustang Island, Texas. The mustangs hadn't roamed here for a century or more, but the flat, windswept barrier island was riddled with brackish wetlands that made a fine home for fish and frogs, which was all that mattered to the heron. As he passed over the relatively barren dunes and reached the southern edge of the sleepy town of Port Mesten, the twinkling lights of a large beach house complex came into view. The bird cocked his head. A flash of color had caught his eye.

With an adjustment of angle and another hefty flap, six feet of wingspan changed course and headed downward. There was something interesting down there. Hopefully something tasty.

He landed with the faintest of whooshing noises on the lawn behind the mansion and folded his immense wings behind his back. He could hear human voices nearby, but they were muffled; no people were visible. A quick look around revealed nothing threatening. His long legs strolled casually towards the object of his attention.

The koi pond, like the rest of the backyard and deck area, was beautifully landscaped. It was bordered with attractive rocks, planted with tropical greenery, and even featured a gently trickling waterfall. Conveniently enough for the heron, the pool also had underwater lights that reflected the koi's shiny orange and yellow scales. The whole yard and deck were brightly lit.

The bird raised one long, stringy leg and stepped into the water. The other foot soon followed.

Gulp.

The human voices grew louder, and the heron paused to look up. He could see figures moving about inside the house through the windows. Dimly, his mind made an association of this feeding spot with a past attack by a human — a woman who had rushed at him, yelling and waving her arms. The heron had flown away then. Territoriality was a thing he understood. Not bothering to eat the food one defended was not. In any event, no human was threatening him now.

Gulp.

The door to the deck opened suddenly. It slammed backward on its hinges as several people poured out onto the deck above, their voices loud. Humans were often loud, but the heron sensed an unusual tension. He froze in place, assessing the risk. The humans continued to make noise. There was shoving, struggling. The heron poised himself for flight, but the humans did not appear to notice his presence. And the colorful fish were unaccountably sluggish.

Gulp.

The heron remained wary. The humans were thrashing about. One picked up an object from off the railing and smashed it over another's head. The human who'd been struck instantly went limp and slipped to the floor of the deck. Still none of them noticed the heron.

Gulp.

The people's movement ceased. The upright ones continued to speak, but their voices were hushed now. After a few moments they all went back inside the house, dragging the limp one with them. They closed the door.

The heron stopped watching them. He craned his neck to advance the last swallowed fish along his gullet, then set about snatching the next one. This was a great feeding spot. He would have to come again.

The lights in the backyard went out, and the little pond went dark. No matter. The heron could see well enough to pick out the last two. After all, they had nowhere to hide.

Gulp. Gulp.

The house was deadly silent now.

The bird craned his neck once more, then gave his wings a contented rustle. His business here was concluded.

He took off and flew away.

Chapter 1

Leigh could barely contain her enthusiasm as the airplane at last popped out from under the clouds, granting her first view of the topside of Corpus Christi, Texas. The sight was less than impressive, given that it was midwinter, raining steadily, and the Gulf of Mexico was on the other side of the aircraft. But Leigh didn't care. She was too happy to be here, or anywhere the temperature stayed in double digits and she had the chance to feel warm sun on her skin. Maybe she was getting seasonal affective disorder, or maybe she was just being a crab, but this last Pittsburgh winter had been getting to her. Vitamin D from a bottle wasn't cutting it anymore, and she couldn't bring herself to do the tanning bed thing. Sometimes, a person just needed *sunshine*.

"Sorry about the rain," Warren said sympathetically. He squirmed in his seat and stretched one long leg out in the aisle, attempting to avert a cramp.

Leigh watched him with a guilty feeling. Her husband had made preparations for this consulting gig a month ago, including securing comfortable exit row seats for himself. But when she had decided to tag along at the last minute, he'd given up those seats to take whatever two were available together. At least on this commuter hop from Houston he'd snagged a spot on the aisle. On the longer haul from Pittsburgh he'd had to choose between window or middle, which in either case meant his knees had been wedged against the seat in front of him for the duration.

"It can't rain forever," Leigh replied optimistically. "I won't allow it. Anyway, it won't snow. And it's supposed to be at least sixty degrees all week. Comparatively speaking, that's tropical."

Warren smiled at her. "I'm glad you decided to come, even if I am working so much I'll hardly see you. It's been ages since we got away together, just the two of us."

Leigh smiled back. He was right, and it was mostly her fault. They had taken many lovely family vacations over the years, but she had never felt completely comfortable leaving the twins behind.

Even now, though the kids were safely stashed at their Aunt Cara's place with multiple grandparents and a great aunt to look in on them, Leigh was nagged by "bad mother" guilt. Never mind that the kids were twelve years old and had practically pushed her out the door. Her son Ethan, who usually replied to her texts with a cheerful "will do," had greeted her last missive of helpful reminders with the comparatively rude, "Yeah, Mom. Geez!" Her daughter Allison had shut off her phone.

Apparently, the kids really didn't mind if their mom spent a few days away on the Gulf Coast, doing absolutely nothing but walking on the beach and soaking up some sun. Who knew?

"You won't be working *all* the time," Leigh encouraged. "This nonprofit may be desperate for your help, but they do expect you to sleep, don't they?"

Warren's brown eyes twinkled mischievously. "They do. And I hope I won't be sleeping alone."

Leigh grinned back. "You will not."

The airplane's landing was smooth, and even though Leigh could swear it took longer for everyone to clear off the plane than they had been in the air, she maintained her cheerful disposition. As they walked to the baggage claim area, she watched out the airport windows, willing the skies to grow brighter. "The sun will be shining by the time we reach the hotel," she said confidently. "I proclaim it."

Warren laughed. "Assuming it's not dark by the time we find the place." They reached the baggage carousel and found a spot in the crowd. The flight had been completely full, and as the conveyor belt cranked into action people stood along the curved track elbow to elbow.

"I hope our accommodations don't fall too far below the high standard to which you've become accustomed," Leigh teased, feeling slightly guilty again. Before her impulsive decision to join him, Warren had made reservations at a comfortable, albeit perfectly boring chain hotel near his client's offices in downtown Corpus Christi. Leigh would have been fine with that, too, as long as she could drive herself to the ocean in his rental car.

But no.

Once news of Leigh's plans had reached her mother and aunts, an inescapable chain reaction of family interventions had followed.

Didn't Leigh remember that their dear cousin Hap lived somewhere around Corpus Christi now? Her great-aunt Eliza's son? The one with the awful harelip that looked so much better after the second surgery and who used to be married to dear, sweet Maureen before she passed away from pancreatic cancer, God bless her soul? And didn't he manage a hotel or something? Surely, he would want Leigh to come and see him and meet his new wife? They might even have a spare room she and Warren could stay in…

The ensuing conversations had been awkward. But in the end, all had turned out well enough. Leigh's cousin Hap — whom she had always liked, but hadn't seen since her Aunt Eliza's funeral over a decade ago — lived with his second wife in a fifth-wheel at an RV park, so he had no guest room. But he did work at a historic hotel on a barrier island about forty-five minutes away from downtown Corpus, and he was sure he could arrange for a family discount, as well as provide Leigh with access to his own car and plenty of home-cooked meals during their stay. Since Warren claimed not to mind the scenic commute, Leigh had been happy to make everyone else happy by accepting Hap's offer. His hotel was walking distance to the beach, after all. She wouldn't even need a car!

"Well, I am used to the lap of luxury on such jobs," Warren teased back. "Nonprofits always put their contractors up in penthouse suites, you know, particularly when they're hiring said contractor because they're in financial straits. That said, you have to admit that Hap's hotel looks — how shall I put it — *quaint*."

"I like places with character," Leigh insisted. "The Silver King is nearly a hundred years old and it's survived four hurricanes and a fire. You could even say it survived five hurricanes, if you count salvaged wood."

"You can't," Warren argued. "But four is impressive enough. I just hope the bedframes aren't a hundred years old, or I'll be sleeping on the floor. Is that your bag?"

Leigh looked down the slowly populating carousel. "That green one? No, I had to bring Allison's, remember? The wheel broke on mine. Look, this is going to take forever. Why don't you go ahead and get the rental car while I wait for the suitcases? We'll get out of here faster."

Warren nodded. "Deal."

Leigh fidgeted in place for another five minutes before her bright blue bag at last came into view. *The Silver King Hotel*. She couldn't wait to see it. It was pure luck that dear Cousin Hap happened to be associated with such a storied piece of Texas history, as opposed to some two-bit, crumbling motor inn. For that matter, once her mother and aunts got involved, she and Warren could have wound up sleeping on somebody's living-room pullout couch just to avoid hurting a relative's feelings.

Truly, she had been fortunate all around.

How odd.

She pulled her daughter's distinctive bright blue bag from the carousel and placed it at her feet, then jumped, startled, to see another woman's hands reaching for it.

"Excuse me!" a cultured voice proclaimed. "I'm afraid you have the wrong bag. This one is mine."

Leigh looked up to see a woman about her own age, well dressed and impeccably groomed. The woman had a large designer travel bag slung over one shoulder and a phone in one hand, and she smiled awkwardly as she rested her other hand possessively upon the suitcase.

Leigh's grip tightened involuntarily on the handle. She looked down at the case again and lifted the colorful plastic Disneyworld ID tag she knew darn well had her daughter's name and address on the other side of it. "No, it's mine," she assured the woman. "Look. See?"

The woman's face promptly drained of color, and her hand dropped back. "Oh. Oh, I'm so sorry. Mine looks exactly like it! How stupid of me. I'm terribly sorry." She lifted both hands in supplication, then backed away.

"No problem," Leigh answered. She caught sight of Warren's bag and made haste to retrieve it. As she headed away from the crowd with both bags in tow, she stole a glance over her shoulder. The woman was now standing with a companion, a very large man with one suitcase already at his side. The woman continued to watch the carousel with one eye, even as she chatted with the man and punched buttons on her phone simultaneously.

Leigh was half tempted to wait around and see what suitcase the woman pulled off the belt next, since it seemed incredible that anyone wearing Gucci shoes on a plane would be traveling with a bright blue bag in an abstract bubble pattern. But she didn't care enough to bother. The woman was obviously distracted. Perhaps she was just a flake.

The rain had stopped falling by the time Leigh met up with Warren and they walked out to the rental car, and as they drove away from the airport the clouds gradually began to thin and the sky to lighten.

"Texas likes me," Leigh announced with a contented sigh. "And so far, I love Texas."

Warren chuckled warmly. "Happy to hear it."

They drove out of the city and across the bay over a causeway before reaching the thin strip of sand and rock that was Mustang Island. To the Pittsburgh born-and-bred Leigh, the most predominant characteristic of Texas thus far was that it was flat. The second most notable descriptor was that it was overwhelmingly, uniformly *brown*. The grass in western Pennsylvania stayed a cheery green all year round, at least when it wasn't white with snow, which made the inland area of Texas seem bleak by comparison. But here on the shore, all was forgiven. The choppy waters of the Gulf changed color with every movement of cloud and sun, the landscape rolled with high sand dunes and low brackish ponds, and tall grasses rippled in the endless wind. The couple cruised through the undeveloped part of the island, passed by the state park, and unhurriedly made their way toward their final destination, the small tourist town of Port Mesten.

The sun was just beginning to dip low in the sky when Leigh's trusty phone app led them along a zig-zagging path of two-lane streets flanked by modest houses, restaurants, beachwear stores, bars, ice cream shops, small motels, and a plethora of RV parks. "That's it," Leigh said excitedly, pointing. "That peach-colored building with the white trim."

Warren parked the car and Leigh hopped out. "It's perfect!" she gushed, looking it over. "Can you believe this place was originally an army barracks?"

"As a matter of fact, yes," Warren replied dryly, popping open the trunk.

"Oh, stop," Leigh chastised. Architecturally, the building was no marvel. For the most part, it was a long, rectangular, two-story block with two levels of porches and an array of doors and windows marching across its face with military precision. But one end of the building featured an octagonal wooden tower complete with a catwalk and cupola three stories aboveground. Both the wooden plank siding and the decorative trim were freshly painted, and rocking chairs and ceiling fans graced the hotel's long, wide porches.

"Surely *that* didn't survive four hurricanes," Warren commented, throwing a skeptical glance at the obviously more modern, yet somehow less sturdy-looking tower section.

"No, I'm pretty sure that's a fairly recent addition," Leigh agreed. "The original tower was destroyed in the second hurricane. There's even a ghost story about it on the website. Some woman was watching for her lover's boat to return in the storm, and she fell to her death from the old catwalk—"

"Enough about ghosts and dead people," Warren ordered sternly, pulling their suitcases from the trunk. "We are on vacation. Well, *you* are, anyway." He threw her a meaningful look, which Leigh had no trouble interpreting.

No funny stuff here, okay? No police investigations. No criminals, no intrigue, no drama. And for God's sake… NO BODIES!

Leigh surprised herself by chuckling merrily. "Oh, I am *so* on vacation!" she assured. "This week is going to be fabulous."

They wheeled their suitcases toward a door at the base of the tower, which a humble wooden sign proclaimed to be the office. As they passed the other cars, Leigh noted license plates from Oklahoma, Indiana, and Kansas. Several of the cars with Texas plates were brand-new and undoubtedly rentals, but among those that seemed legitimately local, a large open-bed pickup stood out. Perching all over it — on top of the cab, along the sides and tailgate, on the hood, and even in the bed — were several dozen large, black birds. The creatures made no sound, but seemed content as they rested, occasionally adding to the already plentiful white bird poop streaked across the truck's midnight blue paint. A few birds sat on the ground nearby, but none perched on any other car.

"Geez," Warren commented. "I wonder what makes that guy so lucky."

The birds seemed, as one, to turn and stare at them. In the distance, a siren howled.

"Weird," Leigh agreed, resisting a slight prickle of the hairs on the back of her neck. "Very Hitchcock. Let's go inside."

Warren made no argument.

Leigh had barely cleared the entrance to the cozy little lobby when a familiar booming voice sounded from behind the counter. "There she is! Francie's little Leigh! Why, I'd know you anywhere, darling! You haven't changed a bit!"

Hap Taylor scooted off his stool and strode toward Leigh with a surprising amount of agility for a man of his bulk. He wasn't quite as tall as Leigh remembered, being a hair under six feet, but he was broad-shouldered and of ample girth. Even so, his head had always seemed overlarge for his body, with a wide, perpetually grinning mouth and sparkling light blue eyes. Leigh always thought he would make a fabulous Santa Claus, had he been able to grow a beard, but Hap was about as hairy as a naked mole rat. For as long as Leigh could remember he had sported only two brownish patches of hair, one over each ear. And both of those had now turned white.

"Cousin Hap!" she said with delight, returning his crushing bear hug. "You always were a liar! I've had two kids since the last time you saw me!"

"And it's a crying shame it's been so long, I know," he said regretfully. "Your mother and the girls have been on me about that. But after Maureen passed, I just couldn't bring myself to get back there." He released Leigh, drank her in with a long, approving look, then turned to extend a hand to Warren.

"Hap Taylor," he said cheerfully. "They tell me we met way back at my mother's funeral, but I'm afraid I can't recall it. Francie's been bragging on you for years, though! Bess and Lydie, too."

Warren shook the proffered hand and reintroduced himself. "It was a long time ago. And they all speak very highly of you, as well."

Hap snorted with laughter. "Well, I guess absence makes the heart grow fonder. Lord knows those three gave me a hard enough time growing up!"

Leigh laughed with him, wondering how Hap's perspective on the family history might differ from what she'd always heard. He was a couple years younger than her mother and Lydie, which made it entirely believable that "the girls" would pick on him. He retold an anecdote Leigh had heard before about his retaliating for some forgotten abuse by tying the sleeping sisters' braids together.

Then he swept a key from off the counter. "Well, don't let me go on all night. Let's get you two settled!"

Leigh noticed that the noise outside had increased significantly. Now multiple siren wails cut through the air, and the birds had begun to squawk.

"I hope that's not your truck the crows have taken over out there," Warren said lightly, voicing Leigh's own thoughts.

"You mean the grackles?" Hap waved a hand dismissively. "My truck's at the RV park. I walk here. But I expect they'll hit it when they've a mind to. Damn things roost wherever they please. They like to pick dead bugs off the front grills. But you leave half a bag of fries or some chips in the back of your truck — well, then you're getting what you ask for!"

He looked at Leigh conspiratorially. "Don't tell Bev I said that, by the way. Cursing the birds. She'll start lecturing me about how it's not their fault because of 'destruction of native habitat' and whatnot — Lord knows I hear enough of that talk already!"

Leigh smiled. "I'm looking forward to meeting Beverly."

Hap's already ruddy face flushed with pleasure. "She's looking forward to it, too. I'm supposed to invite the two of you over to dinner tomorrow. We would have done it tonight, but Bev had to be up at her sister's place today, and we didn't know for sure when you'd get in—"

"Please," Warren interjected. "Don't put yourself out. You don't have to feed us. Although of course we'd love to join you for dinner tomorrow. Don't you need a credit card for check-in?"

Warren already had his wallet out, but Hap waved the offer away and led them toward the door. "We'll worry about that when you leave. You're tired now, let's just get your—" Hap stopped in midsentence as he pushed open the door and the sound of multiple screaming sirens filled the small lobby. Deep furrows crossed his brow as he stared out into the street. "Well now," he said uneasily. "You don't hear this much ruckus around here too often. I wonder what the devil's going on?"

The grackles squawked louder.

Absolutely nothing, Leigh willed.

Hap held open the door for them. They had just picked up their suitcases to follow when the hotel's desk phone rang. "Oh, excuse me just a minute," Hap said apologetically, darting back inside. "It might be one of the owners. I was expecting—" He cut himself off as he picked up the phone. "Silver King Hotel. What can I do for you?"

Leigh felt Warren's arm slip around her waist. "You okay?" he asked. "You look a little... uncertain."

"Of course I'm okay," Leigh insisted, wishing for the thousandth time that her husband couldn't read her so well. "I just have a thing about sirens." She paused a moment. "And maybe about creepy black birds with yellow eyes that cluster in one spot and stare at me. But I'm still good. Texas is good. The sun will come out tomorrow." She looked up into his handsome face and found her happy mood rekindling. "Nothing is getting me down this week, I promise you. I haven't taken this much pure 'me-time' since before the kids were born. I intentionally didn't bring any work along so that I wouldn't even be tempted! I am on vacation with a capital V."

"Glad to hear it," Warren said tenderly. His brown eyes sparkled, and he leaned down and kissed her. At some point, Hap hung up the phone with a bang, and the couple parted.

"I don't believe it," Hap mumbled.

"What's that?" Leigh inquired, not particularly caring. She was eager to get to their room.

"That was my buddy Carl," Hap answered. "His daughter, Bobby Jo, works down at the police station."

Leigh was only half listening. But there was a word in there she didn't like.

Hap whistled. "Never in my life... other places, maybe. But little ol' Port Mesten? Good Lord above, what's the world coming to?"

Warren looked up. He didn't appear to have been listening, either. "What was that?"

Hap cleared his throat. "I'm sorry, I don't mean to upset you. It's just the darnedest thing..." He took a handkerchief from his pocket and wiped his brow. Then he pointed one finger in the general direction of the ocean.

"A body just washed up on the beach."

Chapter 2

I am not involved.

The words were Leigh's new mantra. She would tattoo them on the backs of both of her hands if she could. Maybe even backwards on her forehead, too, so that it would come out right when she looked in the mirror. But of course she couldn't do any of that, because it would make her look guilty of something. And she wasn't guilty of anything. *Nothing at all.*

Yes, for the first time in the history of Port Mesten, a recently deceased corpse had washed up right on the main tourist beach. And yes, that event had coincided exactly with the arrival — for the first time ever — of one Leigh Eleanor Koslow Harmon. So what? Such a convergence of timing meant nothing. To believe that it did, one would have to be both superstitious *and* paranoid.

Leigh was not involved.

The Texas sun was shining brightly this morning, just as she had willed, and Leigh was determined to make the most of it. After waking up alone in the room (Warren having left for work at the crack of dawn) she dressed hurriedly and threw some essentials into her backpack. Today she planned to do some serious sightseeing, all on foot. This was one vacation during which she would *not* gain weight!

She stepped out of the cozy second floor room Hap had assigned them and onto the long veranda, then locked the heavy door behind her. With its creaky floorboards and small-scale spaces, the historic building definitely showed its age, but it was sparkling clean and the furnishings more than adequate for a good night's rest. Leigh walked down the stairs and made her way to the tower lobby, where she found Hap waiting for her with another cheerful grin on his face.

"Good mornin' to you!" he greeted, reaching under the counter to produce a plate of pastries and fruit. "Got a little welcome gift here from the missus. Hot coffee and tea over by the door!"

Leigh's stomach rumbled as her eyes took in the plump

blueberry muffins. Well… walking required energy, did it not?

"I love Bev already," she gushed, pouring herself a cup of java and then accepting the plate. Hap came out from behind the counter to top off his own cup, then they sat down together on the lobby's wicker furniture. "Oh, my," she said, noting the oddly sized pieces of translucent paper that were tacked up on the walls all around them. They looked rather like onion skin and were covered with handwriting. "What are these things?"

"Tarpon scales," Hap said proudly. "You know, the fish? Port Mesten used to be famous for tarpon. Big, shiny devils they were. Six, eight feet long some of them, jumping straight out of the water. They'd fight you when you hooked them — that's what made the sport. Didn't taste too good, but everyone wanted to come wrestle a silver king, just the same!"

Hence the hotel's name, Leigh realized. She leaned toward the wall nearest her to see that the huge scales had been signed and dated by people who had stayed and fished here, all the way back to the late twenties. It was an interesting concept. Still… her personal decorating tastes, such as they were, did not extend to fish skin.

"I read a little about this hotel on the website," she explained, trying not to wolf down the delicious muffin as quickly as she wanted to. "It's one of the oldest buildings in Port Mesten, right?"

Hap nodded. "That's right. The house the museum's in now is the oldest. The original building on this spot was built back in the 1880s to house the men working on the jetty. They used lumber from the old civil war barracks to put it together. That building got mostly wiped out by the hurricane of 1919, but what was left standing got rebuilt into a hotel in the twenties. They knew a little bit more about how to build them sturdy by then, you see. The business has had its ups and downs since, particularly when the tarpon started drying up, but it's lasted through all four hurricanes since, and it's always been a hotel!"

"What happened to the tarpon?" Leigh asked, moving on to muffin number two. *Heaven.*

"Nobody really knows for sure," Hap answered, scratching the top of his bald head. "They just disappeared. Started in the late fifties. By sixty-five, tarpon sport fishing was dead. Some folks blame the drought and the dams, or too many boats, or too much fishing. Probably it was a little bit of everything…"

As Hap launched into an amusing series of fish stories, Leigh finished off her second blueberry muffin and then found herself staring lustfully at the third and fourth. Clearly, they had been meant for Warren. But he wasn't here. She chomped into number three. "So, have you ever wrestled a tarpon yourself?" she asked as soon as her mouth wasn't full. "Mom said you loved to fish."

Hap smiled, but shook his head. "I fish plenty, but I've never seen a tarpon. Bev and I only moved here eight years ago now. She knew the old owner, Dick Patson. But he died not too long after we started working for him. That's when Cort bought the place. Of course, he's gone now, too."

Leigh caught a sudden, sharp look of sadness in Hap's wide blue eyes. "Cort?" she asked softly.

"Cortland Finney," Hap answered. He looked at her expectantly. "You've heard of Cortland's Famous Fish Rub, haven't you?"

Leigh shook her head. More coffee was needed to wash down her third pastry. The fruit looked good too, but… priorities.

"He passed away a little over a year ago now," Hap continued. "Port Mesten's favorite son. Homegrown millionaire. Or billionaire, rather! He and his wife started out with a little diner here on the island, then grew it into a whole chain of restaurants and gift stores. Surely you've heard of Texas Todos?"

That name did ring a bell. "You mean the little gift stores in the airports that have all the Texas-themed stuff?"

Hap grinned. "That's right. Cort and Debra built themselves a real empire. They sold off the restaurants a long time ago, but the gift stores and online business have been bringing in a pretty penny as long as I've been around." His expression turned sour, and his voice lowered. "Nobody knows what'll happen now, though, with the kids taking over. You ask me, I wouldn't trust a one of them as far as I could throw them. Pack of damn jackals…" His voice trailed off as he glanced toward the door. But just as quickly, his good humor returned. "Well, listen to me going on and on like the town gossip, when you're here to get some sunshine! More coffee?"

Leigh accepted gratefully. However, she was enjoying his gossip. "So who owns the hotel now?"

Hap made an obvious effort to maintain his cheer. "They do. The kids. Well, they're not kids anymore, I suppose. They're all around forty. Their mother passed away before Cort did, and word has it the couple always agreed to split everything four ways after they were gone. Which sounds fair, but of course it's been a mess."

"Why's that?" Leigh asked, sipping the steaming cup. She was completely stuffed, but it was worth it. She would simply walk every minute between now and lunchtime.

"Because there's only one thing the four of them hate more than an honest day's work," Hap declared. "And that's each other."

Leigh nodded. "I see the problem. But mom and dad didn't?"

Hap chuckled without mirth. "Hell, no. They thought the world of those kids. Always figured they'd grow up and straighten out someday. What's worse is, Cortland really did seem to think he was immortal. He knew he needed to split up everything proper, but he always figured he had more time. I heard the will he died with was twenty years old."

Hap was thoughtful a moment, then his voice lowered again. "By the way, I'd appreciate it if we kept this conversation between the two of us. Like Bev keeps reminding me, the Finney kids are the owners now, so I'd best stop my ranting about them. It's an awfully small town, at least as far as permanent residents go. And Sharonna stays here in the penthouse sometimes. So don't get me into trouble."

"I wouldn't dream of it," Leigh assured, rising. "There is zero chance I would do anything to jeopardize my odds of getting more muffins."

Hap laughed. He offered to refrigerate her leftovers should she desire a midafternoon snack, then he supplied her with a map of the town and a water bottle and wished her on her way.

Leigh stepped outside and inhaled deeply of the warm, seaside air. The breeze was stiff, but a thin jacket was all she needed to feel warmer than she had in months. She looked across the parking lot for the ill-fated pickup truck, but both it and the creepy grackles were gone. Only a handful of cars remained now, and the only birds she saw were a soaring gull overhead and several brownish sparrows hopping around in the grass near the curb. The sun shone brilliantly, showering some real honest-to-God warmth on her pale, UV-deprived face, and she smiled inside and out.

Bliss. Now this was the vacation she had imagined.

Ignoring the map in her pocket for now, she set off in the general direction of the beach. The Silver King Hotel, which fronted a two-lane thoroughfare and was probably once the only structure on it, was now wedged in among a variety of other commercial establishments. A seafood restaurant and pizza parlor were across the street, but the hotel's closest neighbors were two curiously dissimilar RV parks. On one side was Mesten Acres, a chaotic jumble of fifth-wheel campers and semi-permanent trailers surrounded by a sad-looking chain link fence. On the other side, two rows of tall palm trees flanked the entrance of the Mesten Grande RV Resort, which Leigh could see little of from where she was standing, but which appeared to cater to the kind of luxury motorhomes that cost more than many Pittsburgh houses. As she crossed the street and strode toward the sound of squawking gulls, she wondered which park Hap and Bev lived in.

Two and a half blocks later, Leigh had reached her destination. The gray waters of the Gulf of Mexico lay before her, churning with an unexpected energy. It didn't look like the Florida part of the Gulf that she had seen before. Here, no defined waves crashed upon the sand with predictable regularity. Nor was the ocean flat, lapping placidly at the beach. For yards out from shore, the water churned in a confused froth of broken wave segments, making a constant roiling noise rather than an ebb and flow sound.

Leigh had no idea what peculiar topography, tides, or wind caused the difference. But she did enjoy the roaring noise. She kicked off her shoes and walked barefoot in the sand. Down the beach to her right she could see a pier, and she turned and headed for it, her thoughts drifting aimlessly as she scanned the sand for interesting seashells.

She had already pocketed parts of two broken sand dollars and was studying a strange piece of giraffe-spotted shell when she noticed a cluster of vehicles beside her. She looked up to see a black SUV emblazoned with a Texas Ranger logo and two Port Mesten police cruisers.

Whatever is going on, she reminded herself firmly, *I am not involved.*

Beside the vehicles stood a dozen or so people. Three men and one woman in uniform were speaking with two men in casual clothes. The rest of the crowd seemed to be hanging around out of pure curiosity.

Leigh felt a sudden chill in the wind. A stray remnant of yellow tape remained connected at one end to a squatty bush not ten feet from her, while its other end flapped about in the scraggly dune grass. *This must be where the body was found,* she realized. The remains would be long gone by now, but that wouldn't stop people from wanting to come here, to look around, to talk about it. She felt a tug of sympathy for the unfortunate soul who had first happened on the grisly sight. But at least it wasn't her.

Resolving to walk right on by, she returned her eyes to the sand and seashells. But she still couldn't help overhearing.

"Do they know who it was?"

"Did you hear?"

"I think they know."

"Did they say?"

"Oh, they *know.*"

"I don't think so."

"I heard it was a man. Like an older guy."

"Wasn't anybody from around here, was it?"

"Is anybody missing?"

Leigh forced her feet to keep walking. She had nearly cleared the scene altogether when she made the mistake of stealing a glance back at the uniformed officers. One of the casually clothed men standing near them happened to be looking her direction, and their gazes met.

The man was around her own age, maybe younger, tall and well built with a square jaw and carefully cultivated nascent beard. His full head of hair shone light brown in the sun, and he was wearing shorts and a polo with designer sunglasses perched atop his head. Unwittingly, Leigh stopped walking. He did not look at all familiar. But his blue eyes went wide with what appeared to be recognition... of her.

He poked the man next to him, a local policeman, and mumbled something without ever removing his eyes from Leigh. Then, with a queer expression that was not quite a smile, he began to walk towards her.

Leigh was flummoxed. She ran his face through a mental inventory, but her brain kept coming up blank. She was sure she had never met him, in Texas or anywhere else. He was an exceedingly good-looking specimen. The kind any woman was unlikely to forget.

So what the hell did he want with her?

He walked straight over, but waited to speak until he was standing quite close. "Hey there," he said in a friendly, albeit tentative voice. He waited for her to respond.

"Hello," she said stupidly.

He paused another moment, watching her as if waiting for her to say something else. Leigh stared back at him.

"Um… you having a good time in Port Mesten?" he asked.

"So far. I just got here last night," Leigh said automatically, then regretted offering the information. Who was this guy? He had neither introduced himself nor expected her to. It was as if he already knew who she was. She frowned a little.

He noticed. "Well, I don't mean to bother you," he said pleasantly, stepping back. "Just thought I'd say hello. You, uh… you have a nice time, you hear?"

"Sure thing," Leigh agreed, playing along. The man turned around. As he began to walk back the way he had come, he threw a perfunctory wave over his shoulder. "See you soon."

Leigh had no response to that. She whirled away from him and resumed her beach trek, keeping her eyes on the sand in front of her.

What the heck? If she were ten years younger, twenty pounds lighter, and a whole lot sexier, she might think the man was hitting on her. But that was utter nonsense. So what could he possibly want? Had he mistaken her for someone else?

She tried out a few scenarios in her head, but no matter what kind of backstory she made up for two people having such an encounter, the conversation was still weird. He seemed to have expected her to say something, or to tell him something. But when she hadn't, he didn't get mad. Instead, he acted almost… well, like he'd done something wrong himself.

Had he realized at some point that he had the wrong woman? If so, why did he say he would see her again?

Forget about it. You're on vacay!

Leigh's eyes caught sight of another shell fragment with the funky giraffe-spotted pattern, and she tucked it into her jacket pocket. She'd never seen such shells. Perhaps they were unusual? She would ask Hap about them later.

By the time she had enjoyed a leisurely stroll to the end of the pier, walked back into town, checked out some artsy stores and some not-so-artsy stores, and had a delicious fish taco for lunch, the incident with Mr. Handsome was forgotten. She indulged in a dish of salted caramel ice cream, then, as penance, plodded over a mile along the main highway to reach a local nature preserve that her map claimed would have alligators.

The temperature had climbed well into the seventies, and Leigh's jacket was now tied around her waist. She reveled in every second of the sun and was delighted when the shadow of a tan became visible around her watchstrap. But after the long walk along the highway, she was equally delighted to spend a few minutes resting on a bench under the canopy of some shade trees at the entrance to the preserve.

She pulled out her water bottle and took a swig. She had been in beach towns before, but Port Mesten in the middle of winter had a vibe she hadn't encountered before. For starters, she was one of the youngest people around; most of the tourists seemed to be retirees. Second, listening to the accents of those tourists, she would guess she was in the upper plains rather than Texas. And third, she'd never in her life been any place where so many people wore binoculars around their necks, including the cheap seats at the old Three Rivers Stadium.

She watched with amusement as a group of tiny birds flitted about from branch to branch in the trees nearby. Two women with binocs glued to their eyeballs were following the birds everywhere they went. One woman had nearly walked into a tree trunk in the process, and the other had actually banged her knee on a fencepost, but they remained undeterred. Leigh could only wonder what they sought to accomplish.

Once sufficiently cooled down, she followed the trail past the trees where it changed into a wooden boardwalk that led out over a wetland. The brackish water was several feet deep with a maze of tall marsh grasses weaving through it, and Leigh was glad that the elevated boardwalk kept her feet clear of any lurking alligators. The wetland was alive with birds of all kinds: ducks and herons and giant white things that looked like pelicans, and although Leigh was no birdwatcher, even she could appreciate their sheer abundance and variety. She reached an observation tower and climbed its wooden stairs. From the top, she should be able to see the whole wetlands, maybe even catch a glimpse of those elusive gators.

The wind was blowing briskly at the top of the platform, but she wasn't in the least bit cold. Less than twenty-four hours in Texas, she thought with a grin, and already the bitter Pittsburgh winter seemed like another world. She watched with awe as several giant white birds swooped down at the far edge of the wetlands and landed on the water of an even broader, deeper-looking pond. "What are those exactly?" she asked the woman standing beside her, who was watching the same birds with an impressively large pair of binoculars.

"American white pelicans," the woman answered pedantically.

Leigh nodded, feeling ignorant. She supposed she could have guessed that. But the woman seemed happy to have been asked. "Have you seen any alligators?"

"Yes," came the delighted answer. "At least I did just a minute ago. Let me see…" The woman readjusted her binoculars in another direction. "There he is! He's poking his head out of the little round pond, just to the right of the entrance. If you follow that tallest tree straight down and over to the right, you'll see him." She pulled the strap from around her neck and offered Leigh the complicated-looking device.

"Thanks," Leigh replied. She raised the binoculars to her own eyes, but following the directions was harder than it seemed. She found herself looking at a blur she was guessing was a car in the parking lot.

"You can adjust the focus if you need to," the woman suggested.

Leigh turned the dial on top until the blob turned into a red Nissan. She began moving her field of vision slowly to the right, hoping to find the tall tree and then move down to the pond.

She stopped.

Khaki shorts. Turquoise polo. Sunglasses. Light brown hair.

Holy hell. It was him again. Mr. Handsome from the beach, now loitering at the preserve. Leaning casually against a Porsche with his arms crossed over his chest. Doing nothing in particular.

"Do you see him?" the woman asked, referring to the alligator.

"No," Leigh mumbled.

The man didn't move. But every few seconds, he glanced up in the direction of the entrance. From where he stood, Leigh was guessing that he could see people preparing to exit as they stepped off the boardwalk. People who, at that angle, would be unlikely to notice him.

He was waiting for someone.

"I think you're looking too far to the left," the woman advised.

Leigh swung the binoculars out over the trees and down. Now she saw water. Blurry water. Her heart beat fast.

"Any luck?" the woman asked hopefully.

Leigh pulled the binoculars down and returned them. "I'm afraid I'm not very good with these things. But thanks anyway. I'll walk down closer and look from there."

She would not jump to conclusions. She would not.

"I am feeling lucky today, actually," Leigh insisted.

Because I am not involved.

Chapter 3

Leigh did keep searching for the alligator. But her heart wasn't in it. She couldn't stop thinking about the man lurking in the parking lot. Knowing he was out there and not knowing if his presence had anything to do with her own presence made her nervous. And the fact that she was nervous annoyed her.

When she realized her teeth had started to gnash, she decided to confront the man and get it over with. But when she emerged into the parking lot, he was no longer in his hiding spot. His Porsche hadn't moved, but of the man himself there was no sign.

There you go, she assured herself. He must have been waiting to meet someone. They had left together in another car, perhaps.

With a breath of relief, she reopened her map and searched out a likely spot for another snack. The fish taco had been low-cal, right? Something fruity and icy would be nice. She was halfway back down the long, hot road beside the refuge when the unwelcome thought occurred to her.

What if Mr. Handsome had seen her coming, and had been hunkered down *inside* his car?

Leigh beat back a shudder. She looked over her shoulder instead and studied the highway. The Porsche was nowhere in sight. *But,* as slow as she was moving, anyone in a car could keep tabs on her with only a periodic check-in. Her teeth began to grind again. This situation was not acceptable.

She considered her options for another quarter mile, resisting the urge to look over her shoulder every other second, until she reached her mark: a chain hotel, one of the nicer ones on the island. It was no luxury resort, but it was the kind of place she and Warren might stay if the kids were with them. *Perfect.*

She wandered to the outdoor pool and leaned over the fence, trying to act as if she were communicating with someone inside. After a few moments, she swung her backpack off her shoulders and started digging around inside it as if looking for a key, then she walked from the pool into a side entrance of the hotel.

So there.

One trip to the vending machines, one diet cola, and half a frozen Snickers bar later, Leigh reemerged from a side-street exit, looked around carefully, and began walking again. She continued on a parallel course for several more blocks before making her way back to the beach, where she plopped down on the sand and finished off the melting Snickers. The sun was shining, she was gloriously warm, and whether Mr. Handsome had represented actual risk or paranoid delusion gradually ceased to matter. Either way, she'd lost the guy.

She had nearly dozed off with her head on her backpack when she heard footsteps crunching in the dune grass behind her. She raised up on her elbows and looked through the brush.

A gray-haired couple dressed in matching blue jogging suits were walking side by side, very slowly and carefully, on tiptoe. They had binoculars where their eyes should be. "Has it got a mottled breast?" the woman whispered.

"Shhh!" the man hissed.

Leigh laid her head back down on her backpack. More birders. They were harmless. At least she supposed they were. Even if they did look like technicolor lions stalking the Serengeti.

"Oh, it's just a house sparrow!" the woman announced with annoyance.

The man swore. "Well, we'll never know now, will we? Can't you keep quiet?"

"I don't need to keep quiet when I can see it's just a house sparrow!" the woman fired back.

The man grumbled again. "Well, I don't think there are any seasides over here, then. Let's go back over the other way."

The woman let out a shriek, then muffled it. Leigh startled at the noise, but seeing nothing hazardous in the immediate area, laid her head back down. She was entirely too comfortable to move.

"Good Lord, Bets, what is it?" the man asked irritably.

"I thought that was a body!" the woman squeaked.

Oh. Leigh felt herself shrink with embarrassment. Sheesh. Were her legs really *that* pale?

"For Pete's sake," the man groused. "The feet moved, didn't they? You're seeing bodies everywhere!"

Leigh considered informing the couple that she was not deaf. But she kept quiet, deciding that she and her corpselike legs would be better off remaining anonymous.

"Well, I can't help it!" the woman whined. "The very thought of it gives me nightmares. To think the poor man was wearing a business suit and a tie! Now how could that have happened? You know he had to have been murdered!"

Leigh tensed. Must the woman use that word?

"I don't know anything about it, and neither do you," the man snapped. "You read too many novels. Guy probably just jumped off a bridge somewhere. Hey, is that a kestrel?"

"There are no bridges over the open ocean!" the woman argued. "Yes, of course it's a kestrel. And I do know something about it. I know what that woman in the breakfast room said about overhearing the police say he was a businessman. Now, how many businesspeople in suits do you see wandering around a tourist town like this? Piffle. I say it was a mob hit. Guy got whacked in the city and somebody hauled his body down here and dumped it off the side of a boat. That's what happened!"

"Okay, fine, that's what happened," the man answered, sounding bored. "Look! There's another sparrow!"

"Does it have a mottled breast?" the woman demanded.

The couple crunched away through the grass again. Leigh stayed where she was until their voices had moved out of range, then she rose stiffly. Her peaceful spot didn't seem so peaceful anymore.

A businessman in a suit? With a tie? Really?

She told herself not to think about it.

She roamed aimlessly on the beach a while longer, collecting more shells and enjoying the constant churning sound of the waves, but she was hopelessly drowsy now and suspected she was sunburned besides. When she could no longer control her yawns, she headed back to the Silver King Hotel, kicked off her shoes, and collapsed across the comfy queen-sized bed. Just a short nap, she thought with contentment. Then she'd take a shower and freshen up before dinner.

She drifted off and must have slept deeply, because the voices that jolted her back to awareness seemed to pop up out of nowhere, with no prelude of footsteps or creaking doors.

"What are you doing here?"

"Why shouldn't I be here?"

"Because I told you to stay away!"

"You don't rule the world."

Leigh's eyes opened. The last speaker was a woman, and she was arguing with a man. Leigh had been in plenty of hotels where she'd heard raised voices in the room next door, but "raised voices" was usually the extent of what one could hear. Being able to understand every word was disconcerting, particularly since these two weren't talking all that loudly.

Leigh raised her head and confirmed that her own door was closed. There was no adjoining door between her room and the next, but the thin plank walls carried sound unfortunately well.

"I promised you I would take care of it. You don't have to be here," the man insisted.

"Says you," the woman retorted.

Leigh laid her head back down. She really was sleepy.

"I'll be watching you," the man said matter-of-factly.

"Spare me," the woman returned. "Maybe I'll be watching you, too."

The man made a disgruntled noise. "It'll all be over soon enough."

"Yes, it will, won't it? Too soon. Thanks to you."

"Don't start!" the man said angrily. "It's not my fault!"

Leigh's eyes popped open again. The couple were talking in riddles. They also weren't talking like a couple. Their tone held an unmistakable intimacy, yet there was a distinctive, acerbic bite to it that Leigh couldn't quite put her finger on.

"Dad put you in charge, didn't he?" the woman snapped.

Bingo. They were siblings.

"I'm not getting into this with you, Sharonna!" the man retorted bitterly. "It is what it is. Deal with it. I'm only here to beg you not to make things worse with your damned drama. Can't you just lay low and keep your stupid mouth shut for a few days? We're each going to get our fair share, I promise you. Just like Mom and Dad wanted."

"What they wanted?" Sharonna practically screamed. "You think *this* is what Dad wanted?"

"Will you *shut up!*" the man answered, his own voice now hushed.

Leigh listened for sounds of a struggle, but all she heard was the tinny sound of insincere female laughter. "You are so pathetically anal. Go away and leave me alone."

Leigh heard a door open, but no footsteps moved out of it.

"Have you heard anything yet?" the man asked. His tone had changed altogether. He seemed to be almost pleading now.

The woman paused a beat. "No," she answered, her own voice flippant. "But really, brother dear. After everything you've put me through, do you think I would tell you if I had?"

The man did not answer. The door slammed hard, and footsteps stomped away.

The woman in the room burst into a fit of giggles.

"I do believe this is the best flounder I've ever tasted," Warren said sincerely, finishing the last bite off his bright green melamine plate with a look of contentment on his face.

Bev Taylor's pink apple cheeks glowed. "Why, thank you, sir," she said jauntily. "I'll give Cortland's Famous Fish Rub partial credit. The rest is all me."

Leigh smiled. Broad and square, with a prominent midsection, Hap's "new" wife of eight years was an almost comical version of himself, just shorter and female. She had the same slightly oversized head, friendly broad smile, light complexion, and dancing blue eyes. Mercifully, however, she did differ from her husband in that her head was crowned with a thick mop of frizzy blondish-gray hair.

"She's a wizard," Hap agreed, relaxing in his sling-back chair. The four of them were enjoying the evening outside, sitting on the patio beside the older couple's fifth-wheel trailer. "You know it's true as much as Cortland himself used to show up here for dinner!"

Bev chuckled. "That was high praise, wasn't it? Lord, I miss that old buzzard."

Leigh sat up a little. She had done her best not to dwell on the bizarre conversation she'd overheard during her nap, which had almost certainly come from two of the squabbling Finney siblings. But her best wasn't good enough. As unlikely as it seemed that her down-to-earth cousins were tight with a billionaire, she was definitely getting that impression. "You knew him well?" she asked.

"Oh, yes." Bev shot a sideways glance at her husband. "Not

everybody around here realized that, though. You should explain, Hap."

Hap squirmed a bit in his seat, then took a swig from his can of beer. His voice lowered. "I don't suppose it matters anymore, but... Well, Cortland was the kind of guy who could go to work at that downtown office of his and hassle with all the suits and do a damn good job of it, but that's not really who he was. If he had his druthers, he'd be sitting on a boat all day with a fishing rod in one hand and a beer in the other, talking about nothing at all. When Deb was alive he'd go home to that big old place of theirs in the evening, but after she passed, he got lonely. He started coming down to the hotel and shooting the bull with me and, well... once he tasted Bev's cooking, we couldn't get rid of him."

Bev chuckled again. "Now, you know there's more to it than that. That man was genuinely fond of you, honey. Because he could talk to you." She looked at Leigh with a face full of pride. "Hap's a good listener," she explained. "I wouldn't say the rich and famous Mr. Finney lived a double life, but some days it seemed pretty close to it. If he got fed up he'd ditch that office, change into some old clothes and come sneaking around here looking for Hap."

"Sneaking around?" Warren asked.

"Well, everybody around here knew Cortland, you see," Hap explained. "And for somebody famous, he sure hated fame. Couldn't blame him with so many folks asking for loans and handouts, once he and Deb made it big. But aside from that nuisance, he just got tired of being Mr. Big. He wanted to walk down the street like anybody else and be left the hell alone."

"That's why he liked it here," Bev cut in, sweeping a hand around the central courtyard of the Mesten Grande RV Resort. The greenspace was nestled in the middle of a maze of gently curving, brightly lit streets filled with motorhomes, each of which had a small paved patio and a plot of grass around it. "This place was Cortland's pet project, you know. He was right proud of it. But the best part for him was that it's always filled with outsiders. So he could sit out here with us and grill some fish or have a beer and no one had a clue who he was."

"Whenever anyone would ask, we'd just call him Uncle Herman," Hap said with a laugh. "He got a kick out of that."

Leigh noted again the depth of feeling in her cousin's eyes. Hap had indeed been close to Cortland Finney. But she could swear she heard more in his strained tone than grief at a friend's passing.

"What did he die of?" she asked impulsively. "Was it unexpected?"

Hap nodded solemnly. "He had an artery rupture near his heart. No real warning, no family history or anything."

"It was such a shame," Bev lamented. "He kept saying he needed to redo his will."

Hap's second uncomfortable squirm did not go unnoticed, either by Leigh or his wife.

"What's eating you?" Bev asked. Then her voice turned sharp. "Don't tell me Sharonna's back! Already?"

"All right," Hap said quietly. "I won't tell you."

Bev made a growling sound low in her throat. For a woman of her size, it was surprisingly deep. And loud. "Nobody on earth gets under your skin like that woman!"

"Peaches, I can think of a whole lot of things I'd rather talk about after a fine meal like this than Sharonna Finney," Hap answered with resignation. Then he threw a somewhat sheepish look at Leigh and Warren. "But she is staying next door to you folks, so if it gets too loud up there, you just let me know and I'll move y'all downstairs."

"You expect her to be loud?" Leigh asked. She knew the answer already, but she wanted to hear Hap say it.

He sighed. "Sharonna doesn't have the best social skills, you could say."

Beverly scoffed. "That's generous. The woman's got a whole host of problems — having no filter on her mouth's only one of them. She'll say whatever comes to her mind, with no thought to anybody else."

"True enough," Hap agreed. "Anyway, she can be annoying. So just let me know, all right?"

"I'm sure it will be no problem," Warren said politely. "I haven't heard a thing."

Hap looked skeptical. "I wouldn't have put you guys up there except it's the second best room in the house, and Sharonna just checked out a couple days ago — I was surprised to see her again."

"It's no problem," Leigh soothed, knowing otherwise. If they wanted peace and quiet, they should definitely switch rooms.

Tonight. She should say so.

"There's something else," Hap said anxiously, sitting up straighter in his chair. "I'm sorry to have to bring up such a thing, but if you're hanging around town this week you're bound to hear it some—"

"They've identified the body, haven't they?" Leigh blurted.

All eyes stared at her. Realizing the non sequitur, Leigh wished she could withdraw the question. Why thinking about Sharonna had put her in mind of the body on the beach, she could not explain. The conversation Leigh had overheard in the room next door had included nothing about a corpse. The fact that she had instinctively disliked both Sharonna and her unnamed brother did not entitle her to add two and two and get twelve.

"Sorry," Leigh stammered. "I just got the feeling you'd heard something since the last time we talked, Hap."

Hap raised his thin white eyebrows. "Well, I guess you're right. I did. Got the word a little while ago from my buddy Carl."

Bev drew in a sharp breath. "It wasn't anybody local, was it?"

"No," Hap said quickly. "It was a businessman from Corpus Christi. Some guy named Ted Sullivan. I never heard of him."

The relief that statement might be expected to bring did not materialize. It was too obvious that Hap was still troubled. "But Cortland knew him," he continued. "Must have. He'd been working in the family business for years. He was a bean counter. Most recently he was their Chief Financial Officer."

The table went quiet again.

"Well," Bev asked, "how did it happen?"

Hap shook his head. "They'll have to do an autopsy. But it's hard to see how a man like that dresses himself for work one day and accidentally ends up in the Gulf of Mexico."

Leigh wondered if Sharonna had known as of this afternoon. But this time she was able to keep her mouth shut.

"Does Sharonna know?" Bev asked. "Is that why she's back?"

Leigh had a feeling she and her cousin's wife were going to get along just fine.

"She was in the lobby when I found out," Hap said. "She came in to complain about some fool thing, and that was when Carl called. Sharonna stuck around to eavesdrop and then practically went hysterical. I couldn't tell if she knew the man personally or not — I didn't think she ever set foot in her daddy's office unless Cort was cutting her a check. But she was upset about something. She went on and on about what a disaster this would be for the business, and then she ran out." He shook his head, perplexed. "God only knows."

Bev stood, giving apologetic looks to Leigh and Warren. "I'm sorry for all this gloom and doom at your welcome dinner, but I had a feeling Hap had something to get off his chest." She stepped behind her husband and began to massage his beefy shoulders. "Now, darlin', you know that woman's not dealing with a full deck. She hasn't been since her mother died, and probably not before then, either. But there's not a thing you can do about it. She's an adult, and as long as she's not hurting anybody the constitution says she's got a perfect right to make an ass of herself."

"I know," Hap said glumly.

"If Cortland couldn't or wouldn't do anything for her, you certainly can't, so stop feeling guilty," Bev continued. "As for whatever happened to this CFO, that's got nothing to do with us. You know Cortland never talked business while he was here. I always figured he had good reason. Didn't you?"

Hap's face went red. "What are you saying exactly? Cort was an honest businessman!"

Bev perked an eyebrow. "You sure about that?"

Hap turned his head to frown at her. "Beverly!"

"Okay, okay!" she recanted, renewing her massage. "I'm just saying. Once you get to that level of success, there's bound to be some funny business going on somewhere or other down the line. And there's no telling what's been happening in those swanky downtown offices since the kids took over."

Hap looked thoroughly miserable.

Bev finished off his shoulder massage with a series of energetic karate chops, then turned to her guests with a smile. "All right, now! Who's ready for dessert?"

Chapter 4

Leigh woke up the next morning with the purest of intentions for a day full of fresh air and healthy exercise. The sky was overcast and occasional rain a near certainty, but she refused to be discouraged. She merely donned her waterproof jacket, put an expandable umbrella in her backpack, and headed out the door. She would stop into the lobby only for a cup of coffee and perhaps a quick bite of fruit, but no more, because she didn't deserve it. Not only did she have two helpings of Beverly's blackberry cobbler after dinner last night, but she'd even had the nerve to creep down to the lobby at 2AM and finish off the last blueberry muffin from yesterday. (Conveniently enough, the millennial supposedly manning the desk had been sound asleep at the time.) She really couldn't help herself. After such a long nap earlier, she couldn't sleep. And she *knew* the muffin was down there…

No matter. Today she would make a fresh start of it.

She opened the door to the lobby and was surprised to see Bev sitting behind the counter instead of Hap. "Good morning!" her cousin-in-law called cheerfully, hopping off the stool and heading immediately for the mini refrigerator.

"Good morning," Leigh returned, her hopes fading fast. "Oh, Bev. Don't tell me you made more of those fabulous blueberry muffins! You really don't have to feed me breakfast every morning."

"Breakfast?" Bev disputed with a motherly pucker of her eyebrows. "I'd say it's halfway to lunch by now!"

Leigh smiled self-consciously. After last night's sugar raid, she had indeed overslept. "I'm sorry if you were waiting on me. All I need is some caffeine and maybe an apple or something, and then I thought I'd check out the museum—"

"Looky here!" Bev said triumphantly, swinging up a platter laden with grapes, honeydew slices, and two gargantuan vanilla-iced cinnamon rolls. "You want me to heat one of these up for you?"

Have mercy. "Oh," Leigh said faintly, her traitorous stomach grumbling aloud. "Yes. Yes, I do."

"Thought so," Bev smirked, popping one of the confections in the microwave.

Leigh thanked her and poured herself a cup of coffee. "Where's Hap?"

"He's over at the RV park this morning," Bev answered. "We trade off sometimes." The confusion on Leigh's face prompted her to elaborate. "Cortland bought the hotel first, and then he bought the land next to it and built the Mesten Grande. Hap and I manage them both, but he does more of the desk duties while I handle the community activities at the park. That was part of the deal we struck with Cortland, so we could move our own place over there. We were on the other side before."

In the considerably less high-toned Mesten Acres, Leigh surmised. "I see."

"Cort owned a lot of real estate around here," Bev continued. "He loved the town, and he invested in it whenever he had the cash to spare. God only knows what will happen to all his bits and pieces now, though."

The microwave dinged, and Bev handed Leigh the warmed cinnamon roll on a plate with a napkin. Leigh sat down and dove in. She *had* been trying to forget the conversation she'd overheard between the Finney heirs yesterday afternoon, but the transcript was firmly lodged in her brain. Although she'd said nothing to Hap about it, she suspected his worries about his friend's legacy were legit. "The kids" were up to no good.

"The will's still tied up in court, then?"

Bev shrugged. "I haven't the faintest. No one knows anything. Bruce — that's the oldest, he's more or less in charge, now — he told us they were going to sell the hotel and the RV park both. But that was nearly a year ago, and we haven't heard a thing since. Still, we might not hear a peep until it's all said and done."

Leigh finished the roll. It was insanely good. But she would *not* eat the other one. At least not now. She distracted herself with the honeydew until a man with a suitcase entered the lobby, ready to check out. Bev went back to work, and Leigh returned the rest of the platter to the fridge, thanked her hostess, and excused herself.

She made it exactly four blocks before dodging inside a

tropically themed coffee shop to use the restroom. When she emerged, she headed to the counter to order a cappuccino and found herself standing next to a uniformed policeman.

Friggin' fabulous.

"Morning, Chief," a girl in a ponytail and work apron greeted him from behind the counter. "What can I get for you?"

"Aw, just a regular cup of joe, thanks, Kathy," he answered. The chief was a relatively unimposing man of middle height and weight, but Leigh still felt a desperate urge to turn tail and run. *Stop that,* she chastised herself. *He hasn't the faintest idea who you are! How could anybody know your name down here?* She forced herself to stay put and act natural as the chief paid for his coffee and moved to the side.

"And what can I get for you, ma'am?" the girl asked.

Leigh cringed. She hated being called *ma'am.* Even if she was getting old enough to justify it. "A small cappuccino, please."

The creepy feeling assailed her just as she reached out to accept her change. She knew, without turning, that someone was staring at her. Moreover, she realized that whoever it was must have been staring at her for some time now, tipping the offense out of random chance and well into the discomfort zone.

Was it the chief?

Please, no.

Her heart pounded as she allowed her gaze to slide ever so casually to her left along the counter, in the general direction of the icky vibes. Her eyes met a pair of beady brown ones, deep-set below a protruding brow bone. The man's hair was dark, his lips pale and thin. He wasn't wearing a uniform, but he didn't look like a tourist, either, as he was dressed in a high-end business casual outfit. His expression was brooding, and his regard was intense. Yet when Leigh pivoted to engage with him fully, his eyes left her. He took the fresh cup of coffee he'd been holding and, without another glance, walked away to a table and sat down.

Well, Leigh thought to herself, trying to shake off the unnerving episode, *at least it wasn't the chief, right?*

But she couldn't let it go easily. Not when the chief himself, after receiving his coffee, went and joined creepy-man at the table for two. And not when, as Leigh waited forever for her cappuccino to be foamed, she caught the brown eyes drifting to her humble figure not one or two, but three more times.

She watched the police chief as well, but he paid no attention to her. He merely relaxed in his chair and chattered away at his inattentive buddy as if it didn't matter whether he was being listened to or not.

When Leigh's drink was finally in her hands, she made her way to the door. Sure enough, the brown eyes followed her every step. Her plan was to go to the museum half a block to the right, but on instinct she hung a left instead, then walked the long way around.

Out of an abundance of caution, she told herself as she panted. She shouldn't be out of breath. She hadn't walked far, and it wasn't hot. What was wrong with her?

She was totally freaked out. That was what.

She swung into the museum's front door and collapsed on a bench. She had not seen the men on the street outside just now. She was safe.

"Welcome!" a thin but perky voice said excitedly. Leigh looked up to see a small, very old man hunched over a metal quad cane in front of her. "We're so happy you've chosen to visit the Port Mesten Museum! Would you like a guided tour?"

Leigh would not, actually, as she preferred to meander about such places on her own. But the friendly little man looked so excited she couldn't bear to disappoint him. She rose to her feet again, and he proceeded to lead her slowly around the main level of what had once been a grand little foursquare home. As he explained the different sections of the museum and what historical delights she was sure to uncover there, Leigh tried hard to get a grip on what had frightened her.

Two days. Two different men. Only one had approached her, while the other had made no effort to. But both of them had stared at her with the same, unaccountable look in their eyes. Not friendship. Not politeness. Not even the hunger of a predator for its prey. Certainly not garden-variety lust.

It was a look of recognition.

They *knew* her. But how could they? And if they thought they did, why hadn't they said so?

Leigh's gaze floated over old sepia-toned photographs of laborers hauling rocks to build the jetties and scrap lumber left in the wakes of hurricanes. She suspected that what her guide was telling her was truly interesting; it was unfortunate that she couldn't take in a word of it.

Was it possible that she resembled someone else in town? She recalled the inane saying that everyone in the world had a double somewhere. She had never believed it, but right now she wished she could. If she looked similar enough to someone local, someone both of those men knew, she would at least have some explanation for their bizarre behavior. Maybe they didn't know the mystery woman all that well, and were therefore unsure if Leigh was her. Perhaps they hadn't seen Ms. X in a while, and didn't want to make a wrong assumption. The idea was plausible, at least.

She began to feel slightly better, and when her guide mentioned the name "Finney" she redoubled her effort to pay attention. "Is this the family?" she asked, straining her neck to see a photograph high up on the wall.

"Why, yes!" the man replied with glee. "That's Cortland and Debra and the kids at the diner right here in Port Mesten, although that building wasn't the original. We have a picture of their very first diner over here — "

He pointed off someplace else, but Leigh's attention was focused on the photograph in front of her, which was part of a display touting the local origin of Cortland's Famous Fish Rub. The photograph had been in color, once, but was now faded to dull swirls of brownish red and blue. A young couple stood in front of the glass door to a restaurant with cars parked close on either side of them. The woman was wearing a mini dress and holding an infant, while the man supported a toddler with one arm. Two preschoolers played peek-a-boo around their legs. Leigh studied the children and surmised a birth order of boy, girl, girl, with a question mark over the infant. The oldest boy and girl had darker hair, whereas the toddler girl's hair looked lighter. The woman was thin, dark, and pretty with a charming smile — she looked as though she were bubbling with energy. Cortland was tall, lean, and fair with a calm expression that indicated a quiet demeanor, but his close-set, brooding eyes also made Leigh believe that he was a man who concealed things.

"Did you know them?" she asked her guide.

"Well, of course!" he said proudly, standing as tall as his hunched spine would allow. "Everyone knew Cort. He spent practically his whole life here. His wife Debra, too. Lovely people, just lovely. They've both passed away now, sad to say. But they were as good as they come. Hard workers and smart as whips, both of them."

"And their children?" Leigh watched the man's eyes closely. She felt a flicker of remorse for setting him up, but she was certain he was too polite to be honest with his words.

She was wrong.

His kind, wrinkled face changed in an instant from beaming with pride to stewing with long-suppressed hostility. His eyes clouded over with concentration and his jaws worked as he formulated a response. "I wouldn't say the children took after the parents, no," he replied finally. Then he forced a smile back on his face. "I suppose that happens sometimes."

He pivoted with his cane and directed her towards another display. "And over here, you can learn all about the glory days of the tarpon..."

Clearly, although the community's disappointment in the younger generation of Finneys was no secret, the residents of Port Mesten did not relish dissing their own, either. Leigh indulged her guide with more friendly chitchat as his tour led them around the circle of the four rooms. The displays moved forward in time, and in the last room Leigh caught herself paying extra attention to the photographs with crowd scenes. She was searching for the faces of the two men who had stared at her. She was also searching for a face like her own.

The elderly guide did not seem to find her appearance familiar. Nor had Hap or Beverly noted any similarity between her and any local woman they knew. But still, Leigh couldn't stop hoping. It *would* make the perfect explanation.

Her official "introductory" tour concluded, and Leigh indulged both herself and her host by making a second loop through the museum alone. She read several interesting stories about the indigenous people, the hurricanes, and the tarpon, then returned to the last room for another look at all the recent photographs. Still, none of the faces struck a chord. Disappointed, she moved on to the tiny gift shop, which consisted of a few shelves of handmade crafts, trinkets printed with the name of the town, and local maps and books. She leafed through a few paperbacks self-published by locals, but all were fiction, and none included any photographs. "Has anyone ever written a biography of Cortland Finney, or the story of the family business?" she asked her guide, who had seated himself behind the counter.

He chuckled softly. "Oh my, no. They wouldn't get much cooperation from Cort on something like that! He was a private person. But now that he's gone, who knows? Maybe someday. Is there anything you'd like to purchase?"

Leigh looked around. The man had been terribly nice, and the museum was free. She really should buy something.

"I highly recommend the fudge," he stage-whispered. "It's made right here in Port Mesten by one of our most dedicated volunteers!"

Fudge had never been one of Leigh's favorites, and the last thing she needed was more sweets, but she could see no gracious way out of it. She picked up a gaily decorated plastic bag of homemade fudge, paid for it, and dropped some extra cash in the donation box as well.

"Let me get you a bag for the that," the man offered. As he leaned to the side, Leigh could see on the wall behind him a framed newspaper article celebrating the opening of the museum, with a photograph of a ribbon-cutting ceremony at the front steps. A man she recognized immediately as a much older Cortland Finney stood prominently in the front row. But it was another face that made her heart skip.

"Here you go!" the guide said, handing over her laboriously bagged fudge with unsteady hands. His torso blocked the image again.

"Excuse me," Leigh said, pointing behind him. "That picture there?"

With effort, the man twisted around on his stool. Leigh dearly hoped he would not fall off the edge of it. "Oh, yes!" he replied. "That was our grand opening. That's Sheff Howard, our first director, cutting the ribbon. Tad Jenkins, head of the Chamber of Commerce at the time. And Cortland Finney. He was a major donor, of course."

"Who is that man?" Leigh pointed impatiently, embarrassed to hear the tremor in her voice. "The one on the far right? Wearing a tee shirt?"

The picture was in black and white, it was at least a decade old, and the faces on the periphery of the action were grainy. But Leigh could swear she knew the beady dark eyes that peered out from under the prominent brow bone. She should, shouldn't she? They'd been staring at her only an hour ago.

"Oh," the old man answered, all enthusiasm drained from his voice. "That's Bruce Finney. Cortland's son."

Chapter 5

Leigh was a good distance from the Silver King Hotel when, after hours of mere spitting and sprinkling, the sky suddenly let loose with a downpour. She had walked out of the museum in a daze, headed for the beach, and kept on walking, hardly noticing the rain. How long she'd walked and how far she'd gone, she had no idea, but water was now pouring off her scanty umbrella and dripping onto her shoes. She needed to turn around. More immediately, some shelter would be nice.

The near worthless umbrella quaked in the wind as she held it close to her face to survey her options. *Aha.* There was a wooden pavilion just ahead, across the roadway. It was open sided, but it was better than nothing.

Leigh tromped across the soggy dunes, over the wet asphalt, and along the road's shoulder until she reached a gravel path leading toward the pavilion. When she saw the small parking area and restroom building ahead, she realized where she must be. The nature preserve she had visited yesterday comprised a wide swath of the wetlands abutting the town, and more than one section of it was accessible with boardwalks and trails. She had obviously reached one of the preserve's other entrances.

The rain continued to pound all around her as she finished the last hundred yards to the pavilion at a jog. Other visitors were emerging from the boardwalk and rushing for their cars in the parking lot, while two women in plastic ponchos preceded Leigh to shelter in the pavilion. Leigh grabbed an unoccupied bench, plopped herself down, and pulled out her phone. She did nothing with it except hold it, but it served as a suitable diversion. She really didn't want to engage right now.

That's Bruce Finney. Cortland's son.

The museum guide's words still rattled her. It was one thing to contemplate, in a removed and theoretical sort of way, the possibility that one or more of Cortland and Debra's ne'er-do-well offspring could have offed their corporation's bean counter. The connection seemed obvious enough. The split-up of the family business was already disputed. If the man had been killed in the corporation's "swanky offices" in downtown Corpus Christi, what would the guilty parties do with his body, after all? The birdwatcher at the beach was right. If the murderer owned a boat — and it was a good bet that the Finney family did — a burial at sea was a pathetically obvious choice. Maybe "the kids" just weren't smart enough to do it right. To go far enough out. To weight the body down...

Leigh stifled a groan. She shouldn't be thinking about such things. But really, how could she not? How could anyone not? She was sure that Hap had considered the possibility. Most likely, all four kids were suspects in the CFO's murder. Still, aside from Leigh's feeling sorry for Hap because he obviously felt sorry for Cortland, she *should* have no reason to care.

But now she did, dammit.

Because Bruce Finney had been staring at her.

Leigh pursed her lips. Then it occurred to her that doing so must make her look like her mother. She forced her mouth into a grim line instead. She'd gone over the available facts a hundred times so far, but no matter how she sliced it, she came up with the same result. Bruce Finney, who might or might not be a murderer, *thought* he knew her. Most likely, because he was mistaking her for someone else. And his assumption couldn't be totally off base, because one other individual in Port Mesten had made the same mistake yesterday.

Neither man had been threatening in any way. Either event, in isolation, could be easily dismissed. She could even forget both of them if she convinced herself that she resembled some perfectly harmless individual who used to frequent the island...

She smiled wryly. Both men were middle aged. Perhaps her double was a blast from their past. A one-time pole dancer in Corpus, perhaps? The thought amused. But only until Leigh remembered one other disturbing similarity between the incidents: Both times, when she'd first seen the men, they'd been talking to cops.

Leigh didn't like *that* at all. Not that she had a problem with law enforcement. Her best and oldest friend was a homicide detective, after all. She just preferred not to associate with the police in any official capacity while on vacation.

Or at any other time.

For the rest of her natural life.

"Have you ever seen a roseate spoonbill?" someone asked.

Leigh glanced out of the corner of her eye to confirm that the woman standing by the balustrade holding a small pair of binoculars was indeed talking to her. Apparently Leigh's effort to appear engaged in her phone was unconvincing. Perhaps because her screen was blank. She gave up and put it away. "I'm sorry. Have I seen what?"

"The roseate spoonbills!" the woman answered excitedly. She appeared to be somewhere in her sixties. She had shoulder-length, light-brown hair that was liberally streaked with gray. Pale blue eyes sparkled through her bifocals, and her stick-thin frame practically quivered with nervous energy. "They're such beautiful creatures. But you have to know where to find them. So many tourists never bother! Here, take a look!"

Leigh couldn't refuse. She rose, took the proffered binoculars, and brought them up to her eyes, fully prepared to lie about whatever it was she knew she wouldn't see.

"Oh, no, not that way," the woman corrected gently. "You find the bird with your naked eye first, then raise the binoculars and focus in. Here, I'll turn the magnification down for you. That will make it easier." She fiddled with the dial, then pointed out over the water. "Way over there. See those specks of pink?"

Leigh did. And amazingly enough, with the woman's help, she soon had a wonderfully clear view of several bizarre birds that looked like flamingos, but had long, dark, spoon-shaped bills. She'd never seen anything like them before, outside of zoos. "Another aptly named species," she commented, admiring the rosy hue of their feathers.

"Oh look, Bonnie, the rain has stopped already!" the woman said with enthusiasm.

A primal groan sounded from behind them. "Oh, for crying out loud, Sue, I just sat my carcass down here!" her companion complained. "Can't we rest a bit? My heel's killing me."

Leigh shot a glance at the second woman, who was seated at one of the benches. Aside from the fact that Bonnie appeared to be around the same age as Sue and was also carrying binoculars, the two birdwatchers could not look more different. Bonnie appeared tall, broad, and "stout," to put it politely, with most of her weight concentrated around her middle. She had very short, spiky white hair and deep-set gray eyes that peered out from a perpetually glowering face. And yet, buried somewhere in the tone of her deep, drawling voice, Leigh detected humor.

"Thank you," Leigh said to Sue, returning the binoculars with a smile. "I needed that." She looked out over the rest of the preserve and noticed that the trail the pavilion was on, which skirted around the outside of the wetland, connected with another elevated boardwalk that headed straight into the center of the marsh. Some distance ahead she could see another wooden observation tower, similar to the one she had climbed yesterday. "Have you seen any gators?" she asked.

"Not here," Sue answered gaily. "The water along this boardwalk isn't deep enough. But there are several regulars over by the south entrance. Have you—" She snapped her binoculars up to her eyes. "Bonnie!" she exclaimed. "Thrasher!"

Bonnie snapped to attention. "Brown?"

"I don't think so!" Sue called back in a singsong. Leigh tried to follow her line of sight but had no idea what the woman was looking at. "It looked more gray! It just went into the grass. Come on!"

"Was its breast streaked? Could you see its bill?" Bonnie demanded.

"What does it matter?" Sue called as she rushed off. "For you, it's a lifer either way!"

Bonnie swore fluently. But much to Leigh's amazement, she immediately hefted her "carcass" up from the bench and hobbled after Sue. Leigh watched, amused, as the women stalked whatever the bird was until it flew out of the patch of shrub it was hiding in. When they pursued the bird to its next location as well, Leigh was left alone with her thoughts again.

Forget about the Finneys, she counseled herself, feeling better now for whatever reason. So she looked like somebody two men in town used to know, one of whom could possibly be a murderer. So what? She knew lots of murderers.

I am still not involved.

Her spirits remained high, even though the trek back to the hotel seemed exponentially longer than the walk out had been. By the time she climbed the last few steps to the second level of the Silver King and opened the door to her room, she was limping on a painful crop of blisters. Cursing her own stupidity at having rubbed her skin raw with soaking wet shoes and socks, she stripped off the offending footwear immediately and limped to her suitcase to retrieve some bandages. She dug out the black travel bag in which she always kept her medical supplies, unzipped the top, looked in, and stopped short.

Something was wrong. She studied the plastic bag of bandages and antibiotic cream that she always carried with her on trips. It was lying right on top. Underneath it was the usual assortment of over-the-counter painkillers, allergy and cold medicines, and topical remedies for rashes and bites. She had the mom-travel-bag thing down to a science. She packed the same way every time, because with the twins she was always scrambling to find something either in a moving car or in a dark room in the middle of the night. The only difference this time was that she'd left the kids' meds at home.

The bag of bandages didn't go on top. That space was reserved for Allison's emergency inhaler. When Leigh had packed this bag and zipped it up, she'd noticed the empty space. The bag had been easier to zip shut.

She fingered through the rest of the contents, and a strong feeling of unease came over her. The items were not as she had packed them. Someone else's fingers had also been here.

Warren? Could he have gotten a hangnail or something?

The explanation was perfectly plausible. But Leigh did not feel better. Her eyes roved over the remainder of her suitcase. At first glance, all was as it should be. But the closer she looked, the more small things she noticed. Her shirt stack was crumpled along the suitcase's edges, as if a hand had been run between her clothes and the inside wall. Her deodorant, usually thrown carelessly on top, had fallen to the bottom at the back. Her underwear and socks were packed more loosely than she remembered — she'd had to jam them down to squeeze in her coat after they'd walked into the Pittsburgh airport from the parking lot.

She dashed to the closet, stumbling on her sore feet in the process. She opened the door to see Warren's business shirts and pants, his extra sport jacket, and both their winter coats, all hanging neatly on hangers. Warren himself had hung everything the night they arrived. Leigh remembered that he had offered to hang her coat right after she opened her suitcase.

The coat was where it should be, hanging neat and square. Her mittens were still in her pockets. The phone pouch in the inner left front panel still held her emergency twenty-dollar bill. But Leigh was not comforted. While every one of her husband's garments faced to the left, her coat faced to the right. If she was hanging it herself, that would happen half the time.

With Warren, it would happen never.

She whirled around and looked at the room as a whole. It was clean; the bed had been made. Housekeeping had clearly been here. Was there any good reason the staff would rifle through her closet and suitcase?

No. Was she overreacting out of sheer paranoia? Warren could have been digging around in her suitcase. Maybe the housekeeper had knocked her coat off the rack and rehung it. The important question was, had anything been taken?

Leigh forced herself to take a few calming breaths. Then, after bandaging up her blisters, she set out on a more systematic search. Everywhere she looked, she imagined that both her things and Warren's seemed just a little bit... violated. The thought of it brought a sick feeling to the pit of her stomach, but try as she might, she could find no hard evidence of tampering. Not one item was actually missing. Warren had left change on the dresser; Leigh had cash in both her coat pocket and in her beach bag, none of which was touched. Her laptop and Warren's tablet remained in the drawer hidden beneath his socks. So *why*?

There was no logical reason. Ergo, nothing had happened.

Leigh heaved out a long, unsatisfying sigh and headed for the bathroom. She would splash some water on her face, get a grip, and then go find Bev. Leigh had been invited to a "Ladies' Tea" at the RV resort this afternoon, and although her original reply had been noncommittal, now she figured she and her blistered feet deserved some carbs. Particularly since she had forgotten lunch.

She freshened up, then looked in the mirror without enthusiasm. She was not in the habit of wearing a lot of makeup on vacation, or anywhere else for that matter. But since the rain had removed most of her morning mascara, she decided a quick touch-up was justified.

She reached for the cosmetic bag on the counter, blindly dug her fingers inside it, then watched in the mirror as her pupils dilated. What the—?

She looked at the square piece of plastic in her hands. It was smoky gray eye shadow. Her eye shadow. And yes, she supposed she had packed it... sometime before the twins were born. She only carried it around in the travel case because she'd never bothered to throw it away. It didn't bother her because she never saw it. It was buried too deeply.

Leigh's pulse raced as she stuffed the eye shadow back down in the bag and pulled out the mascara she'd been expecting to find. *Items may shift in flight.* Sure, that was it. Why not?

She applied the mascara hastily, stabbed herself in the cornea with the wand, waited five minutes for her eye to stop watering, then reapplied. Finally, in utter disgust with herself, she locked the door of the hotel room and hurried down the creaky steps and across the parking lot.

Her feet were killing her. Luckily, the RV Resort was only steps away, and Bev was easy to spot through the open windows of the small, modular building that served as a community center. The resort's activity director was buzzing about singing to herself as she arranged tables and chairs for the tea. Leigh knocked on the door as she opened it.

"Oh, come in! Come in!" Bev said happily. "I didn't think you were going to make it!"

Leigh gave the short version of her day, minus the more disturbing stuff.

"Oh, pull up a chair and have a seat then," Bev replied, referencing the blisters Leigh had limped in on. "I've got some salve I can loan you later. Works wonders, believe me." She offered some early refreshments, but Leigh declined. She felt guilty enough not offering to help with the hostess duties, but she truly was desperate to sit down.

Bev took a step closer, then peered at her with concern. "Did something happen to your eye?"

Leigh squirmed with embarrassment, then explained.

Bev chuckled. "I've done that. Sorry, honey."

Leigh returned the understanding smile, even as a new wave of coldness crept over her. She had put on mascara this morning, had she not? And yesterday. She *had* to have left it on top of the case afterwards.

"Something wrong?" Bev asked. "You look like something's bothering you."

Leigh gave up. "I could be wrong. But when I went back to my room just now, I got the distinct feeling that someone had gone through my stuff. Nothing was taken" — she added quickly, in response to Bev's sharp intake of breath — "which makes it all the more unbelievable. I keep trying to talk myself out of believing it. But… I just can't."

Bev stepped up beside her. A folding chair squeaked on the concrete floor as she pulled it out and sat down. "You mean that your things were… what, moved around?"

Leigh nodded.

"And you're sure nothing was taken?"

"Positive." Leigh explained about the cash and the valuables. "I know you probably trust your staff. So this is awkward. But I don't see how it could *all* be coincidence."

Bev's apple cheeks had colored to an angry red. "I trust Rosina, our head housekeeper, implicitly. I promise you this isn't about her. Although there's a tiny chance that her newest hire could have been up to some funny business…" She considered a moment, her brow creased deeply in thought. "No. I'm sure that's not it."

Bev's cheeks turned an even darker red, and Leigh sat up in alarm. "What, then?"

A low growl erupted from Bev's thick throat.

"*Sharonna.*"

Chapter 6

"Sharonna?" Leigh repeated.

Bev blew out a breath of consternation. "That sneaky little she-devil! It had to be her."

"But… why?" Leigh asked, her voice squeaking. She already had an unwelcome random association with one murder suspect. Wasn't having the privacy of her room violated bad enough without having the perpetrator be another Finney sibling?

"Oh, Lord only knows *why*," Bev said dismissively. "There's no point in asking 'why' where that woman's concerned. For all I know she's closet bi and thinks you're cute!"

When Leigh didn't respond, Bev turned to look at her. She smiled thinly. "Sorry, love. Didn't mean to distress you. It's like this. You hadn't been out the door five minutes this morning before Sharonna pops into the office all bubbly like, acting as if she and I are the best of friends. She's complimenting my hair and my shoes, when every other time I see her she's screaming that her washcloth's folded backwards or the soap's the wrong color. So right away I know something's up. Then sure enough, she starts in asking questions about you."

"About me?" Leigh breathed.

Bev nodded. "She'd seen you coming out of the lobby, and she said she thought she knew you. She was sure you'd met before, but she couldn't place you. She wanted to know if you were staying at the hotel, when you got in, where you were going…"

Leigh felt as though her blood had frozen. "She… You—"

Bev waved a hand. "Don't you worry about that. Hap and I take our guests' privacy seriously, no matter who's asking. I told her I didn't know you from a gnat's behind and that you'd just wandered in looking for a bathroom."

Leigh exhaled with relief. But the feeling was short-lived.

"But now I'm thinking she already knew better," Bev continued. "Maybe she saw you come out of your room earlier. Maybe she went back into the office after I clocked out and started hassling

Manny."

"Manny?" Leigh repeated, her spirits ebbing back to another low point.

Bev gave a sharp nod, her expression deep in thought. "He does afternoon and evening shifts. He's no fool; she couldn't get into the database on his watch, no matter what she said. He's got his own password and he knows better than to give out personal information. He might tell her you were a relative of Hap's if he knew that, but I'm not sure he does." Her blue eyes turned to Leigh with sympathy. "But one thing I suspect Sharonna *could* do is wrangle the key out of him. She could tell him she wanted to get up into the cupola — she does go up there to sketch sometimes, and if he gave her the master set, she could open your door, too. Or she could distract him away from the desk and just take the keys. She knows where they're kept. She does own a partial stake in the hotel, after all."

Bev scratched her chin for a moment, then slapped her hand on her thigh with a curse. "That's it. I'll bet you anything. She knew what room you were staying in, and she got the key and let herself in!"

"But..." Leigh resisted. "My makeup? My coat? My freakin' underwear? What could Sharonna possibly hope to accomplish by fingering through all that? Even if she thought she knew me? It makes no sense!"

Bev gave an open-handed shrug. "Honey, nothing that woman does ever makes any sense. She's a beautiful thing, or at least she used to be, before she got that world-weary 'used up' look about her. From what I understand, she was an adorable baby and an absolutely enchanting little girl. Her mother doted on her and her daddy worshipped the ground she walked on. Spoiled rotten, as you can guess. The younger sister doesn't look a thing like her; Janelle is what you'd call 'plain' and she was sickly as a child, and I hear the parents have always favored Sharonna pretty shamelessly. Listening to Cort talk, I don't doubt it. It was always Sharonna this and Sharonna that, but he hardly ever mentioned poor Janelle. And she's the one who's always worked in the business. Sharonna just flits around wasting her parents' money."

Leigh was trying hard to stay calm and think clearly. If Bruce knew Leigh's supposed mystery double, then was it such a stretch that his sister Sharonna would recognize the same face? Of course not. The two were close in age; at some point they must have gone to the same high school. They probably still traveled in some of the same circles. Bruce worked at the family's corporate offices in town; surely Sharonna had to visit there at least occasionally.

Leigh's mystery double was tied to both of them, somehow. Which put Leigh on the radar of two potential murderers.

Awesome.

"Bev," Leigh asked in as solid a voice as she could manage. "Do you think I should worry about Sharonna?"

Beverly's mouth twitched. "I doubt she's up to anything besides garden-variety nosiness. She's the type that bores easily and invents her own drama to amuse herself. But just the same, we should move you to a room in the back where you won't run into her again. We'll watch for her car to leave and then I'll help you move your stuff. I suppose you want to give the police a call?"

Leigh's blood ran cold all over again. "Um... that won't be necessary."

"Now, don't be pulling punches just because we're family, Hap and I," Bev said determinedly. "If you feel the need, why, you go right ahead and call."

Leigh hesitated. Trying to convince some local police officer that her inappropriately slotted cosmetics, refolded underwear, and experience of having random local people stare at her were *not* paranoid delusions held about as much appeal as running herself through with a flounder gig.

"I mean it," Bev insisted. "You have every right to complain. Sharonna's been allowed to get away with entirely too much bad behavior already, if you ask me. The only thing is..." Her expression became troubled.

"What?" Leigh asked.

Bev let out a scornful sniff. "I do worry that it wouldn't do you any good. Not here in Port Mesten, anyway. You see, our Chief of Police, Del Mayfield — he isn't a bad guy, but he's a good friend of Bruce Finney."

Leigh's mind flashed back to the scene in the coffee shop this morning. *Of course he is.*

"Not that there's any love lost between Bruce and Sharonna, mind you," Bev explained. "Shoot, Del and Sharonna have had a few go-rounds themselves, from what I understand. But if you're looking for impartiality when it comes to the Finneys, let's just say Port Mesten's finest is probably not the best place to go looking for it."

"Got it," Leigh answered, feeling oddly relieved. No crisis short of facing the barrel of a revolver would make her subject herself to the official company of any town's finest, but Bev didn't need to know that. All that was needed here, surely, were a few simple precautions. And maybe a little background research.

"Don't let me keep you from getting ready for the tea," Leigh said, forcing herself to her feet. "Surely there's some way I can help you without having to walk. Can I fill a coffee pot or something?"

Three minutes later she was at work in the small kitchen, stacking cups and dishes on a cart. "Tell me," she asked with as casual a tone as she could muster. "What do you know about the other two Finney kids?"

Bev finished loading a mixture of biscotti and lemon bars onto a platter, then licked a spot of yellow goo off her finger. Her brow puckered with thought. "I've only seen the younger girl once that I can remember, and that was at her daddy's funeral. She's a mousy little thing, for sure. Fair and pale; I've heard she's had troubles with bulimia. But nobody around here really knows her. She lives in Corpus Christi; if she ever came down to visit her parents, she wasn't out and about. All I ever remember Cortland saying about Janelle was that he was afraid she'd never get married because she spent all her time in front of a computer."

Bev's expression soured. "Cort was a sexist old fart, pardon my French," she grumbled as she washed her hands and dried them on her smock. "He valued looks and spirit in a woman. Didn't see much to be proud of in a plain, quiet daughter, never mind that Janelle was the only one who actually seemed to *want* to work with him in the business." She took the cart from Leigh and began to roll it out into the dining area. Leigh hobbled to the counter that separated the rooms and leaned over it to continue listening.

"Some people say she's the brightest of the bunch, but sadly that doesn't mean much. I've heard more than one old-timer around here say that you could add up the IQs of all four of those kids and still not equal their parents." Bev shook her head sadly. "Just lousy rolls of the dice, I guess."

"What about the younger son?" Leigh asked. Through the windows she could see two women walking toward them on the path, and she suspected they were headed to tea. Her time was limited.

Bev, seeing the women also, finished setting up the serving table as she talked. "Oh… *Russell*." She shook her head with disapproval. "Cort always talked about him like he was a teenager still sowing his wild oats, never mind that he was pushing forty when Cort died. Never worked, never married, never even had a permanent residence of his own, as far as I know. Just took advantage of dear old dad and whatever friends would have him. He's not worth talking about." She tossed a hand in dismissal, then crossed to hold open the door. "Hey there, Brenda, Joyce! How are you two doing? You and Wayne all ready for that cruise, Joyce?"

Leigh tried to put her anxiety out of her head long enough to indulge in a little social frivolity sweetened with carbohydrate, but the first guest at the Mesten Grande ladies' tea turned out to be even more uptight than she was.

"I don't know," the heavily accessorized, leathery-skinned Joyce said miserably. "We may have to cancel. Wayne's hip has been bothering him."

"Oh, it has not!" her more casually dressed friend Brenda argued. "He told me himself he was fine! You're just making excuses."

Bev guided the women to the serving table. "Now Joyce, you're not still worried about your motorhome, are you? Why, it'll be as safe here as in your own driveway. Probably safer, because all the neighbors will be keeping an eye out, plus we've got the cameras–"

"That's not what's bothering her," Brenda interrupted, stacking three lemon bars on a plate. "It's her cat she's worried about. She doesn't want to leave it, and the cruise ship says no cats, no exceptions, even with that therapy-cat certificate she bought online."

Joyce immediately turned teary. "She just gets so *lonely*, poor thing!"

As Bev simultaneously poured drinks, offered to visit Joyce's cat daily herself, and welcomed three more guests, Leigh's mind trained back on her own troubles. If Bruce and Sharonna had been the only people in Port Mesten to mistake her for her mysterious double, it might follow that the double was associated only with the family business. But that wasn't the case. Mr. Handsome at the beach had recognized her, too. So there must be a local connection, even if this mystery woman wasn't known to Hap, Beverly, the museum docent, the chief of police, or anyone else Leigh had randomly run into thus far. Perhaps someone whose time on the island was in the past?

Leigh stepped back from the counter and pulled out her phone. She had typed in three words when mother-guilt hit her like a bag of wet sand. *You terrible, horrible parent!*

She put her phone back down. But her analytical side had its own opinion on the issue. *Will you knock that off? What possible risk is this posing from fifteen hundred miles away? Besides, you know it would make her day!*

Leigh started typing again.

> By any chance, can you get access to old high school class photographs online?

She hit the send button before she could change her mind. Her daughter Allison, just home from school, texted back immediately.

> Depends. What do you need?

Leigh typed back quickly. Everything would be fine. The mother-guilt thing was an emotional overreaction.

> Port Mesten, Texas. Late 80s or early 90s, not sure. Looking for anybody named Finney.

"Leigh," Bev called from the dining room, "where'd you get to? Hobble on in here and meet the folks!"

Leigh silenced her phone, repocketed it, and obeyed. Despite her angst, she was starving, and the lemon bars smelled fabulous.

"Hey there," a perky voice greeted her, and she recognized Sue the birdwatcher from the pavilion. Bonnie sat in a chair beside her.

"Well, hello," Leigh greeted. "Did you find that... whatever it was?"

"Curve-billed thrasher!" Bonnie boomed with triumph, even as she scowled. "About damn time, too, even if it did cost me a broken ankle."

"You barely twisted it," Sue remarked matter-of-factly. She turned back to Leigh. "So you're staying here in the Grande, too? Are you with a better half?"

Leigh was able to make small talk without touching on any uncomfortable subjects, but she could not stop willing the phone in her pocket to vibrate. A good twenty minutes had passed before she remembered that she had turned that function off earlier when her battery ran low. She grew twitchy with impatience waiting for an appropriate break in the conversation during which she could pull her phone out and check it, but Joyce was now openly distraught. The cat lover seemed certain that her Snowbell would expire from grief if left alone overnight, and Leigh couldn't excuse herself without seeming rude. Luckily, when two different women offered to cat-sit Snowbell in their own RVs at the exact moment some exciting bird decided to perch on the satellite dish next door, Leigh was offered the distraction she needed.

She whipped out her phone and clicked into the message thread.

> Only yearbook I can find is 1989, but it has two Finneys, Bruce and Sharonna.

Leigh's heart beat fast. The internet was an amazing thing. Below Allison's text were two copied pictures. Both were black and white, mugshot-type class photos. The first was of a boy, clearly recognizable as the man with the prominent brow bone that Leigh had seen in the coffee shop. His face was thinner, his hair was wilder, and a goofy grin made him look like a total idiot, but his features were unmistakable. The girl in the second picture didn't look like a high schooler so much as an entrant for a beauty pageant. Dark hair billowed around her face in a giant fluffy cloud, her cheekbones were perfectly sculpted, and her dark eyes glittered like showy, precious gems. She gazed up and to the side with her chin cocked slightly downward, her generous, well-defined lips tilting up a tiny bit at the corners, as if to say, "Yes, you know I'm gorgeous!"

Oh my. So this was Sharonna. Allison had followed up with another text.

> The boy was a junior and the girl was a sophomore. No

extracurriculars, which is kind of weird. You want me to look up
anything else? I'm bored.

Leigh looked around the dining area and found two separate
conversations going on. The birders couldn't seem to agree over
whether the sparrow across the lawn was a savannah or a
grasshopper, and Joyce was back in tears again because she didn't
think Snowbell would be comfortable staying in a strange RV.

Leigh squelched her conscience again. Allison said she was
bored, didn't she?

I don't suppose you could flip through that yearbook and see if
any of the girls look like me? As in, is there anybody in there who
could be mistaken for me now?

Leigh sent off the text and put her phone away again, confident
that Allison was on it. Not being particularly interested in either
live conversation, she decided to take a few dirty dishes back to the
kitchen for Bev. While she was at it, she noticed that there was one
more piece of biscotti than there were lemon bars left, so she kindly
took it on herself to make the portions equal again.

After several more minutes of discussion, the bird had been
identified by consensus as a savannah sparrow, and Joyce had come
up with the idea that, rather than relocate her cat, one of her friends
should come over and sleep with Snowbell at night. This
proposition proved not nearly as popular, and as the women began
to make excuses for why they couldn't leave their own pets and
spouses, Leigh slipped her phone out of her pocket again.

Allison had replied already. Port Mesten must have been a small
high school.

Um... I'm guessing no. These three are the closest. I mean,
people change, but... Well, see for yourself. Still, like, just... no.

Leigh exhaled slowly as she scrolled through the black and white
pictures that followed. What Allison had said, in teen-speak, was
accurate. The girls in the photos all had dark hair and dark eyes and
basically oval faces, and they lacked really obvious identifying traits
like giant noses or buck teeth. But none of them looked similar
enough to Leigh to be confused with her.

Strike that idea, Leigh thought with discouragement, even

though she knew it was a longshot. Then again, this was just one yearbook. The younger two Finneys weren't even in it. Speaking of which...

> Can you find me present-day pictures of Janelle Finney and Russell Finney? They would be a few years younger, grew up in Port Mesten. Janelle works in Corpus Christi at Finney biz, don't know about Russell.

Leigh hit the send button with a feeling of optimism. Why hadn't she thought of this before? She and Warren had given Allison access to various databases for her twelfth birthday, and the girl enjoyed her research. Was Leigh's asking for her help so terribly wrong, just because the people in question could be criminals?

Yes, you terrible mother!

Leigh forced herself to rejoin the conversation in the dining room. Joyce had finally found someone in the group willing to leave her own motorhome and sleep over with Snowbell for a few days, and she was smiling for the first time all afternoon. "Oh, I am so relieved!" she gushed. "Snowbell will be so happy, she'll cuddle up with you all night long. And I did *so* want to go on the cruise. Really, I did!"

Everyone's mood lifted, and the next time Bev passed around the goody platter, it came back empty. Leigh hobbled over to pour herself a second cup of tea, obsessively checked her phone again, and was amazed to find that she already had texts waiting.

She debated whether she could politely read them. None of the other women were fussing with their phones at the moment, and the conversation had become more lively and all-inclusive. But she needn't have worried, because before she could take her seat again, Joyce had realized that Shirley couldn't possibly move in with Snowbell, because Shirley had two cats of her own, and if Snowbell smelled other cats in her bed she would certainly begin to pee all over everything...

Leigh read through the texts. The first was a screenshot of Janelle Finney's profile from a business networking site. It listed her as VP of Financial Strategy for Finney Enterprises, Inc., with various other, lesser titles in her resume, all with the family company. The profile was devoid of any extraneous information. The picture was of an unsmiling woman with very short, fair hair in a boyish cut. Her shoulders were thin and hunched. She wore dark-framed glasses that dominated her long face, and her chin was pointed with a prominent cleft. She couldn't possibly look less like her older brother and sister; although Leigh could see a definite resemblance to the pictures she'd seen of Cortland.

When she scrolled to the next image, her breath caught in her throat. *Not a hundred percent sure about this one,* Allison's accompanying note explained. *No link to sibs. But geographical area fits.* The photograph was from a social media site. It was a snapshot of a man sitting in a boat holding a bottle of beer in his hand. He was wearing nice casual clothes and appeared to be having a great time.

Leigh stared at the familiar cocky stance, the half-grown beard, the chiseled jaw. Her blood ran cold.

Hello, Mr. Handsome.

Russell Finney. Sibling number three.

So, she had not been recognized by a random local stranger after all. There was nothing random about him. Three people in Port Mesten had mistaken her for the same person. All three of them had been Finneys.

All three of them could be murderers.

Leigh slipped the phone back into her pocket with a shaky hand. She would text Allison her thanks later. Right now, she had to think. Whoever this accursed mystery double was, the woman was causing Leigh way more trouble than any innocent party deserved to have on vacation. And it was going to stop.

Now.

First order of business: Leigh's appearance. If this woman looked like her, then Leigh wouldn't. How hard could that be?

Second order of business: disappearing. Bev was right, she needed to switch rooms immediately. Unfortunately, the master keys Sharonna had managed to steal before could probably give her access to any room in the Silver King Hotel, which was legally owned by all four of the individuals Leigh wanted to avoid. She and Warren should stay in Corpus Christi, like they had planned originally. She would have some awkward explaining to do, but she could still drive back to visit Hap and Bev during the day…

Leigh frowned. Her instinct for self-preservation was strong, but she was also angry. Angry at the injustice of being uprooted when she hadn't done anything wrong. She *liked* staying here near the beach, dammit — being in a walkable tourist town, hanging with Bev and Hap, and eating Bev's delicious food. Now that she'd gotten a taste of family hospitality, the idea of staying in a generic city hotel held no appeal. Besides, from a purely practical standpoint, if she was going to spend any time in Port Mesten and someone was determined to tail her, could they not tail her to any hotel, even if it was in Corpus?

She made a split-second decision, and her jaws clenched. She would disguise herself — just enough. And, regrettably, she *would* leave the Silver King. But she would not leave Hap and Bev, and she would not go far.

"Joyce?" she said brightly.

Eyes liberally streaked with mascara looked up at her mournfully.

"If there's room in your motorhome for two," Leigh offered, "my husband and I would love to cat-sit Snowbell."

Chapter 7

Leigh adjusted Bev's floppy sun hat on her head, making sure the brim obscured as much of her face as possible while still permitting her to peer out. Her hair was covered by a bright scarf, and she wore a lightweight summery button-down shirt and casual capris. On the beach in Port Mesten she would blend right in, even if her headgear did put one in mind of a more fragile lady who was decades older.

Leigh was not on a beach in Port Mesten, however. She was not on a beach anywhere. She was sitting at a table in the main cafeteria of the twenty-eight story luxury office tower which housed the headquarters of Finney Enterprises. And she felt like an idiot.

But there was no turning back now. She had risen early and commuted into the city with Warren, and she'd occupied herself pleasantly enough all morning with a driving tour of the bayfront area and a visit to the Texas State Aquarium. Corpus Christi was an easy city in which to pass a day, even with blisters on her feet. But she had not come primarily as a tourist.

Her main objective had been a gut-level desire to get the hell away from Sharonna Finney. Since Joyce and Wayne weren't vacating their motorhome until later today, Bev and Hap had relocated the Harmons to a different room in the Silver King last night. Sharonna had been nowhere around during the moving process and, if she bothered to ask, would be led to believe the couple had checked out. Still, Leigh had slept uneasily, even behind a heavy slide bolt no master key could open. This morning she and Warren had packed their bags and left them at Bev's place, so nothing remained at the hotel for Sharonna to snoop through, whether she discovered their ruse or not. Still, Leigh did not care to run into the woman in the parking lot.

Leigh's second objective in coming to Corpus Christi was harder to justify. But as much as she wanted to stay away from the Finneys themselves, her curiosity over the existence of her mystery double was eating her alive. Who the heck was this woman, and did she really look that much like Leigh? All through the sleepless night, her brain had mulled the possibilities. This doppelganger knew at least three of the four Finney sibs. But since no one else in Port Mesten had yet to recognize Leigh, the odds seemed high that her look-alike knew the family through the business, rather than their hometown. What harm could there be in Leigh's placing herself where she might happen to see a random sampling of Finney Enterprises employees? As long as she herself was disguised, there would be no risk to it. Besides, she had to eat lunch somewhere, didn't she?

She reached out and dipped another french fry into her white-paper ketchup container. The fries had gone cold long ago and were soggy to begin with, but she was too bored to leave them uneaten. She'd been picking at her lunch for an hour now and hadn't spied a single candidate, and she was frustrated with her own disappointment. She'd known that her chances of seeing the woman were slim. Even if she did work for the family business, there was no guarantee she would be eating lunch in this particular place, either today or ever. But Leigh had been hopeful anyway. Finally, with a sigh of disgust, she tossed her dirty napkins on top of the remaining three broken fries and scooted back her chair.

Just as she rose and grabbed her tray, she saw a familiar face walking toward her. But it was not her own face. It was a face from one of the photographs that Allison had texted last night. The photograph of Janelle Finney.

Leigh sank back down into her seat. Janelle hadn't noticed her. The corporate exec, who was wearing a gray pencil skirt, matching suit jacket, and understated pumps, had emerged from parts unknown without a lunch tray and made a beeline for some man two tables over. She was standing over him now, talking earnestly, while tapping her finger at a folder tucked under her arm.

Leigh couldn't hear any of their conversation, but Janelle wasn't smiling. The man to whom she was talking had his back to Leigh, but the other faces at the table appeared uniformly uncomfortable, perhaps sympathetic.

Delighted with her luck, Leigh continued to study the youngest Finney daughter with impunity. Janelle was so thin she was practically skeletal, with blue veins standing out in her neck and running across her temples. Her fair hair was cut too short and styled too severely to flatter her already angular features, and the contrast of its hipster styling with her more conservative outfit and black-frame glasses was jarring. Her thin lips wore a frown, and the deep grooves around her mouth gave one the idea that such a position was their default. Her conversation with the man at the table seemed to be growing increasingly heated, but Janelle did not sit and he did not stand.

Leigh toyed with the brim of her hat as she pondered. She could easily believe this woman to be the type who lived at the office, so it made sense that Hap and Bev would rarely, if ever, find her haunting her old hometown just for kicks. And if Leigh's mystery double was a part of Finney Enterprises, there was no question that Janelle would know her.

Hmmmm. Should she?

Leigh threw a glance around the crowded room. She was perfectly safe here. What could happen? All she needed to do was register a reaction. Once she had the information in question, she could get up and leave. If she had any more trouble with the other Finneys, at least she would have a better idea why.

Her hands moved to remove the floppy hat. Then she untied the scarf. Her hair had to look like hell at the moment, but she couldn't obsess over that. What she needed to do was get Janelle to look her way. But inconspicuously, of course.

She gave her hair a quick fluff, then faked a cough. Nobody paid any attention. She tried a fake sneeze next, but that didn't work either, except that the man next to her glared and moved his tray away. When Janelle drifted to the side slightly, it was clear the conversation was nearing its end, and Leigh got bold. She stood up, lifted her tray, then "accidentally" lost hold of it, allowing it to fall back onto the table with a clatter.

Janelle looked in her direction. Leigh allowed their gazes to meet, trying to keep her own expression innocent and apologetic, even as she studied the other woman's pale blue orbs. *Does she know me? What is she thinking?*

The answer to the first question was obvious. One look at Leigh's face and Janelle's pupils dilated, her cheeks flared, and her body froze in place.

Oh, yeah. She knows me.

But the reaction, although conveniently unmistakable, was way too dramatic to be comforting. If the mystery double was a normal employee of the company, Janelle would recognize her, but not be surprised to see her. Could she be surprised that she was dressed so casually? Or... was it more that Janelle had just seen the same woman five minutes ago, three floors up, dressed entirely differently?

Oh, crap.

Perhaps this experiment wasn't such a great idea after all. Leigh picked up her tray again. It was time to make her exit. She stepped back from the table, scooted her chair in, then dared another look at Janelle.

The executive was still staring at her like a statue. But in the next second, Janelle regrouped. She swallowed, straightened her back, and readjusted her jacket. Then, with her eyes intentionally holding Leigh's, she gave one subtle but clear sign: a sharp nod.

What the...

Leigh kept watching, but Janelle's gaze moved away and she began talking to someone else at the table. Utterly baffled, Leigh carried her tray to the conveyor belt and loaded it on. She had to walk right behind Janelle to get there, but the businesswoman made no move to intercept her. When Leigh turned from the conveyor belt, she caught Janelle watching her again, surreptitiously.

Leigh found the nearest door and used it. This whole thing was getting entirely too weird. If Janelle knew her as a coworker who was dressed inappropriately, why wouldn't she just approach Leigh and say, "Hey, what's up with the outfit?" Janelle's initial bewilderment would make sense if she were literally seeing double, but what of the crazy nod afterward? How did that make sense? The gesture was so emphatic, yet so covert, Leigh could swear Janelle was trying to send her a secret message. But whatever she had to say, why didn't she just say it?

Leigh walked down a half flight of stairs to a mezzanine, then paused to stare over the railing at the people milling about in the busy lobby below. The scarf stayed in her pocket, but she put Bev's floppy hat back on and pulled it down low. She'd had enough cloak and daggers for one day. It was time to go back to anonymity. Maybe check out the Museum of Science and History and hang with some mannequins for a while.

She turned to look for the nearest staircase leading down to street level, then jumped a little. Janelle stood at the base of the stairs Leigh had just come down. She was watching Leigh silently.

Leigh stared back for an uneasy two seconds. Then, thoroughly creeped out, she began walking the opposite direction. She found a staircase leading down and took it. She mingled with the buzzing crowd in the lobby, made her way to the revolving front door, and exited. She walked half a block in the welcome sunshine, then spied a concrete bench by a palm tree and parked herself. She needed to think.

This was nuts. *She* was nuts. She would put her scarf and sunglasses back on and spend the rest of the week incognito if she had to, but whatever was up with the Finney kids and Faux-Leigh, she wanted nothing to do with it.

A cool shadow passed over her as someone briefly blocked the sun. Then Janelle sat down beside her.

Leigh sprang up. "Why are you following me?" she demanded, jumping away.

Janelle's baby blue eyes widened again. She looked almost embarrassed. "Don't you want me to?"

Leigh's answer didn't come for a beat. It took a while for her to process the question. Her pursuer seemed genuinely perplexed. How weird was this? "No-oo!" she stammered.

Janelle's face flashed with annoyance. "Okay, fine then!" she snapped, rising from the bench and whirling back toward the building. "You know how to reach me." The last words were stage-whispered over her shoulder. Leigh stood watching, paralyzed with confusion, while Janelle strutted to the revolving door and re-entered the building without looking back.

Chapter 8

Dawn had broken. But the change in ambient light made little difference to the ibis as it stroked its long, curved orange bill through the mud at the bottom of the marsh. Crustaceans could be stirred up in such a manner with or without the aid of his eyesight. If the dark hours had any benefit, it was merely that the area was quieter, with no humans gamboling about.

This morning, however, the ibis was aware of a difference in routine. The sun itself had not even appeared, yet there were already multiple humans nearby. He snagged an insect with his bill, lifted and swallowed the creepy-crawly with a gulp, then straightened his feathered white neck for a look-round. At the moment, he could see nothing concerning. He had noted one human earlier on the boardwalk, but one human on the boardwalk was of no concern. More unusual was the low-pitched cry he'd heard a moment ago, which was followed now by grunts and huffs, and the slapping and splashing of human feet in the wetlands.

The sounds made the ibis nervous, particularly since they seemed to be coming closer. Suddenly, a group of ducks twenty yards away exploded from their roost in a cacophony of squawks and flapping. Immediately alert, the ibis stretched his wings and fluttered up. He pinpointed the source of the disturbance, then returned to ground a safe distance away.

Humans. The ibis did not bother to wonder why two of them were running through the middle of the wetlands instead of staying on the boardwalk as the others did. He had no incentive to ponder why they might be out so early, how their bodies could be charging the very atmosphere with perceptible fear and rage, or what made one flee while the other gave chase.

The ibis did not care. He settled his wings behind him, then began rubbing his head along his back, oiling his glossy white feathers. But he could not preen in peace. The noise from the humans not only continued, it got louder. The people were moving in his direction.

The ibis stretched out his neck again and cocked one eye in the direction of the noise. He was on the edge of a rise now and could see fairly well out over the mud flats. The humans were touching now, struggling. More waterfowl vacated the area. The ibis heard a human cry, a smacking sound, a groan. The figures weren't upright anymore. They had disappeared into the tall grass. More birds took to flight, making as much noise as the humans were making.

The ibis stretched his wings and readied himself, then caught sight of a juicy worm on a grass stem. *Snap.* Swallow. The ibis returned its attention to the area where the humans had gone down. The noise seemed to have stopped. Wait… there was another worm. *Snap.*

Many worms here. *Snap, snap, snap.*

The ibis heard more human sounds, but these were more distant, and not alarming. They were coming from the boardwalk, like human sounds were supposed to. Low voices, free of tension, with the usual hollow plodding of feet on wooden planks.

One of the humans near the ibis stood up straight again. The figure was quiet now, and much of the charge around him seemed to have dissipated. The ibis watched as the human slunk away, this time making very little noise.

When the figure had moved completely out of sight, the bird lifted its long orange legs and waded back into the water. Those last few worms had been a little dry. He stuck his bill back into the silt and began to poke around for another crustacean.

If he was aware that the second human remained, lying motionless on the ground concealed behind the tall grass, the fact did not concern him.

Chapter 9

"Cats hate me," Warren griped.

"Don't be ridiculous," Leigh assured, stroking the purring white bundle of fur that had forsaken the cushiony cat bed in the wee hours of the morning in favor of Leigh's ribcage — and had not stirred since. "Only Mao Tse hates you. This is Snowbell."

Warren threw his wife a skeptical look as he adjusted his tie. He had to bend over to see himself in the mirror, and the shower had been a little tight, but otherwise he was as content as she was with their new lodgings in the deluxe forty-foot, Class A, quad-slide motorhome. Joyce and Wayne, it turned out, did everything first class. "I thought this was supposed to be a romantic vacation," he reminded. "If I want a hostile cat sleeping between me and my wife, I can get that in Pittsburgh."

Leigh laughed. "Snowbell loves everybody. You just didn't properly introduce yourself, that's all. Come and make friends. Scratch her behind the ears."

Warren made a face, but did as she asked. The cat yawned and stretched contentedly.

"See there!" Leigh insisted. "She accepts your right to exist. How could you possibly compare her to Mao Tse?"

He smirked. "Good point. Well, I'm off. Don't get into any trouble today."

Leigh hid her face behind the cat. He was joking. It was something he said most days. She'd told him about the Finney sibs seeming to recognize her, and he knew about Sharonna's snooping, too. But either he wasn't listening closely or he was distracted by the stress of his consulting job, because as far as she could tell, he didn't seem to register the connection between those incidents and the body found on the beach. Which was just as well.

"So, what are your plans today?" he asked as he grabbed his briefcase.

"Would you believe a morning bird walk?"

He laughed out loud. "Since when did you become a

birdwatcher?"

"Since Bev bribed me with more of her cinnamon rolls," Leigh confessed. "It's one of her community activities. Once a week the ornithology nuts get together and do a morning walk, either at the beach or on one of the preserve trails, and then they get together for brunch."

"Well, the brunch sounds good, anyway." He leaned in to kiss her goodbye, watching Snowbell warily as he did so. When the cat made no reaction he smiled and petted her behind the ears again. "Amazing," he muttered. "Later."

Leigh smiled down at Snowbell as he walked out. The cat looked back at her with eyes half-lidded. The feline was, in Koslow Animal Hospital lingo, a "domestic medium hair" as opposed to a purebred. But otherwise, Snowbell was as upper crust as everything else in the motorhome, including the remotely controlled awnings, the electric fireplace, and the four big-screen TVs. The cat's bright white hair was freshly shampooed and smelled like baby powder, she wore a soft blue collar studded with rhinestones, and her eyes were a striking shade of aquamarine. According to Joyce, she was deaf in one ear. But since Mao Tse's ability to hear had always been voluntarily "selective," Leigh scarcely noticed the difference. Personality-wise, the cat was an absolute darling. Since the moment Leigh had moved in last evening, Snowbell had accepted her new heating pad/servant with equanimity, displaying no angst whatsoever over the change of personnel.

Leigh leaned over in bed and looked at the clock. "Time to get moving, Snowbell, my dear," she said lazily. "I've got to bandage up these blisters if I'm going to earn those cinnamon rolls." The cat was not happy about losing her pillow, but when Leigh slipped out the door of the RV some time later, she was able to leave her charge happily consuming her prescribed breakfast: two different brands of commercial cat food (with gravy) plus a touch of fresh minced shrimp.

Leigh stepped out onto her hosts' spotless patio and admired what looked like another gorgeous day. It had rained hard earlier in the morning, but now the sky was clearing up, there was little wind, and the air was comfortably mild. She smiled as she walked by the wooden sign that was posted in the grass beside the patio. *The Nelsons. Edina, Minnesota.* Underneath the main sign two more hung by chains, one of which read "Joyce and Wayne" and another smaller one was pink, shaped like a fish, and read "Snowbell." A plastic yellow pinwheel was stuck in the ground beside the sign, and it turned lazily in the slight breeze.

RV living. Why not?

Leigh headed out to the wide, curving lane and began walking past other patios, yard signs, and funky lawn decorations and on toward the community greenspace in the center of the park. A few people were out breakfasting on their patios, and all acknowledged her with a smile and a friendly nod of the head, if not a called-out greeting, even though most had never seen her before. She turned a corner and met up with Sue and Bonnie.

"Well, Good Lord almighty," Bonnie drawled dramatically, peering at her through squinted eyes. "I thought for a minute there you were Jackie Onassis. You get yourself sunburned or something?"

Leigh's hand flew up to her scarf. She had sworn she was taking no chances today. Her hair was covered, she was wearing Bev's floppy sun hat, and yesterday she'd walked through a giant shark's mouth to shop in a beach store that sold the gaudiest sunglasses on the planet. She figured that if she wore this getup while hanging around with a bunch of birdwatchers, she'd almost certainly be taken for a woman decades older, particularly while limping on her blisters.

What she hadn't considered was how ridiculous she was bound to look to anyone who actually knew her. Although Bev was aware that she was trying to avoid Sharonna, Leigh hadn't discussed her encounters with the other Finney sibs. Not that she didn't trust Bev and Hap, but even to her own ear, those experiences sounded delusional, and trying to convince people she wasn't crazy had never been a favored pastime. Besides, there was no need. Her association with the Finneys was officially at an end now. Full stop.

That said, she didn't relish lying to the birdwatchers. They were such an earthy, unassuming group. These two women, in particular, she suspected could roll with some punches. "Honestly?" Leigh replied. "I'm trying to disguise myself. There's someone on the island I don't want to run into."

Bonnie huffed out an exaggerated sigh, took Leigh's arm in hers and gave it a pat. "Honey, say no more. Just hang with us. We've all got our little issues. Don't we, Sue?"

"Oh, that we do," Sue said evenly. She tilted her head back and raised her binoculars to her eyes. "Turkey vulture."

"Well, looky there," Bonnie said as they slowly drew within sight of their destination. A small crowd had already gathered just outside the community center. "Everybody else is here already."

"Good morning," Bev greeted them all pleasantly. "Well, I think that's everyone, unless... Did anyone see Stanley walking this way?"

"No," Sue answered. "I rapped on his door, but he didn't answer. I figured he was ahead of us."

"I expect we'll see him there, then," Bev replied. Her eyes rested on Leigh, and her brow furrowed. "You need binoculars."

"Oh, no," Leigh protested, "I'm —"

"Just a minute." Bev hurried next door to her own fifth wheel, then emerged seconds later with an extra pair. "Now you can do this right!" she said with perfect seriousness as she hung the strap around Leigh's neck. "All right, birders!" she cheered. "North entrance this morning. Who's driving?"

Twenty minutes later, Leigh found herself reconnoitering with the group near the same pavilion where she had met Sue and Bonnie the day before yesterday. The birders did not all stay together on their walks, she learned, but split into smaller teams to take the various paths in different directions. Apparently they had a system where those with cell phones group-texted each other with the identification and location of their finds, but Leigh let this critical information drift in one ear and out the other. All she wanted this morning was a peaceful, soul-recharging nature walk in a comparatively warm climate. If she could feel more sunshine on her skin, so much the better, but since the sky had clouded over again, she supposed her earlier optimism about the day had been misplaced. Everyone else must have seen a grim weather report, because all the birders had donned either a raincoat or a poncho, and the preserve itself was practically deserted.

No matter. Leigh's waterproof jacket was tied around her waist again, and extra socks and blister bandages were now official staples of her backpack. She would maintain her optimism.

She started out in a small group with Sue and Bonnie, but when the two practically broke out into a fistfight over whether they were looking at a greater or lesser yellowlegs, Leigh quietly withdrew and moved ahead. The tall observation tower she had noticed before was a good ways ahead along a winding trail that alternated between wooden boardwalk and gravel path. The surrounding wetlands varied from sandy plains with tall grass and some shrubs, to mud flats that might sometimes be submerged but weren't now, to wide expanses of brackish water that ran only a few inches deep, to ponds with enough depth to suit eight-foot alligators. The area where Leigh walked now seemed to have none of the latter, although she suspected that once she reached the tower, she would probably be able to spot some.

Overall, this trail was higher and drier than what she'd seen at the other entrance, with much of the boardwalk leading over nothing but wet mud. The occasional streams of water Leigh passed over were quite shallow, with no ducks and only some very tiny fish and bugs swimming in them. She suspected that on another morning, the giant mud flats could probably show some interesting animal tracks, but the recent downpour had left them as smooth as brownie batter.

Leigh heard some excited commotion from the couple ahead of her, and she looked up to see them fixing their binoculars on something in the distance. But whatever bird they were looking at, she still couldn't see. She looked down instead to study a school of tiny fish that swam in the scant two inches of water streaming beneath her feet. She smiled as the sun peeked out briefly, warming her arms.

This nature-walk thing was good therapy for her nerves. She should do it every morning.

The couple ahead soon began to natter at each other in less pleasant tones, and Leigh slowed her steps several times, hoping they would move on before she reached them. But she could not stall forever, and when she finally caught up with the woman she was surprised to find that the man was no longer on the boardwalk.

"Come back here!" the woman screeched. "Come back, you dad-blamed fool!"

Leigh looked up to see a man who appeared to be somewhere in his seventies standing in the mud about thirty feet away. He was facing the other direction, his binoculars trained on a large, long-legged bird that strutted along the side of a distant stream. The tracks leading from the boardwalk to him seemed to get deeper as they went. His feet were now invisible from the ankles down. "It's *got* to be a reddish egret!" he exclaimed.

"Well, good, then *get back here!*" the woman ordered.

The man stared through his glasses another few seconds. "With the sun at that angle I couldn't make out the colors — it could have been another tricolored heron — but I thought I saw the red neck for that one second, and then when he did that little hopping dance — did you see that? That as good as clinches it right there!" He swung around his upper body, attempting to pivot, but his ankles failed to move. The smile on his face turned to shock as he lost his balance and pitched sideways.

"Walter!" the woman screamed. "Your hip!"

"I'm all right!" the man called back unconvincingly. He had caught himself before he fell, but the twisting action must have cost him, because his face was contorted with pain.

"Oh! Oh, no..." the woman said worriedly as she looked at Leigh. "He's supposed to have surgery on that hip as soon as we get back. He should have had it done last fall." She turned back to her husband. "You need help?"

"No," he insisted stubbornly. But Leigh could see otherwise. Both of the man's feet were still stuck in the muck, and although he could put his weight on the left and move the right one around a little, any attempt to pull up on his left foot made him visibly wince.

"I'm coming after you," his wife insisted, laying her giant bag down on the boardwalk.

Leigh looked at the woman and cringed. Although she might not qualify as morbidly obese, her exaggerated pear-shape would fit right in with the women of Leigh's family. Her hips and thighs were so broad she waddled when she walked, her feet were impossibly tiny, and she looked like she might not be able to step the six inches off the boardwalk without losing her balance and injuring the knee she already had in a support brace.

"No," Leigh said quickly, putting a hand on her arm. "Let me. I think I see a way he can get back easier." Without waiting for an answer, she hustled a bit farther down the boardwalk until the mud flat ended and the grass began. Then she removed her headgear, shrugged off her backpack, and sat everything down out of her way. In this particular part of the wetland the shallow water, sandy mud, and solid grasslands swirled together in whorls like a giant maze. Grassy swamps and brackish ponds could be nearby, but Leigh chose to believe that any alligator-deep water was out of range.

She stood on tiptoe to see out over the brown marsh grass and plot what looked like her safest course to reach the stranded birder. He was standing just a few steps from the edge of a grassy area that looked to be more solid; if she could reach him without having to cross any of the mud flats herself, they shouldn't have any problem returning. But she knew that the wet, sandy soil's appearance could be deceptive. Standing in one place too long, like the man had done, was asking for trouble. The amount of water around one's ankles was a constantly shifting dynamic, and what seemed like solid ground one moment could become a lake the next.

She stepped off the boardwalk and was relieved to find that the footing here was stable. But once she was fully within the grass, she could no longer see her target.

"Walter!" the woman cried. "Walter!"

"Stop yelling, Barb!" the man called back peevishly. "Where do you think I'm going?"

"Then stop squirming around!" she ordered. "You're just making it worse! She's coming to get you, just hold still!"

Leigh felt like a colonial bushwhacker as she pushed the tall grass aside with her arms and plodded forward. The brush was so thick she could only see a few feet in front of her, and she had to assure herself repeatedly that alligators liked more water than this. After walking essentially straight for several yards, she was pleased to find that she had emerged from the thickest of the brush right where she had expected. The thin strip of grass in front of her did indeed connect to the larger "island" near where the man waited. But her smile soon faded. On closer inspection, the grassy strip didn't look so promising.

"Be careful, now!" the man called to her. "Don't get stuck yourself!"

Leigh felt for the fellow, whose head she could just see over the brush. He must find the situation humiliating, an emotion with which she was well acquainted. "No guarantees," she called back. "If a rescue squad has to come with rope and pulleys, we might as well make it worth their time, right?"

She thought that he laughed dryly, but she couldn't be sure, because his response was covered by the sound of a splash as the clump of grass on which she placed her foot instantly collapsed into three inches of water.

Dammit! She knew this was a bad idea. The grass here was like cattails; it wasn't rooted in anything solid. She scrambled around in the muck trying to regain her previous foothold, but the shelf on which she'd been standing also seemed to have collapsed. The sucking mud was only a couple of inches deep, and she was capable of shuffling her feet to keep moving, although it took some effort. Her main problem was finding a portion of bank solid enough to hold her weight as she scrambled back to drier land.

"Are you okay?" the woman called frantically. "Where did you go? Should we call for more help?"

"Leigh, is that you?" Sue's voice shouted.

"Yes, it's me," Leigh called back, working hard to keep her voice chipper as she sloshed along, each foot sinking to a different, unpredictable depth in the muck. Her calves would definitely be feeling this tomorrow. "No problem! Just give me another minute. I'm having to go the long way, that's all."

Just as she was beginning to think the bank would never present a satisfactory entrance ramp, and that she would have no choice but to go horizontal and thoroughly soak herself, she was saved by a piece of trash. She didn't know what the soggy piece of fabric used to be, and she didn't care. All she knew was that it was conveniently resting on top of a clump of vegetation, and that the combination of both things beneath one foot should give her enough purchase to leapfrog out of the wet zone. She sloshed over, took a breath, stomped on the mushy mess, and went for it. Her other foot landed and slid, but she caught herself with her hands before falling. *Land ho!*

She stood upright and slapped her muddy palms together with satisfaction. "Hang in there," she called to the man, whose head she could see again. "I'm still coming." Done with shortcuts, Leigh stood on her tiptoes, mapped out what looked like safest course, and returned to bushwhacking.

"Keep talking," she called out a few moments later. "I think I'm almost there!"

Walter didn't have to answer, because before the words were

even out of her mouth, she could see him standing in front of her. He smiled broadly.

"She made it!" Barb's voice rang out.

"Hooray!" multiple voices cheered.

Leigh stepped to the edge of the grass and looked toward to the boardwalk to see almost all of the birding group clustered around applauding. "Oh, my," she said under her breath.

"Indeed," Walter said dryly.

Leigh grinned. "Let's get this over with, shall we?"

"Please," he agreed.

Leigh found a suitably solid foothold a few feet away from him, and they agreed on a plan. She would take hold of his arms and, with some of his weight distributed onto her, he would try to dislodge his left foot from a more comfortable position. The ploy worked beautifully, albeit at the expense of his shoe, and once he was free Walter turned immediately to hobble off into the tall grass, ignoring the shouts of praise and encouragement emanating from the boardwalk.

Leigh was only too happy to let him lead the way. He moved like a man in a great deal of pain, but since it was obvious he would rather expire than ask for more assistance, she didn't offer any. He followed her trail of beaten grass with determination, walking at a faster pace than he probably should have, judging by his muffled grunts and stifled winces. Leigh said nothing until he neared the spot where she had jumped out of the water. "You'll want to start a new path here, since my shortcut was a fail," she advised. "If you bear right, I'm pretty sure we can stay on dry ground the whole way."

Walter, who was several inches taller than she was, straightened up and looked around. Then he bore to the right.

"Where are you?" a voice called from the boardwalk.

"Walter? We can't see you anymore!"

"We'll come out farther down," Leigh shouted back. "Don't worry, we're playing it safe."

Their progress slowed. Walter's hip injury was obviously getting to him.

"Alligators like more water than this, right?" Leigh joked.

Walter chuckled. "I certainly hope so."

They kept moving, slowly. Leigh tried not to think how

ridiculously far they were having to walk on solid ground to reach the same place Walter had gotten to within seconds by stepping out over the mud flats. But they were getting close, now. The chattering voices on the boardwalk were guiding them in.

"Hey, here's another trail!" Walter said with sudden optimism.

"That should make it easier," Leigh agreed, wondering what other idiot had been out thrashing around in prickly overhead marsh grass. She was starting to feel itchy. Weeds had never agreed with her.

Walter stopped short. "What is it?" Leigh asked. She was in no mood for another detour. She wanted a hot shower. Not to mention those cinnamon rolls.

He made no response. Leigh stepped around him. Ahead of them was a small, irregular area where the grass was cleared already: pushed aside, shoved over, mashed down. On top of the trampled grass lay a man with sunken, bloodshot eyes and a face that was grayish-purple.

Chapter 10

"Don't go any closer," Walter ordered, holding out his arm.

Leigh looked from the grotesque figure sprawled on the ground to the grim, set expression on her companion's face. She had no motivation to argue. She stood still while Walter slowly leaned in for a closer look. "He's gone," he whispered.

Leigh took another look for herself. She saw the body of a man who appeared to be in his sixties or early seventies, wearing duck shoes with casual slacks, a polo shirt, and a rain jacket. Everything he wore was sopping wet and smeared with mud. The jacket was torn and half pulled off. A bedraggled rain hat lay crumpled on the ground near his feet. A pair of binoculars was still attached to his chest by a harness-like contraption, but the straps had been pulled off-kilter, and the disturbed grass and chewed-up ground nearby bore witness to a struggle.

"Are you all right?" Walter asked her gently.

Leigh turned in surprise. No matter how long she lived, no matter how many more corpses managed find their way into her airspace during that period, she sincerely hoped she would never reach the point where she was "okay" with tripping over one. However, having the sympathy of someone who assumed this was a new experience for her was refreshing.

"There's nothing we can do for him now," Walter continued calmly. "Let's backtrack a bit so we don't disturb anything, then we'll wind around to the boardwalk and call the police."

Leigh allowed herself one more look at the ghastly purplish face. The man's head was tilted up, exposing the hollow of his neck, and even with his skin already discolored the bruising around his throat was obvious. This was no heart attack. The man looked as if he'd been strangled by someone's bare hands.

Leigh nodded.

Walter turned them both around and started off in a direction parallel to the boardwalk.

"Where are you?" Barb shouted with frustration. "Did you get lost?"

"Coming dear," Walter called back soberly.

Leigh began to have a sneaking suspicion. "Are you a policeman yourself?" she whispered as they moved.

"No," he answered. "I'm a pathologist. Well, a retired one, anyway."

"I see," Leigh replied, stunned. Her karma for corpses, as had been proven many times over, was both immutable and inescapable. But this time she'd been granted a bona fide guardian angel.

The power of positive thinking?

"There they are!" a voice called. Leigh looked out through the gradually thinning blades of grass to see Sue, Barb, and the others collecting on the boardwalk a few paces away. They cheered again as Walter preceded her out of the brush, and he managed to stand tall. But unfortunately, whatever injury he had done to his hip earlier made it impossible for him to step back up onto the boardwalk without assistance. Again, Leigh felt for him.

"Thank the Lord," Barb opined. "I thought we'd never get you out of there. What took you so long?"

Walter shot a glance at Leigh. He seemed to be saying, "Don't you worry, honey. Let me handle this."

Leigh returned the slightest of nods. Perhaps the feminist in her should resent his natural assumption that her delicate sensibilities should be protected.

Meh. She was good with it.

"There's something I need to tell everyone," Walter announced. "I have some very bad news."

Leigh raised an eyebrow. There was something personal in his tone, something she hadn't expected. The other birders could sense it, too. They quieted immediately and gathered around.

"I'm afraid that Stanley has passed away," he explained. "I'm guessing just a few hours ago. I'm not sure how he came to be off the boardwalk when it happened, but that's where he is, still. We just came upon him, right over there. We'll need to call the authorities. I'm sorry, everyone."

After a few initial gasps, the group fell silent.

Stanley? Leigh searched her brain for the reference. Of course. Stanley was the birder the group had decided not to wait on this morning. He must also live in the Mesten Grande, because Sue said she had knocked on his door. But the others weren't worried about him at the time, presumably because he often headed out earlier by himself.

So Stanley had been a birdwatcher. A perfectly innocent birdwatcher had taken a peaceful, early morning walk in the preserve… only to be strangled to death?

It couldn't be!

"Poor Stanley," Bev said finally, breaking the long silence. "I didn't know he had a health condition. Nothing serious, anyway."

"Are you sure he's dead, Walter?" Barb questioned.

The pathologist threw his wife a long-suffering look. "I'm going to call the police now."

Leigh kept her mouth shut. Being able to do so was a privilege she thoroughly appreciated.

"Oh, this is all so sad," Sue said with sympathy, approaching Leigh. "I'm sorry you two had to be the ones to find him, but I am glad that someone found him quickly. How awful." She looked around the group. "Does anyone know anything about his family?"

Bev spoke up as Walter connected with the police and walked away with his phone. "I know he was a widower," she explained. "He told us he bought the motorhome the year his wife died, and he's been coming down here every winter since. He never talked about family to me. The only other thing I know is that he was from Kansas City."

"He wasn't much of a talker, except when it came to birds," Bonnie offered. "But for a guy from Missouri who was afraid of airplanes, he sure as hell had an impressive life list!"

"He worked for it," Sue praised. "He'd go out at dawn every single day, rain or shine. He was determined to catch a crested caracara this winter."

"Well, maybe he got that tick after all," Bev said determinedly. "Maybe it was more excitement than his heart could handle. We might as well assume the best for him."

With that statement, the cluster of birders began an improvised group eulogy for a man whom none of them, sadly, appeared to know very well. Not knowing him at all, Leigh gradually slipped to the periphery. Other visitors to the preserve periodically approached on the boardwalk, doubtless wondering why the crowd had gathered, but by silent consensus the birders maintained a huddle and didn't look in the direction of the body. When Walter finished his call, he came to stand by Leigh.

"They'll probably want to take your name and ask us both some questions," he advised. "But you shouldn't have to hang around too long." He offered a small smile of encouragement.

Leigh smiled back tentatively. She had no doubt that — unless he was lying about being a pathologist — Walter was fully aware that Stanley must have been murdered. But she could understand his reasons for not saying so. It wasn't his job to tell anyone the "how," whether he happened to be capable of surmising it or not. Even giving details about the "what" would serve no useful purpose. An autopsy would be done by the proper authorities; the news would come out then. Stanley's family had the right to be notified first, anyway.

Leigh's eyes strayed to the grass that edged the boardwalk. The place where she and Walter had emerged was easy to spot. They'd made a trail of trampled grass so obvious it could be followed by a blind person — literally, and with a minimum of effort. But as far as she could see to either side, there was no other opening like it. If Stanley had walked directly from the boardwalk to where he lay now, he would have left his own trail of trampled grass.

So where had the victim and his assailant come from? She and Walter had met their trail maybe a dozen feet from where the body lay. But it hadn't appeared to be coming from the boardwalk. If it had, they would have followed the trail in that direction to begin with and never seen the body. But no, they had merged with the existing trail, because it had been coming from farther out in the marsh, just as they were. Stanley and his assailant had come from the wetlands, they had struggled, and Stanley had fallen.

Where did his assailant go afterwards? Not back to the boardwalk. At least not the shortest way. Leigh tried to remember if she had seen another trail leading away from the body, but no helpful images came to her. Her attention had been focused elsewhere.

She looked up to find Walter's steady gaze studying her. He had to wonder how much of the truth she suspected. Would most people register the significance of ecchymoses around the throat? Most people wouldn't know that the dark, discolored areas of broken blood vessels were called ecchymoses, but you didn't have to know what they were called to think of strangulation when you saw them.

"My dad is a veterinarian," she explained in a whisper, although she wasn't sure why she felt the need. "I helped out in his clinic a lot of years."

Walter's level gaze continued to study her. When he nodded solemnly, Leigh got the feeling they understood each other.

A siren sounded. Port Mesten wasn't a big place, and it did not take long for the local police to arrive. As Leigh expected, the first officer on the scene followed her and Walter's existing trail into the weeds looking confident, only to emerge a few moments later with his phone to his ear calling for backup. The Texas Rangers arrived soon afterward. The police immediately closed the entire preserve to other traffic, but the birding group was allowed to remain nearby during the initial questioning. Leigh found herself glad for their moral support. She recognized the police chief, Del Mayfield, but thankfully he had no Finney with him, nor did he show any sign of recognizing her. Not that he should, based on their brief encounter at the coffee bar, but stranger things had happened to Leigh.

Walter introduced himself as a retired pathologist and was interviewed extensively. He showed the Rangers exactly where he had gotten stuck originally, and what path he and Leigh had taken to walk back out again. He described how they had found the preexisting trail and joined it. He assured the authorities that he had established immediately by visual inspection that the man was dead, and that neither of them had touched the body. He also admitted, within hearing only of Leigh and the police, that he had been careful not to disturb the scene because he suspected foul play.

When the detective in charge finally turned to Leigh, he had almost nothing left to ask her. He needed a few points to be clarified about the path she took in reaching Walter to begin with, and he wanted her contact information. Other than that, he did not seem too terribly concerned with her. He was respectful, but in a dismissive sort of way, as if she were just one more unimportant bystander. Then he thanked her and told her she could leave.

It was her best police experience ever.

"Come on, sugar," Bev said warmly, throwing an arm around her. "Let's get you back home and get some food in you, shall we?

We've all had a tough morning. No sense in starving ourselves on top of it."

Leigh smiled weakly. If she was a better person, she probably would have lost her appetite. But the older she got, the more she took after her corgi. Stress or no stress, she could always eat. And right now, anything that came from Bev's oven sounded fantastic.

"Those Texas Rangers must think Port Mesten's going to hell in a hand basket!" Bonnie groused as the group finally began to move toward the parking lot. "Sleepy little place, nothing ever happens, and then *this*... twice in one week!"

"Oh, you can't possibly compare the two!" Sue chastened, as if even discussing the subject were inappropriate. "A man dying of a heart attack is an entirely different situation from... that other thing!"

"Well, of course it is. But when the Texas Rangers have to come out—" Bonnie's voice dropped out suddenly. "Wait a minute. Why did the Rangers come, anyway?"

Leigh felt her jaws clench. Walter had caused everything to proceed so smoothly, she almost had herself believing the worst of the unpleasantness could be avoided — at least until after she and Warren were safely back in Pittsburgh.

"I suppose it's standard procedure when a body is found in a public place like that," Sue answered. "After all, if nobody was with him, they can't be certain of what he died from until they've done an autopsy."

Bonnie harrumphed. "Well, I suppose that makes sense."

Leigh relaxed a little. But not much. Bonnie's suspicions hit too close to home. More than one townsperson had recounted that before the body of Ted Sullivan washed up on the sand, there hadn't been a murder in Port Mesten in nearly a decade. Now, within one week, she knew that there had been two.

Statistically speaking, what were the odds of two such homicides *not* being connected?

Leigh tried hard not to think about it. She didn't need to think about it.

She was not involved.

Chapter 11

"Are you ready for your walk?" Leigh asked.

Snowbell replied by leaping into her snazzy pink and black stroller the second Leigh had popped it fully open. However, after a quick turn around and a derisive flick of her fluffy white tail, the cat promptly leapt back out again.

"What?" Leigh asked, baffled. She looked into the carriage area of the ridiculously plush pet stroller, which had large netted windows for airy viewing, as well as a removable plastic overlay for inclement weather. "Oh," she remembered suddenly. "Right." She dug into the storage compartment underneath and pulled out a waterproof pad, then spread it out in the buggy. "Now, your highness?"

Snowbell hopped obligingly back in the stroller, sat up straight, and curled her tail primly around her bottom. *Ready.*

Leigh rolled her eyes as she zipped the cat inside. In explaining why the stroller should always be lined with a pad, Joyce had merely said, "Snowbell doesn't like the other kitties." Why Snowbell herself cared whether she sat on a waterproof liner was an open question.

Leigh moved the stroller to the doorway of the RV, stepped around it and outside, and then lifted it down the steps as she had been instructed. Joyce had insisted that Snowbell never be carried outside in anyone's arms, but should be secured in the stroller first. When Leigh had asked why, she'd gotten the same oblique explanation she'd received about the pad.

She locked the door of the motorhome and headed out. It was midafternoon, and although there had been no heavy rain since early morning, the sky was still gray and cloudy. It seemed that everyone who lived in the Mesten Grande, however, felt a sudden need to experience the great outdoors. No doubt this was because a half-dozen law enforcement types had descended on Stanley's motorhome and had been streaming in and out of it for the better part of an hour, occasionally carrying boxes or bags.

Or so Leigh had been told. Bev had texted during her nap to inform her of the development. Leigh did not consider the deceased's affairs to be any of her business, officially. However, she *had* promised Joyce she would walk the cat every day.

She pushed the stroller down the lane and around a bend without incident. She was wearing the floppy hat and scarf, but had left the sunglasses behind. Bonnie had been right about the Jackie Onassis look; wearing shades on a cloudy day only made her look more conspicuous. The half disguise wouldn't fool any of the birdwatchers who had been with her this morning, but it should sufficiently mask her identity as far as any stray Finneys were concerned. She didn't know where Stanley's RV was parked, but everyone's attention seemed to be focused in the same general direction, and that was where Leigh steered the stroller. Because... well, because Snowbell liked people.

She wound around another curve and saw several official-looking vehicles blocking the street ahead. "Leigh!" Bonnie's husky voice called earnestly. "Over here!"

Bonnie, Sue, and several men were clustered on a patio near a red painted sign that read, "Hank and Bonnie Gresham, Edmond, Oklahoma." Leigh studied the assembled men of potential husband-age, wondering who went with whom, but since the men were deeply absorbed in their own conversation, no introductions were made. "Have you heard the latest?" Bonnie stage-whispered conspiratorially.

Leigh braced herself. She moved closer. "I'm not sure. I've been taking a nap."

"It's only a rumor!" Sue interjected critically.

Bonnie, who was seated in a patio chair that seemed dangerously flimsy for a woman of her size, looked at her friend with a melodramatic expression. "Think what you like, Little Miss Sunshine, but I heard that the police as much as confirmed it." She turned back to Leigh. "Word has it that Stanley's death wasn't an accident. They say he was strangled to death."

"I don't believe it," Sue snapped.

Leigh hesitated. For the information to leak this fast, it almost had to have come from the police. "But why?" she demurred.

"Why indeed," asked one of the men Leigh didn't know. "Stanley wouldn't hurt a fly. You ask me, between him and that other one, we got a serial killer on our hands."

Another of the men made a rude sound, apparently in objection.

"Well, why else is anybody going to strangle a guy like that?" the first man defended. "He was, what? Seventy? It's not like some thug would have to kill him to get his wallet!"

"I'm sure he wasn't strangled," Sue said flatly. She was standing up, but not standing still. She kept shifting her weight from one foot to another and twitching her arms. Even when her words made her seem at ease, the woman was jumpy as — ironically — a sparrow.

"I heard he was strangled with his own binoculars!" the first man lamented. Much speculation followed, but Bonnie soon quelled the debate. "No way. That didn't happen, because Stanley didn't wear a neck strap," she said decisively. "He was a bino bra guy. Must have had a pinched nerve in his neck or something."

"What's a bino bra?" one of the men asked.

"Shoulder harness," another answered. The new speaker was a particularly hefty soul who occupied another too-flimsy lawn chair. He was holding a cigar in one hand and a beer in the other, and he sported a gray beard so long its tip rested on a roll of his belly fat. "I've got one of 'em, but I don't like it. Gives you man-boobs."

Bonnie scoffed. "Well, something does." She tossed her head in the man's direction. "My husband Hank. Hank, this is Leigh."

Leigh nodded. "Nice to meet you."

"Hey, you saw the body, didn't you?" Hank demanded hotly. "What did it look like? Was he strangled with something?"

"And yes, he's always this charming," Bonnie added sarcastically.

Everyone's eyes had turned to Leigh. In her mind she could see again the harness-like straps twisted across Stanley's torso. She could see more than that. But she didn't want to. She made a split-second decision. "I can't say," she lied. "I really didn't see much."

Sue jumped to her defense. "Walter Kreger's the one you should be asking."

Hank scoffed. "He's not saying much of anything, I heard."

"Wait! Isn't he a doctor or something?" another man asked.

Snowbell chose that moment to mew. Her voice was well-mannered, but her displeasure was clear.

"Well, I should keep moving. Snowbell's word is law, you know," Leigh explained, delighted with her charge's timing. She said goodbye, escaped without further introductions, and set off in the opposite direction from the roadblock.

The winding streets with their angled slots for the variously sized RVs offered more yard space per resident than most RV parks, but everything was still so close together that it was difficult not to eavesdrop on each and every passing patio conversation. Leigh not only kept hearing the "M" word as she walked, but the term "serial killer" kept popping up as well. Some people were so disturbed they were considering leaving Port Mesten. Apparently, at least one couple had already checked out of the park.

Concerned, Leigh rolled Snowbell onto the narrow asphalt path that led through the community greenspace, then stopped at Bev and Hap's patio. No one was at home, but in the park office building next door she could hear Bev talking on the phone. It sounded like the poor woman was dealing with a second early checkout.

Snowbell politely mewed another complaint.

"Yes, dear," Leigh agreed, pushing the stroller again. She could hear the conversation on the next patio before the people came into view.

"Do you really think that's a possibility?" a woman asked, her voice full of fear.

"Of course!" a man insisted. "It's the only thing that makes sense!"

Leigh recognized the voices of a Canadian couple who had been with them on the bird walk this morning. She remembered that they were longtime snowbirds in Port Mesten, but she couldn't recall their names or much else about them.

"Walter said Stanley had been dead 'a couple hours,'" the man continued. "Well, it makes perfect sense that he went out at dawn then, like he usually does. And you know where he goes. He likes to be up in that observation tower so he can keep an eye on the skies all around, as well as the wetland. You can see part of the beach road from there, too. So there's no telling what he could have seen. But I bet you anything, somebody else saw *him*."

"Oh, but it's such an awful thought!" the woman cried.

Leigh stopped moving. The man's words struck a piercing chord in her brain. *Of course.* Stanley had been awake and looking through his binoculars at a time when most people were at home and sound asleep. Someone quite far from that observation tower could have thought their actions were invisible, only to look up and see the silhouette of a man. A man with greatly magnified vision.

"But what could he have seen?" the woman asked. "I mean, nothing ever happens in Port Mesten!"

The man let out a scoff. "Didn't they just find another body a couple days ago?"

Leigh's feet started moving again. It was bad enough imagining that Stanley had met his end for doing something as harmless as birdwatching alone on a peaceful, rainy, quiet morning in the wetlands. Connecting his murder with that of Ted Sullivan and whatever the hell was going on with the weirdo Finney sibs really was too vile to contemplate.

She approached the couple's patio at a normal walking pace. She knew they would recognize her from this morning, but with luck they wouldn't assume she'd overheard anything. They would just say hello and change the subject. She pushed the stroller ahead of her, and as the patio came into view Snowbell leapt up onto all four paws. The couple were sitting on a rocker loveseat; a fat brown tabby was curled up on the woman's lap.

None of the three people got a chance to say anything. Snowbell went — to choose a singular word — *nuclear*. The fluffy ball of white exploded into hisses, growls, and screams, and the stroller rocked violently as the cat tore up, down, and around the netting like a crazed hamster inside an exercise ball.

"Snowbell!" Leigh cried. Was she having a seizure?

"Oh, not again!" the woman said with a laugh, getting to her feet with the tabby in her arms. "Take her away, Leigh! Nothing else will help!" She turned her back so that her own cat wasn't as visible, but the tabby's back paws and tail still hung languidly out past the woman's side. Whatever was going on with Snowbell, the tabby obviously didn't give a damn.

Leigh said no more, but followed instructions and got moving. "Calm down, Snowbell!" she chided as she jogged away with the stroller. "That mean, horrible cat's all gone now, okay? Sheesh!"

Snowbell performed a few more full revolutions inside the carriage before her head appeared in the window, looking back the way they had come. She was panting.

"Really, he's gone," Leigh assured. "Would I lie? I mean, about this, anyway?"

Snowbell stared out the rear window until they left the greenspace altogether and returned to their own street. Then the cat returned to her original spot in the front of the carriage, curled her tail around her bottom, and began to daintily lick a front paw.

Leigh groaned. She hurried back home, keeping her eyes downcast in an effort to avoid any further "friendly" conversation with her new neighbors. She didn't see Warren sitting outside until she reached their patio herself. "Oh!" she said with surprise. "You're back early!"

Her husband rose. He tried to smile at her, but his effort was half-hearted. Probably because he knew he had zero chance of fooling her when his forehead was covered with stress creases.

"What's wrong?" Leigh asked warily. "I thought you had another full day at the office today."

"I have a full day's work to do," he answered. "But the woman I was working with had another meeting all afternoon, so I decided to finish up here."

Leigh didn't buy it. The motorhome was nice, but its design was hardly optimal for spreading out paperwork. "Keep going," she said warily.

"Can we talk inside?" he replied.

Leigh had no argument with that. Warren helped her carry the cat stroller back up the steps, and as she leaned down to unzip the top she realized exactly why Joyce had insisted on the waterproof liners.

"Lovely," Warren remarked as Leigh rolled up the soiled pad and stuffed it into the covered trash bin. Snowbell, who had leapt from the stroller immediately, was now contentedly grooming herself in the center of their king-sized bed.

"Snowbell doesn't like the other kitties," Leigh parroted. She collapsed the stroller, returned it to its storage compartment underneath the RV, then shut the door behind her. "Now, I repeat. Why did you come home early? For real this time, please."

Warren's brown eyes bore into hers. "I was worried about you."

"Why?" Leigh asked, feeling suddenly indignant. No way did he know about this morning already. Her name wouldn't be in any news reports in Corpus Christi and she was the only person in Port Mesten who knew his cell number.

He blew out a breath. "Allison sent me a text. She fired it off the second she got home from school today."

Leigh was confused. Allison couldn't possibly know anything. "Why was she texting you? I told her I'd let her know if I needed any more research on the Finneys."

"Yes, well, she said she was really bored last night. And she figured you probably weren't telling her the whole story about why you were asking. So she kept digging into the family, and of course it didn't take her long to pull up the story about the body of the Finney Enterprises CFO washing up on the beach in Port Mesten."

Leigh realized, grimly, that Warren was worried about something else entirely. "That whole business happened before we even got here," she said defensively.

A smile tugged at Warren's lips. "She's aware of the timing, I'm sure. But under the circumstances, she decided to make up a complete dossier on the family. She planned to surprise you with it later today, but she ran into a few things she didn't understand, and she forwarded the links to me. They were financial stories about the family business."

Leigh frowned. She'd been trying very hard to stay out of this mess. How dare her own husband and daughter act like she was already in it? "So?" she demanded.

Warren shook his head. "I haven't had a chance to look into it yet. But after skimming the articles, I can tell you that the public face of what's been going on with the family company doesn't jibe at all with what Hap's been telling us. To hear the media tell it, ever since Bruce Finney took over for his father, business has been booming."

Despite herself, Leigh raised an eyebrow. "Hap said Bruce was an idiot. He said they were all idiots. How could the business be doing better? Particularly if the four of them don't get along?"

Warren shrugged. "A valid question. I thought I'd look into it if I finished up early enough tonight. But when I got here and stepped out of the car, the first thing I heard was how another body had been found at the nature preserve. And how it was a man who lived in this park. And how the rumor was that he had been strangled."

He had the gall to look at her expectantly.

"Is that all you heard?" she prompted.

"Yes," he replied, still studying her.

Leigh's face felt hot. She crossed her arms over her chest. "So why are you looking at me like that?"

His brown eyes smiled at her, even as his expression remained sober. He said nothing.

Seconds ticked by.

Leigh uncrossed her arms and threw her hands to the side. "For your information, I was not the first person to find his body!" she informed resentfully. "I was the *second* person, by a solid two and a half seconds, and I am considering that progress. So don't go bursting my bubble!"

Warren stepped forward and folded her in his arms. Leigh appreciated the gesture despite her pride, and she leaned into his chest with a sigh.

"Sorry," he said simply.

"It's whatever," she replied glumly. "But otherwise, I am *not* involved. You hear that? I am *on vacation.*"

Warren was silent for several beats. "Okay."

A knock sounded on the door.

Chapter 12

"Sorry to barge in on y'all like this," Hap apologized as the three of them seated themselves at the motorhome's expandable dining table. "But I thought this was a conversation best had in private." He squirmed uncomfortably in his chair, and Leigh found herself doing the same.

What now?

"I had a little talk with Sharonna today," Hap began, not helping Leigh's nerves in the slightest. "Several, actually. The whole situation with her snooping in a guest's room isn't acceptable, whether you're willing to file charges or not, and it can't happen again. So I decided I'd try to get to the bottom of it. But with Sharonna that's not easy, and I'm not sure I understand a damn thing more now than I did when I woke up this morning. But what she told me, I figure you two have a right to know."

Leigh needed a cat. She got up and scooped Snowbell off the bed, then returned and placed the unresisting lump in her lap. The cat immediately began to purr. *There, that's better.*

"Go on," Warren said, leaning forward.

"Well, first off, there's no question she did it," Hap explained. "Manny confirmed that she asked him for the key to the cupola Tuesday, and that she brought it back about two hours later. She said she was going to do some sketching, and he didn't have any reason not to believe her. We've never had a problem like this before. When I caught up with her yesterday, she admitted getting the key from Manny, but claimed she'd accidentally left the whole ring sticking out of the door the while she was sketching, and that anyone could have taken it out and put it back. Unfortunately, she made a pretty solid case for herself, since we both knew she probably would do something that bone-headed."

"And yet she thinks pretty quick on her feet," Warren noted.

Hap's thick lips twisted into a frown. "More like she had overnight to get her story straight," he argued. "She'd been hiding out until then, avoiding me. But I couldn't leave it like that, so I told her I was going to have a talk with Bruce about the situation."

Leigh remembered the tense conversation she'd overheard through the wall her first night at the Silver King.

We're each going to get our fair share, I promise you. Just like Mom and Dad wanted, the man had said. Bruce? His voice was higher and more nasally than the younger brother, Russell, who had spoken to Leigh at the beach.

What they wanted? Sharonna had spat back at him. *You think this is what Dad wanted?*

"Well," Hap continued, "When I mentioned her brother's name, Sharonna straightened up and got serious real quick. Said there was no reason bringing Bruce or anybody else into it, that the hotel was her baby since she practically lived there, and that she could handle the situation herself. She claimed she'd hire a locksmith to rekey all the guestrooms and said she'd personally report the situation to Del Mayfield."

Hap paused and scratched his head. "Since she is part owner and technically my boss, that was hard to argue with. I didn't think she'd tell the chief bupkis, but since you guys were safely checked out already I figured I'd give her the rest of the day, and then I'd go see him myself first thing this morning."

"And did you?" Leigh asked.

Hap's eyes, which were looking distinctly bloodshot, seemed regretful. "I tried, but I got delayed here at the office, and by the time I got to the police station they'd all been called out to the preserve."

Leigh did not need to ask why. She had seen Del there herself.

"What Manny had to tell me this morning complicated things," Hap went on, sounding increasingly discouraged. "You see, for Sharonna, doing something stupid and screwball on impulse and then lying to cover it up is par for the course. She's been pulling that sort of nonsense her whole life. But what she did last night was different."

Leigh buried her hands in warm cat fur, absorbing the soothing rumble beneath her fingertips.

"Right around midnight, she showed up at the front desk with a bottle of imported beer and started acting like Manny was the hottest number in South Texas," Hap explained. "Now, don't get me wrong. I've heard my own wife talk about what a looker that boy is. But Sharonna's never given him the time of day before, and truth be told I've never seen the woman chase after any man. She's too used to being the one getting chased. But she starts cozying up to Manny nevertheless and tells him she's decided to take more of an interest in the Silver King and she's thinking it's about time she made him manager. Then she practically crawls in his lap and begs him to show her how the computer works, because — get this — she always thought it would be fun to be a desk clerk."

Warren made a whistling sound under his breath. "Subtle."

Hap sighed and looked at Leigh. "Don't you worry, honey. Manny may not come from money, but he's sharper than five Sharonnas. He told her the server was down, and then he got out some old logbooks and pretended like he was having to figure out a bunch of bills with a pencil and a calculator." Hap chuckled bitterly. "He said all he had to do was make an honest effort to explain to her how all the charges were itemized and how to add the tax and everything, and she found an excuse to get out of that office right quick."

Leigh let out a laugh, but the sound was hollow. She could sense that Warren was growing more anxious as well.

Hap leaned forward. "The thing is, trying to trick Manny into giving her access to that computer was devious. Sharonna planned it ahead of time. She also knew she was taking a risk, since I was watching her. That means that whatever information she wanted, she wanted it bad." He paused and exhaled loudly. "Until this morning, I thought her picking your room to rifle through was sheer bad luck. No rhyme or reason to it. But now I know better. I checked in with Rosina and found out Sharonna's asked two of the maids if they knew exactly when you checked out and what kind of car you were driving."

"What?" Warren cried.

"They didn't say anything," Hap assured. "Rosina has them all pretending they can't speak English whenever they get inappropriate questions, and Sharonna's never learned a word of Spanish." He turned to Leigh. "The long and short of it is, Sharonna wants to know where you've gone. For whatever reason, she seems a mite obsessed with you. You have any idea why that might be?"

Warren let his hands drop down onto the tabletop with a thud. "It's not just Sharonna, Hap!" he informed, throwing an accusatory sideways glance at Leigh. "It's Bruce and Russell, too! They both acted like they recognized her when they saw her!"

"Are you kidding me?" Hap exclaimed.

Now both men were staring at Leigh wide-eyed, and she wished she could take her cat, slide down under the table, and keep going. After her disturbing lunch at Finney Enterprises yesterday, she had treated herself to a fabulous boat cruise, during which she had put her blistered feet up and spent the afternoon watching bottle-nosed dolphins playing in the channels. She had told Warren all about it on their drive home and then he'd turned in early... could she have neglected to mention her little adventure with Janelle?

She cleared her throat and braced herself. "Actually, all four of them seem to know me," she admitted.

"What?" Hap shouted, bolting out of his seat. "What do you mean they 'know' you? Why didn't you say something?"

"Yes, why didn't you?" Warren added sardonically.

"Because it didn't seem like that big of a deal!" Leigh insisted. "It's not like anybody was threatening me. It's just that I look like somebody all the Finneys know... or at least somebody they used to know." She described, in terms as brief as possible, her encounters with the other three siblings. "There really was nothing sinister in any of it. I wouldn't have given it any thought at all if it weren't for the murder of that CFO. And I have no reason to believe that any of that is related to what happened to Stanley, either," she finished defensively.

The men settled gradually back down into their chairs.

"I don't know what to make of Stanley's death," Hap said quietly. "I'm still hoping the rumors are wrong and that he died of natural causes. But Leigh, honey, I don't care for the rest of it one bit. I haven't even finished telling you about Sharonna."

Leigh could feel Warren tense up again. She raised an armful of cat and buried her face in the fluff.

"The local police had their hands full all day," Hap continued. "So I never did get to see Del. But I did confront Sharonna again this morning. I told her I knew what she was up to with Manny, and she broke down like a child. Cried a river of tears, begged me not to tell the police or Bruce about it. When I pressed her for an explanation she told me that you were a classmate of hers from Ole Miss, and that you'd been blackmailing her for years over something that happened when you were both in college. She admitted she went through your room, but insisted she was only looking for what belonged to her. I asked her if she found it and she said no, that's why she needs to know where you've gone now."

Leigh lowered the cat. "Wow," she said after a moment. Could Sharonna possibly be telling the truth? "Did she actually go to Ole Miss?"

Hap shrugged. "Cortland said once that she failed out of college, but I don't remember him saying where."

"What did you tell her?" Warren asked.

"Nothing," Hap replied. "I couldn't. She has no idea you're family. As far as she's concerned I don't know the two of you from a hole in the wall."

"Well, that's for the best," Warren agreed.

"Except that I couldn't convince her that it was a case of mistaken identity," Hap replied. "Then again, for all I know, her whole story's a lie anyway."

"Would all three of her siblings know a classmate of hers from her college days in Mississippi?" Warren asked.

Hap pulled a handkerchief from his pocket and wiped the sweat from his brow. "Lord knows. I can't say that would be impossible. But it seems more likely to me that she made the whole thing up."

For a long moment, the inside of the motorhome fell quiet. The only sound was the loud rumble of Snowbell's constant purring.

"Hap," Warren asked finally. "What is your perception of how the Finney family business has been doing since Bruce took over?"

Hap shook his head. "I have no idea. But I can't imagine it's going well. Bruce is all bluster. He talks a good game, but he's a know-nothing. Cortland was always trying to pull him more into the business, teach him the ropes, but Bruce was the type that always acted like he knew everything already. With Cortland dying so suddenly like that, I expect Bruce got thrown in way over his head."

Warren looked intrigued. "So you wouldn't say the son was chafing at the bit to take over?"

Hap laughed out loud. "Are you kidding? All Bruce has ever wanted is to live well and look like somebody important. Hell, I don't think he even cares about power. If he wanted to go into an office and order people around, he could have been doing that anytime in the last twenty years. He acted like he was allergic."

"Not a keen business mind, then?" Warren pressed.

"Born lazy and dimwitted to boot," Hap said uncharitably. "And Sharonna and Russell were never any more interested in learning the business than he was. Janelle was game, but Cortland never took her seriously."

"Do you think maybe she's the one running things now?" Warren asked.

Hap's brow creased. "I don't know her. And I can't say Cortland had an unbiased view. But he told me more than once that although Janelle had a good head for math, she 'lacked her mama's common sense.'"

"Interesting," Warren said thoughtfully. "So you can't see the four of them making a success of the company in their father's absence?"

Hap scoffed. "It'd go belly up in a week if the four of them were actually running it. They couldn't pluck a chicken together. Cort's people are still managing things, I'm sure." His face darkened. "Except for the CFO, now."

He stood up again and put a hand on Leigh's shoulder. "Listen, darlin', I don't like the thought of you getting accidentally tied up in anything those Finney kids have going on. Neither Sharonna nor any of them know you're family, and they don't know you're staying here, and we aim to keep it that way."

"The local police know," Leigh reminded. "They got my information this morning. But I'm sure Del Mayfield didn't think my face looked familiar. For what that's worth."

"Del's a decent guy," Hap said quickly. "He may let his buddies off the hook for some minor shenanigans here and there, but he's not going to stand by and let innocent people get hurt."

"Good to know," Leigh replied, trying not to sound as skeptical as she felt.

"You're safe as a bug in a rug right here with us," Hap assured, giving her shoulder a squeeze. "None of them kids have a reason in the world to be hanging around an RV park with a bunch of snowbirds. And if you wear that get-up Bev was describing when you go out, you could walk right in front of them and they'd never know it. Especially if you hang a pair of binocs around your neck and mosey along with the other birders."

"That's my plan," Leigh confessed.

"Good," Hap said amiably. He headed for the door. Leigh rose and walked with him, Warren right behind her. Hap was about to say goodbye when her conscience got the best of her. Her nature was to downplay the unpleasant, particularly when people were worried about her. But Hap was going to find out the truth sooner or later, and since he was doing his best to help, the least she could do was provide him with all the facts.

"Hap?" she called, stopping him on the steps.

He turned around.

"Stanley Hutchins was murdered."

Chapter 13

Leigh scooted her chair closer to Warren's, which was already jammed up against a window of the Mesten Grande's Community Center. She wanted desperately to open that window, but Bev had closed and locked every one of them before the meeting started. "Everybody doesn't need to hear our business," the activities director had said stubbornly. Unfortunately, despite the early evening hour and the cooling temperature outside, the air inside was already stuffy from sheer density of people.

As the crowd continued to grow, Leigh was beginning to wonder if there would be anyone left outside *to* overhear. When Bev had called an emergency meeting of what she termed "serious birders only" to discuss "an urgent ornithological matter," Leigh had expected roughly the same group she had met on the walk this morning. But evidently, Bev had advertised this gathering beyond the tony gates of the Grande, reaching out to birding enthusiasts all over Port Mesten.

Leigh still wasn't sure what was going on. All she knew was what Hap had told her, that he and Bev wanted to do something for Stanley, something that might help Leigh's situation as well. Leigh and Warren had been invited to come to the meeting early and take seats up front. Everyone else who attempted to enter would have to prove their credentials first.

"No, I'm sorry," Sue said without emotion, waving the would-be entrant to the side from her post at the door. "This event is for serious birders only."

The thirty-something woman rejected, who was wearing a swimsuit coverup and flipflops and whose hair was still wet from a swim, propped her hands on her hips with indignation. "But I heard this had something to do with the murders!"

"Well, maybe it does and maybe it doesn't," Bonnie said haughtily from the other side of the entrance. "But anyone who can't tell a northern shoveler from a mallard sure as hell ain't going to find out!"

NEVER MURDER A BIRDER

Furious, the woman whirled and stomped off. Sue smiled at the next man in line, who could easily pass for ninety. "Hello, sir," she chirped. "Do you know what this is?" She held up one of several color-printed pages that were covered with pictures of various birds. She pointed to a particular specimen.

The man lifted his spectacles and pulled his head back a comfortable distance from the paper, then said without hesitation, "purple gallinule."

"Thanks for coming," Sue said pleasantly, stepping out of his way.

Warren whispered in Leigh's ear. "You sure they're not going to wise up at some point and kick the two of us out of here?"

"It could happen," Leigh admitted.

When it seemed that the little room could hold no more people, and Leigh and Warren had both given up their seats to more elderly attendees, Bev at last shut the door and called the meeting to order. "I'm Bev Taylor, and I'll be brief," she began. "Yesterday morning, one of our own was doing something he had every right in this world to do. He was out in a public nature preserve, watching the birds."

"Amen!" someone shouted. Leigh looked around with surprise, as did several others, but just as many rumbled their agreement.

"He went out at dawn," Bev continued, "because he found the birding the best then. It was a nasty, rainy morning, but Stanley Hutchins went out anyway. And by now you know what happened, my friends. Stanley Hutchins was murdered. Someone chased the poor man down and strangled him to death."

Silence descended. There were a few awkward coughs.

"Now, I know all of you didn't know Stanley. But that doesn't matter. Fact is, Stanley wasn't carrying anything valuable, and as far as anyone knows he wasn't a drinker or a gambler. Heck, he didn't spend enough time with other folks to make enemies! He was just another snowbird, minding his own business. Stanley was *us*, my friends. He was you and me. And while a lot of people out there hear 'two deaths in one week' and immediately start thinking 'serial killer,' people like us see things a little differently. And we're all gathered here tonight because we're thinking the same thing. Aren't we?"

"Damn straight!" said a man in the back.

"I think he saw something!" cried a woman.

"That's what I think! Something he wasn't supposed to see!"

"Had to!"

"It's witness tampering!"

"Could have been any of us!"

"I'm scared to go out alone anymore!"

"That's just it!" Bev declared, slapping her hands together. "Somebody out there looked at Stanley and thought — well, he's seen me. But he's just one scrawny little old man, I can shut him up easy enough! The murderer saw a man with binoculars and a funny hat and decided he was a weak, vulnerable, loner!"

Bev stood as tall as her diminutive height would allow and puffed out her chest. "Well, guess what? I say we're not nearly as weak and vulnerable and alone as we look, because we birders have always got each other!"

Wild applause broke out in the airless room.

"Nothing can change what happened to Stanley," Bev continued, winding up now like a Southern preacher, "but we can do our damnedest to make sure that whoever did this gets exactly what's coming to them, and that anyone else who gets the same bright idea will think twice before taking on one of us again!"

The crowd cheered, even though a few of their faces, like Leigh's own, bore looks of confusion.

"How can we do that?" someone shouted.

"By doing what we do best!" Bev shouted back. *"Watching!"*

The room broke out in dozens of separate conversations, and Bev had to literally jump up and down to regain everyone's attention. "We are in the perfect position to be the eyes and ears of law enforcement!" she explained. "If anyone can spot fishy things going on around Port Mesten, it's us! Stanley was alone, but together we are an army of witnesses! We are everywhere! We can see a whole lot more than anyone realizes we can. We can be in constant communication with each other and with the police. And we might as well be invisible, for all the attention anyone pays us! We, my fellow birders, are like a neighborhood watch *on steroids!*"

"Hear, hear!"

"She's right!"

"Of course we can!"

"Let's do it!"

"Vengeance!"

Bev was unable to hush the room this time. Chaos continued until Bonnie stood up, put her fingers in her mouth, and made an ear-splitting whistle that nearly rattled the windowpanes.

"Thank you," Bev said, wincing a little. "Now, anyone who's on board with fighting back, you just sit tight right here and we're going to talk about what we can all do together to make this town safe again. Anybody who's not comfortable with the idea of being in a neighborhood watch type of group, that's fine. But don't go blabbing about the project to anyone outside this room, because we need to stay inconspicuous. And please go ahead and leave now, because it's hot as bloody hades in here."

More grumbling resounded, and perhaps a half-dozen people made their way out the door. But their absence was scarcely noticeable. "Now that we're committed," Bev continued, "here's a little primer on how watch groups work, and how to stay safe. Could everybody by a window pull their blinds down for me?"

Hap flipped off the lights and turned on a projector. Since it was already dark outside, Leigh figured Bev's goal was to shield their activity from prying eyes. She tried not to think of the heat that the machine was adding to the room as Hap played a training video describing the do's and don'ts of crime watch groups. Leigh attempted to crack open the window nearest her about five minutes in, but she was halted immediately by a vigilant Sue. By the time the video was finished, both Leigh and Warren were dripping with sweat.

"Now, here's the thing," Bev began soberly. Her face was in shadow now, lit only by the blank screen of the projector. "We're going to operate a little differently from your average neighborhood watch. In a neighborhood, you want the criminals to know you're watching, because that helps to deter crime. What *we* want right now is to solve one. We want to help the police figure out what's going on in Port Mesten, and we want Stanley Hutchins' murderer rotting in jail."

"Yes, ma'am!"

"I'm in!"

"Once that's accomplished, then we can make it crystal clear to everybody else out there that messing with one of us is not to be tolerated… that *no birder is ever alone!*"

"Amen!"

"You said it!"

"Let's do it!"

Another round of cheers went up, but Bev patiently shushed the crowd again. "So to begin with, we have to be discreet. No one can know what we're doing. As far as the general public is concerned, we're just watching the birds. Got it?" There was a general rumble of assent. "We will be reporting any suspicious criminal activity to the police, of course," Bev clarified. "But that doesn't mean they need to know about our little group... *per se.* When you report, you'll report simply as concerned citizens."

Warren's eyes slid over to look at Leigh. She could tell he was getting uncomfortable. And not because he'd lost five percent of his body weight to dehydration.

"Why can't we work with the police?" someone asked.

"We are working with the police," Bev insisted. "As individuals dutifully reporting anything and everything you see that could possibly shed light on Stanley's murder. But we're going to ask you to watch for something else, too, and that something is... well..." She turned toward Hap and made a gesture.

He rose stiffly from his chair by the projector and came to stand beside her. "Hey, y'all. Hap Taylor, here. What my wife is trying to say is, well..." He looked uncomfortable, but forged on. "You see, if you take the tourists out, Port Mesten is a mighty small town. So small that the permanent residents almost all know each other, and that includes the police. Now, I'm not saying that anyone on the police force is guilty of anything. But I do think it's harder to be impartial as a lawman when you're dealing with people you've known since kindergarten."

"You think Stanley was murdered by a local?" a woman called out.

"I have no idea," Hap said miserably. He was perspiring so heavily that rivulets of sweat ran down his temples. "But there's a second situation going on right now with one of our own that I believe this group can shed some light on. Maybe it's related to Stanley's death and maybe it's not, but we need to find an answer either way." To Leigh's horror, he extended a hand in her direction and looked right at her. "Leigh, honey, you want to come on up here?"

No, Hap. No, I definitely do not.

Warren gave her a not-so-gentle shove. Leigh glared at him, then dragged her feet to where Hap was standing. Her cousin smiled and put a moist arm around her as his wife took a seat. "This here's a dear friend of mine and Bev's. Her name is Leigh. As some of you already know, she happened to be with Walter when he came across Stanley's body this morning. But mighty strange things have been happening to her even before that. She's never been in Port Mesten before this week, but ever since she got here, four local people have been following her around and snooping through her stuff. Now, none of us have the faintest idea why. But the fact is, all four of those people have the last name of Finney, and they're all connected to the businessman whose body washed up on the beach Sunday afternoon."

The room began to buzz with muttering, and Leigh wished she could disappear. The goal was not implausible; such heat could surely reduce her to a puddle eventually.

"Now remember, we're not accusing anybody of anything, and we can't say that the weird things happening to Leigh have anything to do with the businessman's murder, much less Stanley's," Hap continued. "But we can't say they don't, either."

"You got that right!"

"Sounds fishy to me!"

"That's why this group has two jobs. The first part is a general watch for any suspicious activity, like it showed in the video. But the second part is even more important — and you understand it's top secret. We need to keep a special lookout for those four people. We want to know if they're in Port Mesten, and if they are, where they're going, and what they're doing. Just what's plainly visible from public property, mind you — that's all we need. Nobody should approach them. We don't want them to suspect we're watching them. But if any of them try anything funny again where Leigh's concerned, we're going to make damn sure the police hear about it."

"You bet!"

"What four people?"

Hap returned to the projector. Leigh stood in an agony of embarrassment as he flipped through pictures of all four Finney sibs, along with descriptions of three of their cars with pictures of similar makes and models. After stressing for the third time that none of the four had necessarily done anything wrong and that all that was being asked of the birders was to make note of the Finneys' public movements and report back to HQ, he returned to his seat and allowed Leigh to do the same.

"He got that together fast," Warren whispered with admiration.

Leigh made no response. Her face was so flushed with both heat and embarrassment that she doubted her muscles would move.

"All right," Bev announced, standing again. Her normally pale face was also red as a tomato and her arms were shiny in the reflected light. "We're going to adjourn this meeting tonight because otherwise I'm going to need an ambulance. But as you leave, sign up on one of the clipboards. Those of you with cell phones, start keeping them with you, because that's how we'll communicate. If you don't have one or you don't text, stick with a buddy who does. After tonight, if you run into somebody and you don't know if they're in the group, you'll use our code phrase: "How about those ivory bills?" The secret response is, "Never say never!" Unless you hear that, you don't say *word one* about 'the project.' Got it?"

"Got it!" multiple people shouted as the whole room applauded again. Leigh had to admire Bev's ability to work a room, even under physical duress.

"Good!" Bev returned. "Then open those windows and prop those doors and let's get the hell out of this sweatbox!"

Leigh did not need to be told twice. She and Warren skipped the clipboard signup and moved to Bev and Hap's patio. "How much of that did you know about?" Warren asked as he fanned his shirt and gasped for air. He had buried himself in paperwork as soon as Hap left their motorhome earlier, determined to finish his paid work that so he could concentrate on Leigh's problems the rest of the night.

"None of it," Leigh admitted. "Hap and Bev must have put their heads together and come up with the whole idea in a matter of hours."

Warren shook his head, sending drops of sweat flying. "Impressive. I'm a little concerned with Hap's distrust of the local police, but I assume he has his reasons. As for the Finney sibs, I have to say, it's an inspired idea. I'll feel a lot better leaving for work again tomorrow knowing that an entire roomful of people with binoculars are keeping an eye on you."

"On me?" Leigh said with surprise. "Not on me. Just on the Finneys."

A wicked smirk spread across his face. "Oh, you think?"

Chapter 14

The turkey vulture flapped her wings once, then caught the updraft and poised herself for a good long soar. She was hungry this morning. At least her feathers were dry, and the weather was warm. She teetered on the thermal, craning her ruddy, featherless neck to survey the ground below. As she drifted along the northwest edge of Mustang Island, her eyes were drawn to the stark parallel lines of the road running along the shore, but her vision registered nothing of interest. The scents that filtered through her brain as she glided with the wind were rich and varied, but equally unexciting.

The vulture kept moving, giving her ragged gray wings a flap only as often as strictly necessary. Whenever she located another warm current, she would ride it up high, then soar out to forage again. Her gaze alternated between scanning for carrion below and watching the surrounding skies for signals of good fortune. So far, none of her kind appeared to be having any better luck than she was.

She flapped, rose, and soared again.

The wind was still devoid of any intriguing aroma when her eye at last caught what she was looking for. Her head turned for further study, and the sight exhilarated her to the core.

The vulture changed direction. She could expend more effort now; its use was warranted. The brethren were gathering, and they were calling. Food had been found. From the looks of the group, quite a lot of it.

She could hardly wait.

The vulture caught what thermals she could and flapped the rest of the way. Catching up with her mates, she immediately joined in their dance — a restless swirl of anticipation high above the ground. Ah, yes… she could smell the carrion now. An unusual aroma… but reasonably fresh. A day old maybe. No more than two. She could see it now also. It was quite large, and none of the brethren had descended yet. If the first vulture on the scene had spotted a single serving, he would promptly have dispatched with it. But when one of the brethren spied an entire banquet table, it was customary to wait until sufficient guests had arrived to fill the seats.

The turkey vulture was hungry. She circled restlessly as two, four, and finally seven more birds joined the flock. Not all her kind, but other, testier ones, too. Then at last, the cue came. One of the vultures descended. He landed on the ground next to the carrion, and she and the rest of the group followed.

They were quickly stymied. The object of their attentions was not as accessible as it had appeared. The vulture hovered a second, trying to find someplace to alight that was dry and still close enough to the food, but all such real estate had been claimed already. She sloshed down in a sticky place and studied her options. The carrion was floating in water. A few birds tried to land on top of it, but then the whole carcass bobbed and shifted, pulling it away from those who'd been close enough to pick at it from the bank. They squawked in resentment. Poor access always heated up tempers. The aroma was *so* intoxicating...

The carcass drifted randomly. When it neared the bank again, it came closer to where the vulture waited, and this time she went for it. Another bird attempted to claim the same spot, but with a ferocious hiss she lifted her wings into a menacing posture and struck out at him with her beak until he backed off.

She was bigger than he was.

And she was hungry.

Chapter 15

"Leigh? Leigh, wake up. We need to talk."

Leigh didn't know where she really was or what was going on, but she knew she did *not* want to wake up. In her dream she was lying in a fluffy bed that was actually a boat, and it was skimming out over the blue waters of the Gulf with happy dolphins leaping out of the water ahead of it. Mao Tse was purring on top of her. A cappuccino maker was set up on one side of the bed and a tray of Bev's cinnamon rolls and muffins sat on the other. She was good.

"Leigh, I know you can hear me. *Wake. Up.* I have to leave soon."

Warren appeared suddenly on the bow of the boat, frowning down at her, and Leigh made the mistake of opening her eyes.

Crap. She'd woken up. But at least he wasn't actually frowning at her.

"Sorry," he said more gently as he buttoned his shirt cuffs. "I know you didn't much sleep last night. Neither did I. But we need to talk before I leave. Then you can sleep all day if you want."

Leigh forced herself to a sitting position, rolling the pliant Snowbell off her chest and down into her lap as she did so. "No, I can't. I volunteered for a patrol with Sue and Bonnie." She yawned, then shook her head to clear it. Now she remembered. After attending the clandestine meeting of the birders, she and Warren had returned to their motorhome to go over Allison's "dossier" on the Finney family. Warren had been in the process of digging further into Finney Enterprises' financials when Leigh had fallen asleep.

"What did you find out?" she asked, alert now.

Warren threw her a sober look. "I can only tell so much by looking at the data that's publicly available. But my hunch is that the birders of Port Mesten aren't the only people keeping a close eye on the Finney sibs right now."

Leigh tensed. "You think they're doing something illegal? With the business?"

"Finney Enterprises' stock is up," Warren said as he finished dressing. "*Way* up. It tumbled when Cortland died, which isn't surprising, then it started a slow rebound, which might also be expected. But then the company started reported some pretty impressive numbers, and the stock went on a significant upswing. It's been climbing steadily ever since. You might see a pattern like that if there was a good reason behind it, like a promising new product or acquisition, or a shakeup in management. But not this shakeup. Not with everything Hap's told us, all of which was borne out by what Allison found."

Leigh nodded in understanding. The bios Allison had cobbled together held many interesting factoids about the sibs, both relevant and irrelevant. But there was no evidence of any hidden corporate or financial prowess. In fact, a close study of Janelle's CV suggested that rather than giving his daughter a leg up, Cortland had probably been pinning his daughter beneath his boot. She had worked for the company for sixteen years at the time of his death, and in all those years — despite variously worded job titles — her duties had never seemed to progress beyond basic accounting.

The vaunted eldest son did no better. Despite seeming to have his father's blessing as successor, Bruce Finney had failed out of two private colleges before eventually getting his business degree — at the age of twenty-seven — from the local state university. His bona fides with the company were so slim that prior to his taking over as President and CEO, he had no online business profile of any kind and not a single career accomplishment credited to his name. In other words, his contribution to the family business had probably consisted of an empty office with his name on the door.

"Well, if the kids didn't mastermind an improvement in the business, then what did?" Leigh asked. "Did Bruce hire new people?"

Warren shook his head. "Almost all of Cort's vice-presidents left at some point during the transition, and Bruce didn't replace any of them. He promoted Janelle to a decision-making position in the accounting department, but other than her, the only one of Cortland's old guard managers to stay on board was—"

"Don't say it," Leigh interrupted.

"Ted Sullivan," Warren finished. "The Chief Financial Officer."

Leigh blew out a breath. "Now conveniently deceased."

"Yes," Warren agreed. "The board of directors is made up of

Cort's old buddies, and they probably would have stepped in if it looked like the business was in trouble. But since the stock values went up, they apparently stayed out of Bruce's way." He sat down on the edge of the bed and reached out a tentative hand to pet Snowbell. The shameless cat stretched, exposing her belly.

"So what do you think is going on?" Leigh asked, not sure she wanted an answer. This was not the first time she had speculated whether the Finneys were a pack of avaricious murderers, but as evidence actually piled up against them, it was becoming more disturbing to do so.

"I think they've been manipulating the stock price," Warren said simply.

Leigh was skeptical. "They don't sound smart enough to do something like that."

"It's not that difficult to *do*, at least not in the short term," he countered. "Janelle could have figured out how to inflate inventory, decrease accounts payable. A little money laundering here, a little debit-memo fraud there — creative accounting can go a long way to increase a company's reported income. The hard part is not getting caught."

Crap. What he said made perfect sense now. "So you think that when the kids took over, the first thing they did was force out all the people they didn't like, and then they figured out some way to make it *look* like things were going great, even though the company was probably tanking?"

"Right. But you can only keep up a charade like that for so long. There are records to keep, auditors to report to. They must have known it was going to come crashing down soon, because according to public SEC filings, all four sibs have recently cashed out. They've rather quietly sold nearly all their shares in the business. Selling out isn't illegal in and of itself, of course. But manipulating the stock price for the purpose of —"

"I get it," Leigh interrupted again. She lifted Snowbell from her lap and placed the sleeping lump in her fluffy cat bed. "And you think Ted Sullivan got in the way somehow?"

"There are any number of ways he could have," Warren suggested. "He could have been helping them, and then demanded a cut for blackmail. They could have been hiding things from him that he found out and then threatened to expose. Or he could have been the mastermind behind the whole scheme, and either they felt he'd betrayed them or they wanted it all."

Warren grabbed the keys to the rental car. "There's no telling which or how many of the four siblings were involved in the decision to go dark in the first place. It's not clear that Sharonna or Russell have anything at all to do with the business. But regardless of who's at the helm, Cortland's will makes certain that all four siblings will share equally in the bounty — or the fallout."

Leigh's mind again replayed a snippet of the conversation she'd heard through the wall of the Silver King. *We're each going to get our fair share, I promise you.*

She barely noticed when Warren kissed her goodbye.

"The good news," he continued, "is that we're not dealing with some subtle sleight of hand from a criminal genius, here. Finney Enterprises doesn't just have a red flag on it, it's got a flashing neon sign that says, 'Get Your Fraud Here.' I have zero doubt that the Texas Rangers already suspect the Finney sibs for the Sullivan murder and I suspect the Feds are well into a financial investigation as well." He stepped to the door. "All of which makes me feel considerably better about leaving you to go to work today. It's only a matter of time until one authority or the other gathers enough evidence for an arrest. If the guilty parties were smarter, they wouldn't even be here — they'd have hightailed it out of the country already. So all you have to do is *stay away from all four of them* and let nature take its course."

"Easy enough," Leigh replied.

He laughed stiffly. "I don't believe that for a minute. But today, I don't have to. I know you won't be alone, whether you try to be or not." He smiled at her as he let himself out the door. "Happy birding."

Leigh sat on the bed a while longer, attempting to digest the new information. But her brain had no intention of cooperating before caffeine, and she soon gave up and made herself a cup of coffee. She was halfway through her first dose when her cell phone sounded with her daughter's ringtone. Allison was requesting a video call, which Leigh despised. There was simply no way to hold the phone where the camera didn't give her either a triple chin or bags under the eyes. She held her phone down on the table in front of her so that the camera would be aimed at her coffee cup — one of several mugs that Joyce had emblazoned with a picture of Snowbell — then answered.

"Aw," Allison cooed. "That's cute."

Leigh peered in at an angle to see that Allison was sitting on her cousin's spare bed with Lenna's three-legged tortoiseshell cat on her lap. "You should appreciate the view. I look hideous this hour of the morning. How's Peep?"

"She's awesome," Allison replied, stroking the cat. "Still likes Lenna best, but we're buds now."

"Mao Tse doing okay? And Chewie?" Leigh inquired, asking about her own cat and dog.

"Mao misses you, but she lets Aunt Cara pet her when you're not around. Chewie's going to gain five pounds, though, because Uncle Gil keeps feeding him under the table. He says he can't stand those pathetic brown eyes staring at him."

Leigh sighed. "So gullible. And how about your brother? Is he—"

"Listen, Mom," Allison broke in. "I only have, like, two minutes before we have to catch the bus, but I wanted to let you know that Sharonna called me last night."

Leigh's blood ran cold. She scooped up the phone and pulled it to her face. *"What?!"*

"Don't freak out," Allison said calmly, still petting the cat. "It's not that big a deal."

Leigh made some inarticulate noises. Allison kept talking. "It was, like, 2:00AM here, which is why I didn't call you right away. And as for how she got my number, I've been thinking about that. My first thought was that she must have got hold of your or Dad's phone. But I suppose you would have known about that."

Leigh managed only a gurgling sound. "But then I remembered that you have my suitcase," Allison continued. "And I'm sure I put my cell number on the luggage tag. So there you go. Any idea when she might have seen your luggage? Snapped a photograph?"

"What did she say to you?" Leigh practically exploded, cursing herself for not thinking of the abominable luggage tags sooner.

Allison had the gall to smile. "It was pretty funny, actually. She seemed surprised at my voice. I didn't bother to sound more grown up or anything, so if she was expecting you, that would have been a surprise. There was a pause, and then she just said, 'This is Sharonna.'"

Leigh waited a beat. "That's all? Just 'This is Sharonna?'"

"That's it," Allison confirmed. "I decided to play dumb, so I said, 'Who?' like I was really annoyed at being woken up in the middle of the night. And then she hung up on me."

Leigh breathed a silent prayer at having given birth to such intelligent children. Although in Allison's case, slightly less intelligence would also be acceptable. "I'm really sorry about this, honey."

Allison smiled and shook her head. "Stop worrying about me, will you? She thinks you used a fake number. You're good. Still, I can't help but wonder what she expected you to say back. What is it she wants from you? You know, if you and Dad would just give me the whole story here, I'm sure I could help you figure things out..."

Over my dead body!

Bad choice of words.

"I have no idea what she wants," Leigh answered. "But it isn't your problem. Don't miss the bus. And please don't answer your phone again unless you know who it is!"

Allison smiled thinly. "Bye, Mom. See you soon!"

The video cut out, and Leigh's teeth gnashed. The child hadn't agreed to anything.

She dressed quickly, prepared and served Snowbell's breakfast, and then walked to Bev and Hap's place. The fifth wheel was empty again, but Leigh found Bev in the small park office, talking on two phones simultaneously. Bev gestured through the glass door for Leigh to enter, and Leigh stepped inside and looked around with amazement.

The tiny office had turned into a fully functional command and control center. One wall was dominated by an enlarged map of the town; the other by a giant, color-coded whiteboard. On the counter lay a series of rosters and reporting logs. Leigh studied the roster on top and saw her own patrol prominently listed. Sue or Bonnie, one, had volunteered their group to keep an eye out for birds and assorted mischief on the beach just north of the RV park. *Perfect.*

Bev hung up both phones. "Morning, darlin'," she said in typical motherly fashion, producing a tray of lemon poppyseed muffins and fresh strawberries from thin air. "You doing all right?"

Leigh's mouth started to water. She'd been doing well with the walking — until the blisters happened, anyway. And she could hit the pavement again, now that her feet were better. Besides, stress burned calories, right?

She took a muffin. "I'm fine. Thank you. These look amazing." She took a bite. They were amazing. She gestured around the room while she chewed. "I can't believe all this. You and Hap are incredible."

Bev's expression sobered. "It's early still, but we're already getting results."

Leigh wasn't sure she found that comforting.

"Janelle's car just showed up at the Finney mansion," Bev reported. "As far as anyone knows, Bruce is there too."

Leigh swallowed an overlarge mouthful. The Finney mansion, she had heard, was a six-bedroom spread on the south edge of town that had been built by Cortland and Debra in the eighties. It fronted the ocean and had a nice tract of land besides, with a giant deck for entertaining, a swimming pool, a tennis court, and a dedicated storage building for the tycoon's boat trailers and collection of antique cars. The house had fallen into Bruce's hands after his parents died, and rumor had it that his third wife Misti had been dumping a fortune into landscaping and redecorating ever since. Despite the size of the house, Bruce's siblings were not known to the neighbors to be regular guests. "I take it that's unusual?"

Bev nodded. "Janelle almost never comes to Port Mesten. But for her to show up on a Friday, during business hours, is especially strange. And there's something else, too. The dawn patrol at the north entrance to the preserve said they saw tracks out in the mud flats. All around the area that was taped off yesterday. *And* right through the middle of it."

Leigh's throat felt dry. By "the area that was taped off," Bev meant where Stanley's body had been found. *Ghouls!* She poured herself a second cup of coffee from the small carafe on the office counter. "What kind of tracks?"

"Boot tracks. Big ones," Bev answered. "Like a tall man. They couldn't have been there long, either. It rained pretty hard overnight, if you recall. It started about midnight, just as Hap and I were turning in. That would have wiped out any footprints the police left yesterday, and the birders were out at first light and didn't see a soul. So whoever made those tracks had to have been running around out there in the wee hours in pitch dark."

The mental image sent a shiver through Leigh's shoulders. "But *why?*"

Bev shrugged. "You got me, honey. I can see somebody poking around out there just out of curiosity, but I can't see them doing it in the dark. And alone. The team swore there was only one set of footprints."

"Did they tell the police?"

Bev nodded. "I had them get in touch with the investigator from the Rangers directly. He'd given Walter his number yesterday, so we used it. No point diluting the message by sending it through the locals first… if you know what I mean."

Leigh did. "I have some news myself," she said miserably. She summarized Warren's theory about the Finneys' financial problems, then described the disturbing call Sharonna had made to Allison's number.

Bev swore. "That skanky little witch! She just won't quit, will she? Rosina told me this morning that she won't leave the housekeeping staff alone, either. Yesterday she was nosing around the hotel with some guy who was translating for her. He was asking the girls in Spanish if they remembered what kind of car you were driving and what type of person you were traveling with."

Leigh's face got hot. "What *type* of person?"

"Yes," Bev said speculatively, stroking her dimpled chin. "That was an odd bit. Rosina said the girls got the idea that Sharonna didn't understand the man's relationship to you. Now, wouldn't you assume that any woman traveling with a man in a room with one bed was traveling with a significant other? *Weird.*"

Leigh thought about the luggage tags. Taken at face value, she and Warren would appear to be traveling as a couple named Warren and Allison Harmon. As far as Leigh knew, there were no other personal identifiers in the room. She kept her purse in her backpack and all Warren's things were with him in his briefcase. If Sharonna believed Leigh was someone else, then it might be reasonable for her to assume they were intentionally traveling with fake names on their luggage. But she might believe the phone numbers were legit, in case the bags got lost. So she'd given it a shot. And when a young girl's voice answered? *Of course!* She would assume the number was fake, too.

Leigh exhaled with relief. Maybe everything would be all right after all.

It took exactly two seconds for panic to set back in. *Warren*. If Sharonna had called Allison's number, she must have snapped a picture of the luggage tag while she was snooping in their hotel room. Had she snapped a picture of Warren's tag also? Would she be calling him next? Sharonna might assume both names were fake, but if she bothered to do an online search on "Warren Harmon" she could quickly determine that he was a real person who lived at the address on the tag. Perhaps it was no wonder she was confused that Leigh's doppelganger was shacking up with a legitimate financial consultant from Pittsburgh!

Leigh started to say something, only to notice that at some point while she had zoned out, Bev must have picked up another call. The activities director had put on a headset, moved to the map, and stood ready with a notebook and pen in her hand. "Okay, go ahead," Bev ordered into her mic. "Uh huh. What time was that? And he was headed which way? Gotcha. Thanks so much! What was that? A lesser black-backed? Where on the beach, exactly? Hey, that's awesome! Congrats to you both!"

Bev stuck a pin in the map, scribbled something on her notebook, then stepped to the whiteboard. "Russell's in town," she reported. "His car was spotted at the Cocoa-Nut Cafe. He just left, heading east. Now I'll alert the other teams to keep a look out for him, too. Ah, this is working beautifully! I feel like I've stepped right into an episode of Hawaii 5-0."

Leigh had to smile at the other woman's enthusiasm. She examined the pegboard map more closely. "Do you know where the other Finneys are?"

"We think Bruce and Janelle are together at the mansion, like I said," Bev answered. "Sharonna's still in her room at the Silver King with the 'Do Not Disturb' sign out. She's never awake this early."

A hundred unconnected thoughts raced through Leigh's sugar- and poppyseed-fueled brain, most of them unpleasant. She needed to think this through. She needed to concentrate. There had to be some way to safely extricate her family from this whole mistaken-identity debacle. And the sooner, the better.

"Bev," she said with determination. "Would you mind if I borrow those binoculars of yours again? I've been meaning to tell you, that salve you gave me worked great on the blisters. And right now, I'm feeling like taking a nice, long walk."

Chapter 16

Leigh stood on the platform at the end of the pier and breathed in deeply of the ocean air. The morning sky showed no traces of the gloomy intermittent rain of late, and her beach walk had been refreshing. She wanted to rest her forearms on the weathered wood of the pier railing and lean out, but although she was not a particularly fastidious person when it came to animal waste, the amount of bird poop on that surface was too impressive to ignore. So she continued to stand up straight, enjoying the churning sound of the waves and the amazing sun-on-your-skin sensation that had lured her to Texas in the first place.

Several fishermen had cast their lines off the pier. The whole area smelled vaguely fishy, but from the general level of activity around her Leigh suspected she was smelling bait rather than anyone's catch. She looked down into the gray-brown water and saw nothing but one floating jellyfish. To her side, two surfers were doing their best to stand on their boards more than three seconds at a time. But although the waves out by the pier were better organized than the churning froth closer to shore, the pulse of the Gulf was still chaotic, and the surfers didn't seem to be having a very satisfying session.

A gust of wind kicked up, and she tightened the strap of her floppy hat under her chin. She was in full disguise again… at least for now. She lifted her binoculars and focused in on a flying pelican. The binocs had proved a helpful addition to her ensemble. With the complete getup, not only did she find herself dismissed as uninteresting by virtually every man and woman under the age of fifty-five, but she also saw some pretty cool-looking birds. She had no idea what any of them were called, of course, but she found she still enjoyed looking at them. She also enjoyed looking at her fellow birders, whom she was quite certain had been following her progress ever since she'd left the Mesten Grande park office.

She swung the binoculars around and focused on a spot up the beach a few hundred yards, where a couple moseyed along consorting with a flock of gulls. The man had his own binoculars to his eyes, and Leigh picked up her opposite hand and waved slightly. The man in her sights smiled and waved back at her.

Warren would be pleased, wouldn't he? At least it made what she was about to do all the more reasonable. She pulled her phone from her pocket and called Bev. "Leigh here, checking in from the pier," she said brightly. "Any news?"

"Bruce is on the move now," Bev said sharply. "Best we can tell, he's following Del Mayfield around. It's like he's got nothing to do with his own time! Janelle's car is still parked at the mansion. Little brother Russell hasn't stopped moving since his first cup of coffee this morning. He just seems to be trolling the streets. Quite honestly, Leigh, we think he might be looking for you. He's driving around with his arm hanging out the side of that sports car of his, scanning up and down every block. Every time he sees a crowd gathered, he slows down and checks them out." She chuckled humorlessly. "It's sheer bad luck he's come nowhere near you so far. If he had, I would have called you."

"Don't worry about it," Leigh proclaimed. "I think the time may have come, Bev. Where is he now?"

Bev paused a beat. "You're not thinking of confronting him?"

"Only in a safe place," Leigh assured. "Look, my running and hiding isn't accomplishing anything, is it? Why shouldn't I tell them straight out that I'm not the person they're looking for? Until I set them straight, they're just going to keep probing. And putting my family in their crosshairs is not acceptable!"

"Well, at least let me send Hap down to be with you!" Bev begged.

"I'd be happy to have the backup," Leigh agreed. "But only if Russell doesn't know he's there. Think about it... the more afraid I act, the more likely the Finneys will be to think I know something about their criminal activities. But if I act more annoyed than anything, they'll be much more likely to buy the idea that I am a completely clueless bystander. In which case they can safely leave me alone!"

Bev muttered under her breath. "I suppose."

"Where is Russell now?"

Shuffling noises sounded in the background. "Last report he was driving around over by the south entrance to the preserve," Bev replied. "But he seems to cycle between there and the busier shopping areas in town."

Leigh considered. Neither place was an easy walk from her current location, and now that she'd made up her mind, she didn't want to miss him. "You know anyone who could give me a lift into town?"

Bev sighed. "Sure. Go and wait out by the pier entrance. Best chance of catching Russell's eye would be to go get a cup of coffee at the Cocoa-Nut and park yourself on one of the tables outside. I'll make sure Hap's nearby. You talk to Russell if you want, but don't you *dare* go anywhere with that man or anybody else, you hear?"

"No worries," Leigh promised. She ambled back down the pier at a leisurely pace, hoping that Hap would not be asked to abandon his post at the hotel desk for her sake. When she reached the parking area she leaned casually against a post and pretended to be studying her phone. When a truck pulled up and stopped within a few feet of her, she looked up expecting to see her cousin or one of the women she knew. When she did not, she quickly buried her face in her phone again.

"Hey there, toots!" a creaky voice called out. "Wanna go for a spin?"

Leigh looked up again. The vehicle in front of her was a dilapidated pickup that looked and sounded like it was held together with wire and duct tape. The individual driving it was a tiny, shriveled man who could be anywhere from eighty to a hundred-and-three. He was wearing faded dungarees, a once-plaid shirt faded to near white, and a cap with a picture of a fish on it and the words "Size Matters." He smiled at her with minimal teeth and gestured for her to get in.

Leigh hesitated.

"How about them ivory bills?" he grinned.

Leigh grinned back and opened the door. "Never say never," she returned. "Thanks for coming."

"Eh, I was already here," he admitted cheerfully.

Leigh hopped inside. The truck reeked with an interesting combination of fish, dog, and some other aroma she couldn't quite identify... until she noted the assortment of distinctive round tins rattling around in the console. *Ah. Chewing tobacco.*

After a round of introductions and five minutes' worth of a surprisingly intriguing discussion about whether or not the tarpon were staging a comeback, Leigh thanked her chauffeur profusely and then hopped out of his truck in front of the coffee shop. She went in and bought an herbal tea — having discovered that finding bathrooms could be an issue on a walking day — and then planted herself at an outdoor table as instructed. She checked in with Bev and learned that although Hap should be arriving any second, three other "operatives" in the area already had her in their sights. Furthermore, by total coincidence, a local Port Mesten police officer happened to be getting his hair cut in the barbershop across the street.

Leigh relaxed in the metal armchair, feeling quite safe. She had removed her headgear and sunglasses, and the feel of the warm sun on her face was bliss. Everything would be fine. Whatever trouble the Finneys were in, *Leigh Koslow Harmon was not, and never had been, involved.* All she had to do was convince Russell of that.

She had been sitting no more than ten minutes when a Porsche 911 Carrera came cruising down the street with Mr. Handsome at the wheel. He spied Leigh immediately, as least as far as she could tell by looking at the mirrored lenses of his designer sunglasses, and then he continued down the street to park. Leigh sat tight while he made his way back to her on foot. She watched with amusement as he sauntered down the street looking everywhere but at her. Only when he reached the coffee shop and pretended to be going inside did he pull off his sunglasses and "notice" her. He lifted a hand to rub at the beard on his rugged, square jaw and gave her a dazzling smile.

Leigh smiled back.

He dropped the door handle and closed the distance between them. "Well. We meet again," he said smoothly.

"I noticed you staring at me again," Leigh said matter-of-factly, cutting to the chase. "Look, I don't know who you think I am, but I promise you, I'm not that person. You are totally mistaking me for someone else."

Russell's smooth brow furrowed slightly. His head cocked to one side. Her words clearly confused him, but the expression did not last long. His blue eyes soon sparkled with understanding, and his lips drew into a sardonic smile. He scanned up and down the street, appeared to see nothing alarming, then pulled out a chair and sat down opposite her.

His efforts at precaution made Leigh grin. She could see at least three people with binoculars pointed their way, and Hap was now inside the coffee shop with his back turned. But it didn't matter, because there would be nothing *to* see. Russell would apologize now and move on.

The millionaire-heir relaxed in his chair and threw her another thoroughly practiced, drop-dead sexy smile. "Listen," he said in a low, husky voice. "I'm not sure what kind of game you're playing. But whatever's happened... if you have what I want, there's no reason we can't still work together."

Leigh's bubble of happiness burst into a puddle. She looked straight into Russell's eyes and he stared straight back into hers. The idiot man was entirely serious.

He didn't believe her.

"I don't know what you're talking about!" Leigh blurted, her voice sounding way more desperate than she wanted it to.

Russell's expression went from calculating to annoyed. He leaned in close and dropped his voice to a whisper. "What happened with the old guy? What's going on?"

Leigh's metal chair scraped on the pavement as she pushed it back and stood. "I told you, I don't know what you're talking about!" she repeated, not bothering to be quiet anymore. "I'm a freakin' tourist!"

Russell stood up with her. He wasn't being quiet anymore, either. "Just tell me what you want, will you?" he replied angrily.

"I want you to leave me alone!"

Russell's face turned red. He did not seem to notice that Hap had come outside and was standing a few feet behind him. Preferring the two men make no connection, Leigh quickly retreated the opposite direction down the street.

She had walked more than a block when heavy footsteps hurried up behind her. She whirled around, expecting to see Hap. She nearly collided with Russell instead. He stopped short and laid a hand gently on her wrist. His unnaturally handsome face was sweating and his eyes caught hers with a beseeching look. "We can get you out of this!" he said earnestly. "I can help you!"

"Hey, Russell!" Hap called from behind them, his booming voice artificially pleasant. "Hold up, there! I got a question for you."

Russell dropped his hand and stepped back, exhaling with a huff of frustration. Leigh suspected he was about to say something else to her, but she didn't care to hear it. She dodged away from him, jaywalked, confirmed that Hap had successfully embroiled the moron in some suitably pointless conversation, and then weaved her way out of sight.

Chapter 17

Russell didn't believe her.

Leigh stomped her way through town until she realized she had no idea where she was. Then she stomped some more. How dare he not believe her? Where did the overgrown playboy get off, thinking *he* knew better than *her* who the hell she was?

It was maddening.

What was even more maddening, she realized as his words replayed in her head, was that he not only seemed to think that she had something that belonged to him, he had the gall to suspect that she... *SHE* was responsible for what happened to Stanley!

Leigh felt a strong desire to go back and wring Russell's attractively tanned neck, but despite her rage and indignation, she was aware of the hypocrisy in that fantasy.

She kept on stomping instead.

Eventually she realized that her phone was ringing. She paused long enough to see that the call was from Bev, then took a deep breath and slowed her steps. "Hi, there."

"Are you okay, honey?"

"I'm fine. Just annoyed. Is Hap all right? Please tell him thanks for me."

"Of course Hap's all right. But where are you trying to go? They say you're headed for the wastewater treatment plant."

Leigh stopped walking. "I am?"

Bev chuckled. "Just sit tight and Hap can pick you up."

"No," Leigh said quickly. "I don't want any of the Finneys to see me with him. Or you. I don't want my family involved in this any more than you already are, just because of this stupid face of mine." She scowled. When and if she ever met this trouble-making doppelganger, she might just ring *her* neck.

She gave Bev a brief summary of her exchange with Russell, remembering to put her disguise back on as she talked. The headgear wouldn't fool Mr. Handsome as long as she was wearing the same outfit from the neck down, but it should protect her from the other three nightmares, none of whom she was up to meeting at present. What she wanted most right now was to relax and make the most of what little time she had left on her rapidly dwindling vacation. Bev had promised them a grilled shrimp dinner tonight, and tomorrow was Saturday and Warren didn't have to work. Leigh *would* have a singularly fantastic time from here on out, dammit!

"I don't suppose I'm anywhere near the beach where I'm supposed to meet Sue and Bonnie?" she asked.

Bev chuckled again. "Um... no. But I'm sure someone can give you a lift. That is, if you're sure you still want to do a patrol? You really don't have—"

"I want to spend time at the beach on a beautiful day," Leigh assured. "And if I have company, no one will pester me."

A half-hour later, after having been picked up on the street by Sue herself and given a ride to the rendezvous spot, Leigh kicked off her walking shoes and socks and wiggled her toes in the sand. She had known exactly what she was doing in signing up for this particular shift. Bonnie's sore heel would keep the group moving at a leisurely pace, and Sue was rumored to make amazing fruit smoothies.

Besides which, Leigh found the women amusing. As eager as they were to help with "the project," neither seemed curious enough about Leigh's personal situation to pepper her with questions. They did not even ask her about her encounter with Russell this morning. They were far more interested in the birds. As the threesome came upon a black bird picking through some trash, Leigh described the Hitchcock scene that had greeted her and Warren when they first arrived in the Silver King's parking lot.

"Great-tailed grackles," Bonnie said with disgust. "You're lucky you only saw one truck's worth of 'em. Some places in Texas, they roost by the thousands. They take over whole parking lots like a cloud of locusts. Only they're a hell of a lot bigger than grasshoppers. And messier!"

"All birdlife is of equal moral value," Sue chided.

Bonnie made a rude noise. "Speak for yourself, Pollyanna. You've obviously never come out of a mall after a long day's shopping to find your brand new Taurus buried in two inches of guano!"

Leigh lowered her eyes and stifled a grin. Catching sight of another one of the strange giraffe-spotted shell fragments, she scooped it up and held it out. "Isn't this interesting? I've never seen a shell like it before. Do you know what kind it is?"

Sue pulled down her binoculars for only a fraction of a second. "That isn't a seashell," she said matter-of-factly. "It's a piece of a crab."

Leigh dropped it.

"Hold the phone!" Bonnie said suddenly, just as she was, ironically, checking her own phone. "Crested caracara sighted!"

Sue pulled her binoculars down again and swung around. "Where?"

Bonnie pushed up her glasses and adjusted the distance between her phone and her eyes. "It's Clem and Jean. They're on the observation tower at the north entrance."

Sue's look of excitement dampened. "Oh, that's... Poor Stanley. He waited so long to see one. And then it happens the day after he dies? Right where he was? That's not right."

"Well now, we don't know that he *didn't* see one!" Bonnie replied. "In any event, there's one there now. Actually, two! And a whole venue of vultures, they say."

Both women turned and looked longingly up the road. "We can come right back here," Sue decided. "It's not that far out of our area, and we haven't seen anything here, anyway." The two looked at each other with eager anticipation. Then they looked at Leigh.

"Um... just let me get my shoes back on," she replied, faking accord. She had no desire to go anywhere near the spot where Stanley had died. "I don't care to go back in the preserve, myself," she admitted once they began walking again. "But I can wait for you at the pavilion or something."

The women looked contrite. "Oh, how stupid of us," Sue apologized. "We didn't think."

"Don't you worry, we won't go... there," Bonnie assured. She was typing away on her phone as she walked. "We won't need to. Jean says the birds are circling pretty far away from them, kind of off to their northwest. So we can probably see them just as well if we keep walking down the main road outside the place."

"Let's go, then!" Sue proclaimed, raising her binoculars back to her eyes. "For heaven's sake, get a move on, Bonnie! How long's it been since you saw a caracara?"

Bonnie harrumphed. "At least two RVs ago. But if they're feeding, they're not likely to rush off, you know."

Leigh got a sudden, sick feeling in her gut. "Feeding?"

Sue turned to Bonnie. "Did they say for sure it's not a kettle?" At Leigh's confused look, Sue explained. "That's where a group of vultures spiral around on the same thermal current. Just because you see several in one place doesn't mean they're hovering over a carcass."

Leigh's spirits rose slightly.

Bonnie putzed around with her phone a moment. "Jean says they're definitely feeding on something."

Leigh felt ill again.

"They've been watching the birds dive down," Bonnie continued, "but they're landing on the other side of some tall grass or something where they can't see them anymore. They can't see that area at all except from up on the tower, but Jean's thinking we should have better luck from the road here."

The women continued walking down the beach highway past the pavilion and parking lot that marked the north entrance to the preserve. "I see them!" Sue exclaimed, her gaze focused on the sky ahead. "Oh, look! There's *two* caracaras!"

"Well, son of a—" Bonnie began, stepping forward with her own binocs pressed to her face even as a Mack truck rolled up toward them. Leigh grabbed her arm and Sue's and pulled them further back onto the shoulder. "We hear it," Sue insisted, still looking through her binoculars.

"Haven't got flattened yet," Bonnie corroborated.

Leigh kept her mouth shut. When the truck had passed by, the women lowered their binoculars just long enough to look both ways. Then they crossed the road and lifted their lenses again.

"It must be something big," Bonnie drawled. "Look at all of them! I don't see any black vultures, though, do you?"

"No, only turkeys. Blacks are rare here," Sue answered. "But you're right, it must be at least a deer. Maybe a wild boar?"

Leigh was definitely feeling sick now. "Maybe we should stop here."

The women lowered their field glasses and looked at her. "Are you okay?" Sue asked.

Leigh didn't know how to answer that question. Her rational mind knew that whatever the vultures had found, its fundamental substance couldn't alter based on whether or not she continued walking forward.

But it still seemed like a bad idea.

"I'm just... trying not to overdo it with my blisters," she said lamely. Her blisters had healed up nicely and she'd been walking all morning without complaint. She looked down the road, and inspiration struck. "Besides, once we get to the next bend, the road starts moving off the other direction. So it's not likely we can get much closer than this without stepping in the mud anyway."

"Oh, but look," Sue replied, pointing. "There's a gravel road turning off just up ahead, see? I bet you anything it goes right along the edge of the preserve. We'll just walk up it a little bit. It looks like it may take us right by that area where the deeper water is!"

Leigh's resolve crumbled. The women desperately wanted to see the birds up close. She had no legitimate reason to refuse.

It was still a bad idea.

They began walking down the gravel lane, and sure enough, after a brief detour through some scrubby trees, the tire tracks wound back around to the edge of the preserve. As the cackles and grunts of the squabbling vultures became louder, Leigh grew more queasy.

"Look at this dumping!" Bonnie groused, scowling at the tire and rusted lawn mower handle that protruded from the grass in the shallow ditch beside the road. "Despicable!"

"Looks like the birds are landing right over there!" Sue called out a moment later as she pulled down her binocs and plunged into some brush beside the road.

"You see either of the caracaras coming down?" Bonnie asked, heading after her. "I've only seen them flying before!"

Leigh moved no closer. But as she studied the area around her, her heart sank steadily into her shoes. She hadn't spent much time driving around the island in a car, but from what she had seen of the inland waterways, most appeared quite shallow. Those that were deeper were in the heart in the preserve, and only accessible by walking. Yet this private road — or service road, or whatever it might be — skirted quite close to the edge of what looked like a decent-sized pond. She gazed out toward the center of the preserve.

There it was: Stanley's observation tower. She raised her binoculars. Jean and Clem were clearly identifiable, standing atop it and waving at her merrily.

Leigh waved not-so-merrily back. Everything she saw, heard, and felt now made perfect, albeit horrifying, sense.

She waited.

A few endless minutes later, Sue and Bonnie reemerged from the grass. Leigh had heard no screams, but she was not surprised. Neither woman seemed the screaming type. In fact, their only concession to their distress was the greenish cast to their faces. "I'm afraid we'll need to call the police, Leigh," Sue said calmly. "It's not a deer. It's... It was a person."

Leigh never went any closer. Listening to the squawks of the vultures and the occasional splashes of pond water were more than enough to put her into sensory overload as they waited for the police to arrive.

The state of the body was evidently such that neither of the women were inclined to discuss details. They reported only that it had "been in the water a while," and that the birds were frustrated and fighting because the wind had only partially beached the object of their attentions, leaving much of it still afloat and inaccessible.

Bonnie and Sue had interesting reactions to the shock. Both were subdued initially, but as the minutes ticked on Sue grew more thoughtful while Bonnie got more fired up.

"I don't know what the Sam Hill this place is coming to!" Bonnie bellowed. "When you can't go out on a perfectly innocent bird walk two mornings in a row without winding up smack dab in the middle of an episode of *CSI?*"

Leigh made no comment.

"The two events are hardly random," Sue said with almost preternatural calm. "Don't you think *this* is what Stanley saw yesterday?"

"What, a flock of vultures?" Bonnie asked obtusely.

Sue threw her a critical look. "You do know that... well, bodies tend to sink at first and then... resurface as they—"

"Oh. I got you," Bonnie said heavily. She swore out loud, looked for someplace to sit down, then swore out loud again. Leigh could understand both feelings. Plunking oneself down on either grass or gravel in this particular location meant getting back up with a seriously muddy rear end — if one got up at all, which in Bonnie's case was not a given. As for the other thing... Leigh didn't want to think about it, either. But she could hardly deny its plausibility.

Someone had used this secluded gravel lane to dump off more than trash. Someone had dumped a body here. They had scouted out one of the few spots where they could carry their load straight from their car to some decently deep water without risk of being seen. Or so they had thought... until they looked up and realized that if they could make out a figure on top of the observation tower across the wetlands, that same person might also be able to see them. Not very well, of course.

Unless he or she had binoculars.

Leigh shuddered at the thought. Had Stanley's murderer run out across the wetlands to confront him? She looked toward the tower and decided that was unlikely. There was too much distance, too much water, and too much mud separating them. If Stanley saw his pursuer starting toward him, he could easily slip away on the boardwalk.

No, it made more sense for the murderer to jump in his car and drive back to the north entrance parking lot. Then he could reach the other end of the boardwalk in seconds and cut off Stanley's only easy escape route. Even if Stanley had read the other man's mind and started running from the tower immediately, he might not have reached the parking lot first. Even if he did, he had no car there. Stanley had walked from the RV park.

The birder also had no means of calling for help. Like many men his age, he wasn't in the habit of carrying a cell phone around, and even if he had screamed or shouted, no one else was near enough to hear him.

Leigh remembered the pattern of trampled grass she had seen yesterday morning as she and Walter came upon the body. The two men's footprints would have been washed away by the overnight rain, but the grass they had trampled showed that Stanley and his pursuer had been roaming around well off the boardwalk. If Stanley had gotten trapped on his way out of the preserve, he would have had nowhere to flee but the open wetlands.

"Police are here," Sue said evenly.

The women stepped off the gravel road onto the least muddy patch of earth available and waited for the cruiser to stop. Behind it trundled another car. Leigh looked through the windshield of the cruiser and saw two officers. The driver was the chief of police, Del Mayfield. Feeling less than totally confident in their saviors, Leigh looked to the second car, hoping to see the Texas Rangers. It was a silver Infiniti Q70.

Bruce Finney's car.

Leigh steeled herself for another confrontation. Bruce opened the door of the shiny sedan and pulled his long legs out slowly. *He has no reason to be here*, she thought with annoyance. *Why does the chief put up with it?*

Del Mayfield did not appear to notice. He and the female officer riding with him got out and strode toward the women. The chief seemed like a pleasant-enough fellow. He was somewhere in his early forties, with a ready grin and no trace of guile. But his attempts at paternalism were, in the present case, sadly misguided.

"Hello, ladies," he said in a soothing tone. "What's all this hysteria about another body? Now, I know it's unusual for a place like Port Mesten to have two such unfortunate events in one week, but I promise you, there's no need to panic every time we see a few vultures overhead! This happens all the time around here. Why, it could just be a dead chipmunk! But if it'll make you feel better —"

"Now you see here!" a red-faced Bonnie boomed, drawing to her full height and puffing up her bounteous chest. "I don't know who you think you're talking to, but I worked as a nurse for thirty-four years, near half of them in an ER, and *I think I damn well know* a human body when I see one! Particularly when it's *wearing clothes!*"

Del blinked. The female officer who was with him quietly departed from his side and headed off into the scrub.

The chief pulled a notebook from his pocket, his eyes still locked with Bonnie's. "And your name is?" He took down her basic information and Sue's, then turned to Leigh. Unfortunately, this time she made more of an impression on him. The chief's brow creased. "I interviewed you yesterday," he said flatly. His gaze was suspicious.

Perfect.

"Leigh didn't even see it!" Sue said impatiently. "Only Bonnie and I did, when we walked around the edge of the pond to get a better view of the birds." She pointed in that direction. "You have to walk around those bushes."

Del seemed torn. His gaze alternated between Leigh and the direction Sue pointed.

"Chief!" the female officer called out, her voice fraught with tension.

Decision made for him, the chief turned and followed the sound of the other officer's voice.

"Bloomin' yokel," Bonnie muttered. "Telling *me* I don't know a human from a flippin' chipmunk!"

"As if that many scavengers would gather for something so small!" Sue muttered with equal indignation.

Bonnie swore, mopped her sweating forehead with a shirtsleeve, then began walking toward the police cruiser. "Well, we might as well make ourselves comfortable."

"Yes," Sue agreed, walking with her, phone in hand. "I'm going to report to Bev."

"Tell her if the Texas Rangers don't show up in five minutes, we're going to call them ourselves," Bonnie scoffed as she leaned upon the cruiser's front bumper. "Incompetents!"

Leigh intended to follow them, but she hadn't quite got her feet moving before Bruce Finney appeared at her elbow. She was not unaware of his presence; she had been keeping an eye on him with her peripheral vision ever since he had stepped out of his car. But she had also been keeping alive the hope that her hat and scarf would sufficiently disguise her. Since Bruce had said nothing and was being ignored by everyone else, Leigh had decided to try ignoring him also.

So much for that. She stiffened in annoyance, but she wasn't afraid of him. Not with Sue and Bonnie only steps away and two purportedly non-corrupt police officers within shouting distance. Still, it was unnatural for him to have moved so close to her. He had placed himself within whispering distance, and whispering is exactly what he did. The second that Sue and Bonnie became distracted with their own conversation, he leaned down to within inches of Leigh's ear and spoke to her as if they were bosom buddies.

"You want to tell me what's going on?"

Chapter 18

Leigh closed her eyes a moment. Really, this was too rich. Bruce Finney, President and CEO of Finney Enterprises, was asking *her* what was going on?

I am not involved.

She whirled around and faced him. "Who are you?" she asked at full voice. "And what are you talking about?"

Bruce's face — which already had a permanent glowering look to it — reddened with anger. At the same time he seemed surprisingly nervous. Bullets of sweat beaded up on his imposing brow, and he seemed to have trouble standing still. "Don't play with me," he hissed back in another whisper. "You said three days! We need to meet."

Leigh stared back at the man, flummoxed. She really didn't know what he was talking about, but she knew a great deal more about him than she wanted him to realize. And since she had never been a particularly good liar, she supposed that her blanket denial had probably just made her sound guilty.

"You have me confused with someone else," she tried again, making eye contact. "I told the other man that, too."

Bruce's pupils dilated.

Aha! Now she had his attention.

"Other man?" he repeated.

"There are two of you staring at me," Leigh returned, feeling gutsier now that she could tell the straight truth. "I told him, and I'll tell you. I am a tourist, I don't know what you're talking about, and if you don't leave me alone, I'm going to the police!"

Bruce's face seethed with confusion and frustration. He shot a glance toward Sue and Bonnie, and when he did, Leigh noticed that both women were standing in silence now, watching them intently. The women did not seem inclined to interrupt the conversation, but it was clear they considered themselves "on call." Bruce straightened. He could get away with nothing threatening, every word he said above a whisper could be overheard. Yet whatever his mission was, he seemed unable to give it up.

"Please," he whispered again, his tone gentler, more persuasive. "I'm sorry to push you. But we *don't have time* for this. Just tell me what to do. Whatever you need."

Leigh's brain tried to process the offer. Whatever *she* needed? Russell's words of a few hours earlier came back to her: *We can get you out of this... I can help you!*

Leigh shook her head in disbelief. This numbskull thought she was a killer, too! If he and his brother were so sure she was some kind of murderess, why the hell didn't they turn her in, instead of offering to help her?

The Finney sibs were insane. Totally bonkers, lampshade-wearing cuckoo birds.

No offense to the actual cuckoo bird.

"Forget the others," he said, his voice dropping so low she could barely hear him herself. "Keep this between you and me and you can be out of here in an hour." He threw his eyes in the direction the chief had walked. "I can make it happen."

"You all right, Leigh?" Bonnie barked.

"I'm fine," Leigh called back, figuring her name would be no secret from Bruce after today, regardless. He could always ask his buddy Del for information about her. And the police had her current address in the RV park.

Dammit. This was all so unfair!

Leigh decided she had had enough of the Finneys. She dropped her eyes and took a step closer to Bonnie and Sue.

"You can't just walk away!" Bruce fired back at her, no longer bothering to whisper.

Leigh whirled around and was stunned to see his limbs shaking. If he had been shaking from sheer anger, she would have ducked and run for cover. But the vibe she perceived from him was far more complex. As frustrated and as annoyed as he obviously was with her, he seemed to be suffering from some deep-seated fear. And whatever he was afraid of, it appeared to be keeping his anger in check.

"I don't know how many times I have to tell you this," Leigh repeated slowly. "But you have *the wrong woman!*"

Their gazes locked, and they studied each other. For one brief, shining moment, Leigh saw a sparkle deep in his dark brown eyes that she thought might signal acceptance of the truth. But before she could be sure, the crackling of brush alerted them all to the return of the police chief. Ignoring Bruce as usual, he walked directly to Bonnie and Sue.

"My apologies, ladies," Del said humbly, looking genuinely miserable. "It looks like the make-believe's on my part today. I really didn't want it to be true."

Bruce swore. Then, without a word to Del or anyone else, he made a beeline for his car and hopped in.

"I've called the Rangers," the chief continued, not seeming surprised by his friend's abrupt departure. "They should be here soon."

Leigh watched as Bruce backed his Infiniti down the road.

Had he believed her? Finally? Could she be so lucky?

She tensed up all over again. Maybe Bruce had believed her. Maybe he had taken off so quickly in order to avoid any further awkwardness between them.

More likely, though, he wanted to avoid the Texas Rangers.

"Don't you worry about us, Bev," Sue said briskly, even as she accepted a coconut macaroon. "We're fine. It's Leigh we're worried about."

"And how!" Bonnie agreed, mumbling through her own cookie. "She's still awfully pale looking."

Leigh felt Bev's sympathetic, motherly gaze on her and flushed with embarrassment. "That's only because I've been wearing your sun hat all week," she insisted. "I'm fine. Really. I keep telling you, Bruce didn't threaten me. He just said a bunch of stuff that made no sense."

Bev put two coconut macaroons on a napkin and placed them in Leigh's lap. The four women were commiserating in the RV park office while Bev worked. Bev had brought in some extra folding chairs as well as her obligatory plate of pastries, never mind that the three others had already had fruit smoothies in Sue's motorhome once the Rangers had finally finished with them. Morning had dragged well into afternoon without Leigh's having any memory of lunch, so this time the carbs were fully justified.

"Nothing any of Cort's kids does makes a lick of sense," Bev said with frustration. She looked down at her phone, then rose to stand by her wall map. She pulled out a blue pin and moved it to another location. "I swear, ever since this afternoon they've been buzzing around this town like a hive of bees!"

"What do you mean?" Leigh asked, feeling ambivalent even as she did so. As much as she longed to understand everything that was happening, and *now*, a big part of her simply wanted to return to her trailer, lock the door, and take a nap with Snowbell until Warren returned.

"Well, Bruce went straight home after he left y'all," Bev reported. "But he wasn't home a half hour before Janelle bolted. She drove straight to the Silver King, looking for Sharonna no doubt, but Sharonna wasn't there because she was out following Russell around. Finally Russell went out to the mansion, but when he saw Bruce's car he left again, and then Bruce left too. Right now all four of them are out in separate cars driving around in circles like chickens with their heads cut off!"

Leigh felt a wave of dizziness. "But why?"

Bev threw her palms up. "Who knows? It's almost like they're keeping tabs on each other — each one afraid the others are up to no good!"

"I don't know them from Jack, and I can tell you none of them are any good!" Bonnie pronounced. "I saw the way that Bruce fellow was hassling Leigh, and I didn't like it one bit. This isn't some idle preoccupation that man's got. Whatever he's on about, to him it's life or death!"

Leigh's jaws clenched. She did not disagree, but nor did she want to hear it.

"I'm with Bonnie," Sue agreed, popping up and beginning to pace. "I think the man is dangerous. He seemed quite desperate for Leigh's help."

"Well, she can't help him!" Bev exclaimed with irritation, taking a macaroon for herself. "So where does that leave her? Leigh, dear, I think it's time you had a little talk with the Rangers yourself."

"And tell them what?" Leigh protested. "We're leaving the day after tomorrow, and I refuse to spend my last day here being interrogated by multiple police departments over something I have nothing to do with and know nothing about! All I want is *one* carefree day on the beach with a husband who isn't working. Is that so much to ask?"

The other women looked at each other.

"Besides," Leigh continued to argue. "I think I may have gotten through to Bruce at the end. He looked like he finally believed me. If he does, maybe they'll all start turning their attention to someone else now."

"It's still a little hard to believe that anyone else could look *that* much like you," Bev said skeptically. "Are you sure you don't have a twin?"

Leigh laughed. "Believe me, if I did, I don't think she would have escaped my family's clutches. My mother is an identical twin herself. She would have strong feelings against separating another pair."

"And you're definitely not adopted?"

Leigh smirked. She had never thought she looked anything like her mother. Yet the number of times she had walked by a mirror lately and fleetingly mistook herself for a middle-aged Frances was disturbing. Besides which, Allison was a dead ringer for Leigh's father. "Um... no."

"Then there must be another logical explanation," Bev concluded.

"I was thinking..." Sue began. But then her voice dropped and she resumed her pacing.

"Will you cut that out?" Bonnie ordered. "You're giving me whiplash! What are you thinking?"

Sue stopped abruptly and stared at Bonnie. "Did you see... the foot?"

Bonnie's lip pursed. She nodded grimly. "Yes. What of it?"

Sue lifted her chin and turned to Leigh and Bev. "I wish I didn't have to bring this up. It may mean nothing. But..."

"Oh!" Bonnie exclaimed with sudden understanding, her hand flying to her mouth.

Leigh was missing something. "What is it?"

Sue flitted about another moment before stopping in front of Leigh and taking her hand. "The body we saw... it was a woman. It was hard to tell much. But we could see one strappy high heel, so that much is certain. The only other thing was... well, we could see hair. Or at least part of it. It was wet, obviously, but... I'm guessing that it was about the same color as yours."

Leigh's hand turned to ice.

Sue promptly used both of hers to rub it. "It could mean absolutely nothing," she soothed. "Half the women in the world have brown hair. I just thought you should know that if there *is* a woman out there who looks like you and is legitimately mixed up in something illegal—"

"My doppelganger," Leigh said tonelessly. "Somebody killed her."

"Now, that's definitely putting the cart before the horse!" Bev chided. She promptly poured Leigh a cup of hot coffee, then handed her a third macaroon.

"But the Finneys couldn't have done it..." Leigh continued, thinking out loud. "They think *I* killed her! But how could I kill myself?"

"Good Lord, now she's lost it," Bonnie bemoaned.

Keep this between you and me and you can be out of here in an hour, Bruce had said. If he didn't realize that Leigh's doppelganger was the victim, who did he think the body was? Did he not believe there was a body? Or did he think Leigh was some random serial killer? He didn't seem to give a hoot either way as long as she gave him what he wanted. But what did he want? What could possibly be so important to him that he would risk working with a raging murderess to get it?

Leigh clapped her hands over her face. "It makes no sense," she said, her words muffled. "And if it makes no sense, it can't be right."

"Maybe I should get you one of Hank's valiums," Bonnie offered.

"No, thank you," Leigh replied quickly, pulling her hands down. "I'm not losing my mind. But I could use a little time alone to process all this. Preferably with a cat on me. Purring lowers blood pressure, you know."

"Of course, dear," Bev said quickly. "You go right ahead."

"We'll walk you over," Sue offered.

Leigh felt like a preschooler as the two older women walked her from the park office all the way to the door of Joyce's motorhome. But she did appreciate their concern. After they made sure she had both of their numbers and reminded her that the Grande had security cameras covering every angle of the park 24/7, they left her alone behind the locked door. Leigh collapsed on the comfortable king-sized bed, and within seconds Snowbell was doing her part at human blood-pressure reduction.

Leigh's mind was far from settled, however. As little as she wanted to believe that the woman whose body had surfaced this morning was her mysterious double, the idea had a disturbing feel of truth to it. Bruce's words to her had been specific. *You said three days.* And he definitely acted as if those three days were up.

With a rush, Janelle's words came back to her as well. When Leigh had asked why the executive was following her, what had Janelle's surprised answer been? *Don't you want me to?* And when she'd first met Russell at the beach, he'd acted as if he expected Leigh to take the initiative.

They all wanted something, yes. But they were waiting to hear from *her*.

We need to meet, Bruce had said.

Leigh's heart beat faster. Yes, of course that was it. They were all waiting for her to set up a meeting *with them!* Sharonna's snooping was still a little irrational, but from the sounds of it, so was Sharonna. The sibs had been waiting for this woman to contact them, and when she didn't, they had gotten frustrated. When they confronted Leigh and she had acted ignorant, both Russell and Janelle had backed off, even though they clearly thought she was lying. Why? Did they suspect their real contact had a legitimate reason to play it coy? To hide her true mission? To watch her back?

Quite clearly, she did. Someone had murdered her.

A fresh wave of dizziness washed over Leigh. Someone had killed a woman who looked so much like her that at least four local people couldn't tell the two of them apart.

Could the murderer?

Chapter 19

Leigh's mind wouldn't settle enough for her to take the nap she so desired. But Snowbell did succeed in purring her cat-sitter into a reasonably comfortable state of semi-consciousness, which Leigh remained in for quite some time before the ringing of her cell phone jarred her rudely back to alertness. "Hello," she answered, seeing Hap's name on her caller ID.

"Hey, darlin'," he replied. "Listen, I've got some news for you. I shouldn't have it, probably, but I do. My buddy Carl's daughter, Bobby Jo — she's going to get herself fired someday over those loose lips of hers — she's saying that the Rangers have got a pretty good idea who the woman was that... well, that you folks found earlier."

Leigh sat up. "The body's been identified? But how could it happen so quickly? I mean... Sue and Bonnie said—"

"Yeah, I've heard the story from Bev, honey," he assured. "I'm sorry you had to be there, but I sure am glad you didn't have to see this one, too. Anyway, the way I understand it, it's not like an autopsy's been done yet or anything. But word is the general description and personal effects match a missing-persons report from Corpus. It's a long way from official, but still, it sounds like everybody down at the station considers it pretty cut and dried."

Loud noises coming from outside distracted Leigh's already scattered thoughts. She scooped up a limp Snowbell — who was rarely bothered by any noise — and stepped to the window. The RV next door was moving out.

Serial-killer hysteria was spreading.

Leigh moved away from the window and refocused. She picked up a pen and note pad and sat down at the dining table. "Please tell me what you know about her," she asked Hap.

"Her name was Eva Menlin. She's from New York City, but she was last seen in Corpus Christi. Her husband was expecting her home Wednesday night and she never got on the plane."

Leigh scribbled furiously. "Could you spell her name for me?

What else do you know?"

"That's it, honey," Hap replied, after giving her the spelling. "Bobby Jo just said that her husband described the jewelry she was wearing or something like that, and it was a match."

Leigh let out a long, slow breath. Thinking of the mystery woman as a real person with a real husband was terribly depressing, whether she was a criminal or not. "Thanks so much, Hap."

"Now, you're not planning on going out anywhere, are you?" he warned. "Bev told me they were making sure you stayed put the rest of the day."

Leigh smiled self-consciously. She never would have imagined that being constantly spied upon by a bunch of retirees with high-powered binoculars would have a relaxing effect, but oddly enough, it did. "I'm staying put," she agreed.

"Good girl." Hap repeated Bev's earlier invitation for the grilled shrimp dinner, then rang off. The motorhome next door loomed large in the front windows as it began to pull out into the street, and Snowbell hopped off Leigh's lap to watch the action. Before Leigh could rise also, however, her cell phone buzzed again. It was another video call from Allison.

Leigh looked around for a focal point other than her own face, and decided to point the camera towards Snowbell. "Hey, honey!" she greeted, trying her best to make her voice sound as though she'd spent the day hunting for seashells and shopping for souvenirs. "How's everybody doing at home?"

Allison, who was sitting outside on her Aunt Cara's screened porch with a suspiciously bloated-looking corgi in her lap, looked into her own phone's camera and scowled. "Mom, seriously. Don't even. You are *so* bad at faking."

"Excuse me?" Leigh said resentfully. "You can't even see me!"

"Don't need to," Allison said tiredly. "So, did you find this last body, too, or what?"

Leigh turned the phone back to her face. It was too much effort to look at Allison from an angle. Besides, triple chin or no, one never knew when a mother-glare might be indicated. "I did *not* find the body!" she protested. "And how do you know about that, anyway?"

"Local news plus internet," Allison answered. "How else am I supposed to keep up with what's happening down there when you won't tell me?"

At the sound of Leigh's voice in the phone, Chewie's giant ears perked, and he raised his head. But when no recognizable sight of his mistress followed, his sausage-shaped body quickly went slack again. "What have you been feeding that dog? He looks like he just gorged on an entire box of dog biscuits!"

Allison rubbed the corgi's belly affectionately. "More like fettuccine alfredo."

"*What?*"

"Mom, don't worry. I already got Grandpa on the phone and had him yell at Uncle Gil. Chewie will be fine. In fact, he may never want to go home again. But that's not why I called. I want to know if you need me to look anything else up. I'm bored here. I need a mission."

Snowbell raced suddenly from the front of the motorhome to the bedroom at the back, looking like a miniature blizzard.

"Eva Menlin," Leigh proclaimed, resigning herself to fate and giving Allison the new information from Hap. "Let me know anything you can find out about her."

Leigh's camera view had moved to a picture of Cara's porch ceiling, probably because Allison was writing in her pocket notebook. "You think she was your lookalike?" Allison asked, sounding ill at ease.

Mother-guilt attacked again. "I don't know," Leigh said quickly. "But there's no need to worry about me. I have a whole army of birders watching my every move, and I'm under lock and key and on camera besides. Really. I'll be fine."

A weird scratching noise was coming from the motorhome's bedroom.

The camera switched back to Allison's face. The girl looked concerned, but determined. "I'm on it, Mom. Just let me get to the computer and I'll get back to you as soon as I can."

"Wait a minute," Leigh said, an odd thought dawning. "Why are you outside, anyway? Isn't it cold there?"

Allison smiled a little. "No, actually. It's been awesome weather here. It's been sunny and in the sixties today."

"That is so… great," Leigh replied.

Allison laughed out loud. "Lame, Mom. Very lame. Bye!"

Snowbell was making an odd growling sound. Leigh had taken exactly three steps in her direction when her phone rang again — this time with a call from Bev.

"Bev?" Leigh said quickly, having a bad premonition. "Is something wrong?"

"No, honey," Bev answered, sounding stressed. The cat made another weird noise back in the bedroom, this one more like a cluck. "It's just that the motorhome in slot #32 is moving out, and it didn't occur to me until right this second, but Joyce asked me to warn her if anybody ever moved in next door to them with a cat—"

"But nobody else has moved in yet!"

"No," Bev continued, "but the Edwards in slot #33 have two Russian blues, and I was just thinking that since there's no longer a motorhome blocking the—"

Leigh dropped the phone. But it was already too late. She reached the bedroom to find a spastic Snowbell tearing from the side window across the top of the bed to the opposite wall. Then the cat scurried halfway up the blind, back down on the bed, across the bed, up the built-in chest of drawers, across the big-screen TV, down the big-screen TV, up onto the bed again, across the spread, down onto the floor, under the spread, out from under the spread, back up the chest of drawers…

Leigh scrambled to the window and pulled down the blind. She raced to every other window on that side of the motorhome and pulled down those blinds. She turned on the sound system and played mood music with jungle birds. She found a can of air freshener and doused the RV in the scent of lilacs. Then she collapsed on the bedroom floor.

"Snowbell?" she called into the bathroom. She was pretty sure the cat had wound up hiding in the shower. But trying to chase her was definitely contraindicated. "The evil kitties are all gone now. It's safe to come out. Are you okay?"

Leigh heard nothing. She stuck her head around the bathroom door and saw Snowbell sitting on top of the closed toilet seat. Her little pink tongue hung out as she panted.

The worst was over.

Leigh crawled back and found her phone. Bev had hung up, but Leigh texted her to say that everything was okay. She was still sitting in the floor when a key turned in the lock and Warren opened the door.

He walked up the steps, looked at her curiously, and sniffed the air. Then he set his briefcase down and loosened his tie. "I'm afraid to ask."

"Don't," Leigh suggested. She got to her feet, kissed him hello, then hurried back into the bedroom, where she hastily rolled the bedcoverings into a ball. "On a totally unrelated note — how would you like to run by the laundromat before dinner?"

"The laundromat? Isn't there a washer and dryer in the bathroom?"

Leigh looked down at the heavy comforter in her arms. No way would it fit in the motorhome's compact little units. "Yes, but... I thought an hour or so at a laundromat would be a fun thing to do on a Friday night."

Warren watched her skeptically as she placed the roll of bedding on the floor by the door. He sniffed the air again.

Leigh forced a smile. "Snowbell doesn't like the other kitties."

Her cell phone rang again. It was Allison. *Already?!*

"Warren," she said apologetically. "I know I should have called you earlier, but I didn't want to distract you — I thought it would be better if you could finish as soon as possible and just come home. But there have been some new developments today..."

He did not appear pleased.

She answered the phone. "Allison? You have something already?"

"Of course I do," came the small, yet confident voice. "Are you ready?"

"Wait a minute," Leigh suggested. She took Warren's hand and led him to the dining table, where they both sat down. She pulled her pen and paper back out and put Allison on speaker phone, then told Warren about the most recent discovery, conveniently omitting her own involvement. "So you see," she finished gently, "it looks like my mystery double's been found."

Warren's expression changed from frustrated to horrified.

"Um... no, Mom," Allison proclaimed. "I don't think so. You can take a look at her picture yourself — I put all the deets in an email for you. But I'm telling you, she looks nothing like you."

Warren breathed out with relief. "Well, that's good news, anyway."

"But that's not possible!" Leigh argued. "She has to be the one!" As comforting as it was *not* to be a dead ringer for a dead woman, she couldn't bear to have all her logical progress undone... again.

"Trust me," Allison insisted. "She has a long, thin face and a big nose and she's just... no. But there's a whole lot else that's interesting about her. Get this, Dad. Eva Menlin has a pretty unusual profession. She's a diamond trader. Like, one of the big ones."

Warren sat up straighter. "A diamond trader?"

"Yep," Allison confirmed. "She lives in Manhattan with her husband, who's a lawyer. He's the one who reported her missing. She was on a business trip in Corpus Christi when she dropped out of contact. Then she missed her flight home. The date of last contact on the report was Tuesday."

Leigh watched her husband's face and could see that an idea was brewing in his mind. "What does it mean?" she asked.

"Did you see anything about her business contacts?" Warren asked Allison. "Any link to Finney Enterprises?"

"No," Allison answered. "But so far I've just looked at the obvious things. Missing Persons' database. Local news reports. Social media. I can do some more digging later, but I wanted to get this to you first."

"Thanks, honey," Warren praised. "This is very helpful."

Leigh thanked Allison also, and then they hung up. Warren had leaned back in the chair, and he appeared to be deep in thought.

"What does it mean?" Leigh repeated. "What is a diamond trader, exactly?"

Warren put a hand to his face and stroked his chin. "In the diamond business, you have dealers in each source country who buy directly from the miners. Then you have buyers who travel to those countries to secure the diamonds. Traders are the next step in the line. They either purchase diamonds from the buyers or they'll fund the buyers' purchase of them. Either way, large amounts of cash are exchanged, so it's a high-stakes, high-trust business. The most successful traders have a long history in the business and a select list of contacts, and the networks tend to be family-related. It's not something you just wake up one morning and decide to do."

Leigh's mind raced, but she still didn't get it. "So what does Eva have to do with the Finneys?"

"It's just an idea," Warren said. "But if we assume that we're right about the Finneys trying to pull off a giant stock fraud, they're bound to have realized by now that they've been colossal idiots and that very soon it's all going to come crashing down around them. In which case, it's quite likely they've also decided that their best chance of staying out of prison would be to skip the country while they still can."

"But they haven't," Leigh noted.

"No, they haven't," Warren agreed. "The disadvantage to fleeing the law is that their assets could be frozen at any moment, robbing them of nearly all their ill-gotten gains. Unless..."

Leigh began to get it. "Unless they could get their money and run?"

Warren nodded. "Bank transfers can be traced. Cash is bulky. But diamonds are small and easy to slip through airport security. If the Finneys decided to bail, that's exactly how they could do it... cash out as quietly as possible, front the money to a trader, collect the diamonds, and disappear."

"But..." Leigh murmured, not sure where her protest was going. She understood what he was saying, but she was still no less confused. "But where do I come in?"

She remembered again all the bizarre comments the sibs had made. She had something they wanted. They expected her to contact them. To set up a meeting...

"Oh, my God!" she cried. "They think I'm the diamond trader!"

"It would make sense," Warren agreed soberly. "But what possible reason could they have to believe that?"

"Allison has to be wrong about the picture!" Leigh insisted. Remembering the promised email, she picked up her phone and clicked into her inbox. "Here it is," she reported. She opened the email and held out her phone for Warren to see.

The picture was a glamour shot of a woman about Leigh's age, with brown hair and dark brown eyes. She wore a suit jacket that was stylish, elegant, and sexy, her hair was in a flawless updo, and she was heavily accessorized with expensive-looking jewelry.

She looked absolutely nothing like Leigh. With or without the fancy getup.

"There's no way," Warren exclaimed. "No way in a million years anyone could mistake the two of you. There must be something else going on."

Leigh's eyes remained glued to the picture. She agreed with her husband wholly. The woman's face was a different shape, her skin tone was olive; one might say she looked vaguely European. But there was something else intriguing about her. Something that rang a bell in a distant cobwebby corner of Leigh's brain.

Eva Menlin looked familiar.

Chapter 20

"Don't you feel better now?" Warren asked, rubbing a hand along Leigh's back as they leaned against the counter at the Laundro-Center.

"Not especially," Leigh replied, wishing the king-size comforter would finish drying already so they could get back to the motorhome and she could take a shower. Being interviewed by detectives always had that effect on her. "But I'm glad we got it over with tonight, anyway."

"You did the right thing," Warren reiterated.

Leigh grumbled. She knew he was right. It could conceivably be helpful to the Rangers to know that the Finney sibs had been chasing the wrong woman all over town. Even if it weren't, Leigh had legitimate cause to fear for her own safety at this point, so working with the authorities was her only sensible course of action.

She still hated it. Somehow, no matter what the circumstances, she always came out of such encounters feeling like a criminal.

So, why didn't you report your concerns to the local police? Why didn't you tell the investigator earlier today that you had been at both recovery scenes?

The truth was just so… messy.

We notice here that you were once arrested for homicide yourself, Ms. Harmon. That's a pretty unusual thing to notice on a background check for an advertising copywriter…

Is it any wonder she put off the pain?

"It might have been the right thing," Leigh agreed reluctantly. "But that doesn't mean it did any good. When you were offering your theories about the diamond trading, I got the feeling he already knew all about that."

"So did I," Warren replied. "But that's good news, isn't it? It means the law is onto the Finneys. They're probably under surveillance even as we speak; maybe they have been all along. Most importantly, the Rangers will be keeping an eye on you too, now, so we can rest easy tonight."

Leigh glanced around the laundromat. It had been empty when

the detective had interviewed them, but another woman had just come in and was starting a load in the far corner. It was an odd location for an official interview, but given the current serial-killer mania, Leigh hadn't wanted to spark panic by having an official vehicle parked outside either the Silver King or the Grande. The newcomer smiled at them as she dumped in her detergent, and upon closer inspection, Leigh could just make out the black loop of a binocular strap disappearing beneath the collar of her bulky windbreaker.

"I do feel well watched-over," Leigh said, returning the smile.

"I just wish you could remember where you've seen Eva," Warren commented.

The reminder of her epic failure made Leigh frown again. "So do I. It's been recently, I'm sure of that. I wish the museum were open — I'm thinking maybe I saw a picture of her there."

"Why would her picture be in the Port Mesten museum?" Warren argued. "She was a New Yorker. Coming here was supposed to be a one-time business trip."

Leigh sighed with frustration. "I don't know. I just don't think I saw her on the beach, that's all. I'm envisioning her all dressed up, like she was in the picture."

"Could you have seen her the day you drove with me into Corpus Christi, then?" he suggested.

Two men walked into the laundromat in a rush, the bells on the door jingling loudly as they entered. Leigh and Warren both jumped, but the men's pastel-colored golf shirts and white Bermuda shorts soon put them at ease. "Heads up!" one of the men said, looking directly at Leigh as he tossed his head in the direction of the street. Then the two of them walked to a row of plastic chairs and sat down.

They carried no laundry. Leigh and Warren exchanged a look of concern, but before either could get a word out, a woman approached the door alone. She peered through the glass, saw Leigh inside, wrenched the door open, and entered. Then, without offering a single sideways glance to see who else might be in the room, she strode directly toward Leigh.

"Hello again," Janelle snapped.

Leigh straightened to her full height, as did Warren, but the gesture felt like overkill. The mousy Janelle had stopped several feet away, she was wearing casual slacks and a thin cotton shirt, and she carried nothing in her hands. The tiny purse slung over her shoulder could have a weapon in it, but unless she was the fastest draw in Texas, it posed little danger to anyone.

"Hello," Leigh returned, deciding to go with civility. If Janelle Finney — who was simultaneously under suspicion by the FBI for securities fraud and by the Texas Rangers for triple homicide — could waltz around Port Mesten acting like she'd done nothing wrong and had nothing to fear, why the hell should Leigh act nervous?

I am not involved.

"What do you want?" Leigh added. She sounded a little flippant. *Good.*

Janelle's impassive face was set like stone. "Let's get something straight," she began in a monotone. "I have no beef with you personally, whoever you are. But I believe you have something in your possession that legally belongs to me. And I would like to have it back now."

Leigh's heart pounded against her sternum. But she reminded herself that she couldn't leap to any conclusions simply because Janelle had hired a diamond broker. Whether one or all of the Finney sibs had dispatched with Eva Menlin themselves, Bruce's ties to Del would ensure that they all had access to at least as much information about the murder investigations as Leigh did. Furthermore, as logical as it might seem that the sibs were working together, Leigh reminded herself that she couldn't assume that, either. Hap insisted that the four were barely on speaking terms, and Bev had claimed as recently as an hour ago that they were still tailing each other in aimless loops around the town.

If the siblings didn't trust each other, they were bound to worry that one of the others might try to abscond with more than his or her fair share of the diamonds. And quite probably with just cause — had Russell and Bruce not both offered to "help" Leigh in exchange for some sort of personal favor?

Leigh felt a sudden shockwave of sympathy for Eva Menlin. Whether this particular business transaction was technically legal or not, it was a risky gig from the get-go. Who in their right mind would want to deliver a large amount of precious gems and bear the responsibility for splitting them equitably among four unethical people who hated each other?

"Listen," Leigh said plainly. "I will tell you exactly what I told both your brothers. I am a tourist. I don't know Eva Menlin. I don't have anything of yours, or theirs, and I never did. I have no idea why you think I have anything to do with any of this, but it's been *your* mistake from the beginning. All I've ever wanted is to be left alone."

Janelle's pale eyes stared back into hers, their dim depths unreadable. Leigh considered herself a fair judge of character, but Janelle was an enigma. She seemed intelligent in some way, but there was certain density to her gaze that signaled an incomplete understanding of the world. The petite figure stood like a statue, staring at Leigh with no expression whatsoever, for a very long time. Then, finally, she issued a question.

"If you're so innocent, then why did you drive all the way into the city to hunt me down at the Finney offices?"

Uh-oh.

Leigh began to sweat a little. The truth was so blasted convoluted that even a lie would be more believable, assuming she could tell it well enough. "Tourists go to the city, too," she said with an attempt at sarcasm. "They also eat lunch, and my husband happened to be doing consulting work in the same building."

Janelle continued her hard stare. "You intentionally dropped your tray on the table to get my attention."

Crap.

"You obviously know who I am, and you know my brothers as well," Janelle continued. "How you got involved with Eva I don't know, and I don't care. I don't care about anything except getting what belongs to me. *Legally.* Do we understand each other?"

Leigh was screwing this up royally. And for next steps, she was at a loss. She wasn't afraid of the tiny woman standing in front of her — at least not at the moment. An additional three people had entered the laundromat since Janelle came in, none of whom, mysteriously enough, carried any laundry. One of them looked like he could be a plainclothes Ranger; the other two were old enough to be his parents. Leigh found the collective presence of the onlookers exceptionally comforting, but Janelle's laser-focus seemed to have screened out her audience entirely, despite the jingling bells that announced the newcomers. Leigh wondered if Janelle or any of the

Finneys even realized they were under surveillance. Were they too stupid to notice? Or too desperate to care?

Leigh decided she'd had enough of the pussyfooting. "Clearly we do *not* understand each other," she said firmly. "Because you're not listening to me. I don't have whatever it is you're talking about. I never did. But because your family insists on threatening me about it, I have just had a nice, long talk with the Texas Rangers. Now they know everything I know. So please be advised that if anything happens to me, or anybody connected to me, the Rangers will know exactly who's behind it. So will you just go away now and leave me alone, please?"

For the first time, Janelle's facade of calm broke. Her cheeks suffused with a ruddy color and her pale eyes burned with malice. She whirled around, startled a second upon noticing the additional people in the room, then stomped toward the door. She was halfway out of it when she shot back over her shoulder, "Just remember, Ms. Leigh Koslow Harmon. *I'm* not the one who was convicted of murder!"

Leigh's face burned. "I... No... *Arrested!*" she stammered. "*Falsely* arrested!"

The door swung shut.

Leigh took a step, but Warren stopped her with a hand on her arm. "Let her go. It doesn't matter."

Janelle got into her car and backed out. Leigh looked around the room, mortified. She cleared her throat. "Um... The charges were dropped, by the way."

The man that Leigh suspected was a Ranger threw her a smirk. He tipped his fishing cap, then started out the door after Janelle.

Leigh thought for sure that, if nothing else, the day's events should destroy her appetite. But when Bev brought out the grilled shrimp kabobs, lo and behold, there it was. The four of them ate heartily at their belated dinner, which Bev served outside in one of the cozy picnic shelters at the county beach park. It was dark, which made the location seem strange for a picnic, but the milieu was enjoyable nevertheless. The sky was clear, it was a warm, moonlit night, and Bev had surrounded them with citronella candles. Several RVs were camped nearby, but the beach was otherwise deserted, except for whatever Texas Ranger sat in the SUV that was parked prominently beside Hap's own car.

Leigh did feel safe enough. The shrimp kabobs were amazing, the churning sound of the waves was heavenly, and the wind was unusually calm. Hap and Bev were delightful company, and their wealth of funny family stories had succeeded in keeping Leigh's mind off the rest of her day for the better part of an hour.

But they could not avoid the unpleasantness forever. Although Leigh had heard nothing from the authorities since Janelle's visit, it was clear from the way the Rangers were following her around that they had reason to believe she was in danger. Amazingly, Hap and Bev, rather than being annoyed by the trouble their cousin had brought down upon their heads, seemed more embarrassed that their hometown was not showing the couple a better time.

"Have some more roasted pineapple," Bev suggested when the group fell quiet suddenly. Her kind eyes were filled with angst. "I would have brought the ice cream, but I was afraid it would melt. We'll have it when we get back home."

"Bev, please," Leigh pleaded, even as she accepted more pineapple. "You have no idea what a culinary fantasy you have made this vacation for me already!" She looked her host and hostess in the eyes. "I do wish you would stop looking like you feel guilty. None of this is your fault. Other than all *that* stuff, I've really had a fabulous time."

Bev and Hap exchanged a look. "Well if that's the case, darlin', you sure as hell need to get out more," Hap teased. "But since you brought up the subject, let's talk. What happened with Janelle earlier?"

Leigh summarized the encounter in between bites of pineapple. "The sibs obviously know exactly who I am, now. They must have looked me up, just like Allison looked them up, as soon as Bruce wheedled my name out of Del. But what really blows my mind is that knowing the truth doesn't even matter anymore. They *still* think I'm involved… and that I have been all along!"

"Of course they do," Warren reasoned. "Look at the evidence from their eyes. You were present when two of the three bodies were discovered, you followed Janelle to Finney Enterprises, and you have what looks like a fishy criminal record."

Leigh flushed again. "I —"

Warren cut her off with a side hug. "I know. But think about it. If they're looking at media stories online, with all the things that have happened in Pittsburgh over the years… Plus, there's no telling how much of your police record Del might have leaked. You know perfectly well that if you were a Finney, you would suspect yourself right now."

Leigh groaned. "I wish the sibs *could* get along. If they'd all acted together, then they would know I was innocent, wouldn't they? But no. One of them — or who knows, maybe two of them? — must have killed Eva and Stanley and taken all the diamonds for themselves. But the others don't know that. So the innocent ones suspect *me* of still having the mother lode. Right?"

Bev dropped her hands on the wooden table with a clunk. "Well, that would point right to Sharonna then, wouldn't it? She's the only one who hasn't approached you to beg for her share!"

"That's true," Warren said thoughtfully. "But if Sharonna has all the diamonds, why is she still here? She should be on the first plane out. Or train. Or bus. She should swim if she has to, but if she doesn't leave soon, it will all be for nothing. The Rangers are clearly closing in."

Hap shook his head. "Sharonna's a loose cannon. I can see her doing something dumb. What I can't see her doing is killing a woman and disposing of her body in a swamp, then chasing Stanley around and strangling him to death."

"Oh, no," Bev said quickly. "I can't see that either. Even if she were strong enough, Sharonna's way too high and mighty to go tromping around in a marsh. She would have to have help."

"Have you seen anyone with her?" Warren asked.

Hap shook his head. "Rosina said Sharonna paid a guy to help her question the maids, but I know him; he's just a local kid."

"Maybe the other sibs are faking it," Bev suggested. "Maybe one of them already has the diamonds, but they're trying to convince the others they don't, and that includes approaching you — just to be thorough."

"I don't think they're that smart," Hap remarked, shaking his head.

"Janelle did seem awfully confident when she came in the laundromat," Leigh mentioned. "Like she didn't care whether she was being watched or not. Like she had nothing to be ashamed of.

She only lost her cool when she found out I'd already talked to the Rangers."

"Maybe that's the moment she first started to doubt herself," Warren suggested. "To wonder if you really *didn't* have the diamonds. Which, again, would make her seem innocent."

"Well, look at it this way," Bev said, patting Leigh's hand. "Whichever of those kids is guilty, that one has those diamonds right now. And as soon as they skip town, or try to, we'll know exactly who it is. Then you'll be in the clear, honey."

"It's not the guilty one I'm worried about," Leigh admitted. "It's the innocent ones who think I've stolen their inheritance. And 'innocent' is a relative term. We still don't know what happened to that CFO. Or *why* they were all so convinced I had anything to do with Eva in the first place, when she looked nothing like me!"

"It doesn't matter at the moment," Warren insisted, attempting comfort. "All that matters is that you're safe. The Rangers are going to be watching you every second, and the Finneys know it. They should also know that no matter what your involvement was with Eva, they stand zero chance of getting either their diamonds or their money back now. If you had — or still had — what they wanted, you would not be working with the Texas Rangers."

"I... suppose," Leigh agreed with hesitation. His words made sense. But she was reluctant to ascribe any sense to the Finneys when none of their actions thus far had been based on it. She envisioned herself walking around Port Mesten with millions of dollars' worth of uncut diamonds hidden in Bev's floppy beach hat, and she laughed a little. "Seriously, can you imagine me as a diamond trader? Me in my wrinkled capris and my plastic beach sandals and my —"

Leigh stopped talking as the image blossomed in her mind.

Gucci shoes.

She stood straight up at the picnic table. "I remember!" she cried out loud. "I know where I saw Eva Menlin!"

Chapter 21

Dawn was still hours away, but the great blue heron was hungry. He flapped his giant wings and turned his keen eye to study the wetlands below. The clear skies and full moon were to his advantage; with luck he could spot some scale shine and secure an early breakfast. He steered his course over the familiar waters that had been most bountiful in the past, but saw nothing to spark his interest. Yet in the distance… what was that?

The bird changed direction. He flew toward the tiny, bobbing point of light that appeared on the mud flats. Its appearance intrigued him; it presented possibilities that his hunger demand he investigate. Still, he sensed a need to proceed with caution. As he neared the apparition, he climbed higher in the sky where he could view it from a safe distance.

His vision trained in, and his interest dissipated. The light was coming from a human. It wasn't normal to find a human here, in this place, in the dark hours.

The heron was not generally bothered by humans. He considered them primarily a nuisance. Over the years he had become an acute judge of which human behaviors were associated with danger and which were not. But predictability was a critical part of that calculation, and any actions outside the norm were inherently suspect.

He flapped his wings and rose still higher. He would not hunt in the wetlands tonight. There would be better, less stressful options.

He flew out of the preserve, crossed the highway, and headed down the coast. The heron surveyed the ground continually as he flew, always on the lookout for sparkles of interest. The pattern of light normally visible in his night hunting grounds was well known to him, and variations of traffic and building lights were part of that pattern. Therefore, the cluster of flashing red and blue lights that appeared around the large beach house below did not disturb him. He had seen such a collection of lights before, at other locations, and they were of no consequence. That other sparkle, however… the tiny glint of bright orange that reflected up from the small, glowing pool of water behind the house... *that* was very interesting indeed.

The heron descended a bit. He took a closer look.

Eureka.

His brain had no need to recall specifics. He knew only that he associated this location with food. He landed on the ground about six feet from the artificial koi pond, then immediately began a safety check. The flashing red and blue orbs were only part of the display here; bright spotlights lit up the yard and the deck, and light shone inside the windows of the house as well. Many humans were about, moving in and out of the big house and the other buildings, too. There was talking and some yelling. Human tension in the air, for certain. But none of the people paid any attention to the heron, and none were currently in the immediate vicinity of the koi pond.

No problem.

The heron approached the small pool on foot, one long leg at a time. When he was three feet away, he stopped short. His eyes had caught a shape on the water that sparked an instinctive alarm. He froze in place and studied the image. He watched and waited for it to move, poised for flight in an instant if necessary.

More yelling in the house. Car engines starting up.

The bird was not concerned with the noise, all of which was distant. The shape of the object still bothered him, but it was bothering him less and less as time went on. He had experienced something like this before, and that memory was not associated with danger. He took a step closer. The object did not move. He took another step.

Eventually the heron drew close enough to the object that his remaining wariness evaporated. He could sense now that it was not alive. He raised a claw and plunged into the water, scattering the fat and sluggish fish whose brightly colored scales were reflected so beautifully by the underwater lighting.

Gulp.

The human chaos around the bird continued, but as long as no person approached, he remained unconcerned. The vaguely familiar taste was delectable.

Gulp. Gulp. Gulp.

Was that all? The heron looked behind him. No. One more glint of gold.

The last remaining koi darted underneath the floating plastic alligator head that Bruce Finney's third wife had installed when she restocked the pond the day before. The heron craned his neck a little.

Gulp.

Chapter 22

When Leigh opened her eyes, it was still dark outside. Despite the purring cat on her ribcage and the promise of a lazy Saturday to sleep in with her husband, she had spent a restless night, and now she was both awake and thirsty. She picked up the lump of Snowbell and transferred her to Warren's chest without either mammal seeming to notice. Both the purring and the snoring continued.

She folded back the covers, slipped out of bed, and crept into the kitchen. After settling herself at the table with a glass of juice and a slice of the cranberry bread that Bev had wrapped up for their breakfast, Leigh heard herself sigh into the silence.

This would all end soon. It pretty much had to, didn't it?

The lead investigator on the case had sat across from her at this very table mere hours ago. Unlike most investigators, he had seemed quite pleased with her. She'd gotten the impression, although he never came right out and said it, that her involvement in this fiasco — such as it was — had provided crucial evidence of a link between the Finney sibs and the murdered diamond trader. Janelle had not brought up the name of Eva Menlin in the laundromat, but Leigh had, and Janelle had not disputed the connection. The very fact that all four of them had been pursuing Leigh was significant.

Being considered helpful to an investigation, for once, was nice. But it didn't stop all the unanswered questions in Leigh's mind from tormenting her. Which of the Finney children had murdered poor, innocent Stanley? And Eva? Was it the same person who had murdered the CFO? Did more than one sibling do it? Could it be all of them? And still the nagging question that had started it all — *why* had the diabolical foursome ever believed that Leigh was Eva in the first place? She took a bite of cranberry bread and tried to think. The lead investigator, nice as he was, did not seem as impressed as Leigh had hoped he would be at the triumph of her otherwise-slowly-dying-from-old-age memory.

So, you say you remembered having seen Ms. Menlin before at some point?

Yes! I saw her in the Corpus Christi airport. In the luggage claim area. We must have been on the same connecting flight from Houston.

I see. Did you speak to her? Did she approach you?

She did. She claimed I had picked up her suitcase by mistake. But I hadn't. It was a very distinctive suitcase, so I thought that was odd at the time.

The investigator had tapped his pen thoughtfully on his note pad. *Did she handle your suitcase in any way? Could she have slipped something inside it?*

Leigh chased down the bread with a sip of juice. The detective's question had disturbed her. It disturbed her still. She had told him that it wasn't possible, that the whole exchange had lasted only a few seconds and that Eva's hands had been in view the entire time. He had seemed skeptical, but hadn't belabored the point. In fact, Leigh was surprised when he let the matter drop. He had seemed to be in a bit of a hurry.

But she could not stop thinking about those few seconds with Eva, replaying them endlessly in her mind. How she wished she had waited around to see if the well-dressed diamond trader really did have an identical suitcase! If not, then she must have had some purpose in interacting with Leigh. What if Eva *had* planted something in Leigh's bag? Something that snooping Sharonna had removed two days later? Had Leigh actually been in possession of millions of dollars' worth of diamonds for nearly forty-eight hours without knowing it?

No way.

If Sharonna Finney had taken the diamonds, why was she still hanging around asking dumb questions about Leigh days afterwards? Why had she not left town? And why would anyone have needed to kill Eva?

Leigh took another bite of cranberry bread, this time a giant one. Carbs helped her think. She still didn't see how Eva could have unzipped the suitcase and put anything inside it. But, sleight of hand was always possible. Magicians were trained to do it, weren't they?

She closed her eyes and pictured the scene again. Eva had put her left hand on top of the suitcase. That one was too far from the

NEVER MURDER A BIRDER

zipper to do anything. But her right hand was more on the side. With that one she could have—

The phone!

Leigh nearly choked. She grabbed her glass and took a drink. Eva had had a cell phone in her right hand. There was no way she could have held the phone *and* unzipped the case *and* put something inside with just five fingers. But she could have done something else, couldn't she?

After Eva had relinquished the bag, she had admitted she was wrong and said she was sorry. She had thrown both hands up in the air and backed away. The phone was still in one of them. She could easily have angled the screen, punched the side button, and snapped a close-up, straight-on picture.

A picture of Leigh!

"That's it!" she cried out loud. She jumped up and ran into the bedroom. "Warren!" she said with a shake. "Wake up! I figured it out!"

Her husband awoke with a start, his pupils dilated with angst. As he took note of the smile on her face, he gradually relaxed back into his pillow. But when his gaze focused forward, he stiffened again. "Why is there a cat on me?"

"She has to be on somebody," Leigh answered. "Listen, are you awake?"

Warren glanced at the darkness outside their window and blinked. "I am now."

"Eva Menlin knew I didn't have her suitcase," Leigh announced. "She created a distraction so that she could take a picture of my face. *A picture*, Warren. Somehow or other, she got my picture to the Finney sibs and told them I was her. Or she was me. Or that I was the one who would set up the meeting. Don't you see?"

He raised up on his elbows. Snowbell rolled downhill a little, but after a slight repositioning, she dozed off again on his midsection. Warren stared at Leigh for a moment, but then his face dawned with understanding. "That does make a weird sort of sense. If she knew what she was getting into with the Finneys, she would want to be in control of the circumstances of that meeting. Otherwise any of the four could try to approach her individually before the group handoff and bargain with her, or threaten her, or worse."

"Exactly," Leigh agreed. "And you know they were watching for her to show up in town, too. What better way to protect herself than to send them out after a decoy?"

Warren nodded. "You're right. It's brilliant, actually. She could send out your picture and say, 'Here I am, I'll be getting in touch, but don't call me, I'll call you.'"

"That must be what she did!" Leigh exclaimed. "If she told them *not* to approach the woman in the picture, it would fit perfectly with the Finneys' reactions. Think about it. Russell came up to me on the beach expecting *me* to talk to *him*. But when I didn't, he backed off like he realized he'd overstepped. Bruce followed the rules a little better, at least at first. Sharonna didn't follow them at all — she searched my room hoping to steal the friggin' diamonds for herself! And at the office Janelle followed me outside because she thought I was trying to initiate contact!"

"All that makes sense, except one thing," Warren said. "How could Eva know you were going to be hanging around Port Mesten, specifically? Getting off a plane in the Corpus Christi airport means nothing. You could have been headed anywhere."

"That's true," Leigh considered, deflating a little. "But she didn't have to send a picture of somebody they'd necessarily run into."

"No," Warren argued. "But it wouldn't have worked nearly as well. Didn't Bruce say something about 'you' promising contact within three days? My guess is that Eva wanted to spend at least one full day in the area herself, incognito, getting a feel for where and how she could arrange the handoff of the diamonds. Ensuring her own safety would be a delicate operation. A diamond trader's professional reputation is their livelihood, so the Finneys could be assured that a pro at her level wouldn't rip them off. But *she* couldn't be assured of the same."

"No," Leigh said heavily. "She could not."

"She was probably aware that the FBI was closing in, and that the Finneys would be antsy. There's no telling if she knew that the CFO had been murdered when she arrived — at that point his body would have been in the ocean, but not yet washed ashore. Maybe she suspected the worst. Maybe he had been the one who hired her; clearly, they used some go-between. Whatever made her nervous, having a local decoy was a godsend. It kept all four Finneys spinning their wheels while she was free to roam around undetected."

Leigh blew out a breath. "I was her patsy."

"Yes," Warren said sympathetically. "But why you? How did she know?"

Leigh concentrated until it came to her. "The Silver King!" she said triumphantly. "We were talking about it when we got off the plane, remember? I don't know what we said or exactly where we were, but she could have been eavesdropping on the jetway or in the halls or right next to the carousel — it doesn't matter. All she had to hear was Silver King or anything about Port Mesten and she'd know she'd found her mark!"

Warren nodded. "You're absolutely right."

Leigh felt a chill. She walked around the bed and crawled back under the covers again. "So… do you think Eva ever called that meeting?"

Warren was quiet a moment. "No, I don't think she did. Her return flight was for Wednesday night. She must have intended to hand off the diamonds by then."

"Stanley was murdered sometime around dawn on Thursday," Leigh thought out loud. "I think he saw Eva's murderer trying to dispose of her body. But she could have been killed anytime on Wednesday, and the murderer was just waiting until dark. Maybe he had trouble finding a likely spot, seeing as how throwing a body in the ocean had just been shown to have its drawbacks."

"You called the murderer 'he,'" Warren noted.

Leigh nodded. "I don't see how Janelle or Sharonna either one could have chased down and strangled Stanley. He might have been old, but he wasn't weak. If either of the women is guilty, they weren't alone. It's a shame it rained so hard, or we would have known from the footprints how many people were involved."

Footprints. The thought seemed to strike a chord, but when Leigh's phone buzzed on its charger in the kitchen, the idea morphed into a wisp and evaporated into her mental fog. That was happening entirely too often these days.

"Let it go," Warren said with yawn. "It's just a text. We don't have to get up for hours yet. If it's an emergency, they'll call." He reached out to pull her in, but Leigh's curiosity was piqued. She slipped out of bed and strode into the kitchen.

Her phone screen glowed with the light of a text from Bev, who had even less reason than Leigh did to be awake at this hour of the morning.

> Attention Birders! We will have an emergency meeting of Team Stanley Saturday morning at 9:00am SHARP. Established members only: NO exceptions. Critical updates must be shared! Dire consequences must be prevented! ABSOLUTE SECRECY IS IMPERATIVE. TELL NO ONE. DELETE THIS TEXT!

Leigh stared at the message, her brow furrowed. What the hell?

Chapter 23

When Leigh and Warren entered the door of the Grande's Community Center this time, they were dressed for a summer afternoon in Death Valley. The morning was warm already, and given the tone of the meeting notice, the windows were certain to be shut tight again.

"Well, hey there, you poor dear," Bonnie greeted Leigh with her usual melodramatic drawl. "How are you holding up?"

"I'm all right." Leigh smiled back at her and Sue both, wondering at their continued concern over her mental health when they had been the ones to stumble upon a uniquely grisly crime scene just yesterday. They were unaware of Leigh's depth of experience in unintentional corpse viewings, but their own constitutions were still remarkable. "What about you? Are you two all right?"

Sue waved off the concern. "I feel for the woman's husband of course," she explained. "But as for the rest, well... circle of life, as they say. Did you know it's a regular funerary practice in Tibet? They call it 'sky burial.'"

"The way they see it, the vultures perform a valuable service," Bonnie chimed in.

"The shame was in the woman's murder, not how nature dealt with its consequences," Sue said practically. "Please, take a seat up front, Leigh. Bev wanted you to be handy."

Leigh hesitated. She had tried to contact Bev this morning, but her cousin-in-law hadn't answered and Hap would say only that they'd both been very busy. He explained that he couldn't talk where he was at that moment, but that everything would be explained at the meeting.

Warren led his wife, her feet dragging, to two open seats in the front row. "More air circulation up here," he purported. The room was filling in fast, and although the crowd was not as large as that at the original gathering, the showing was impressive for a meeting called on a Saturday morning with only a few hours' notice.

Bev soon emerged from a crowd of birders in the kitchen. She gestured for everyone to sit down and for Sue and Bev to close — and presumably to guard — both doors. The windows were already shut and the blinds pulled. "Thank you for coming," Bev announced, her booming voice and commanding presence once again belying the short, stout frame and apple-pie face that would otherwise scream "pushover."

"It's been an eventful night, folks," Bev began. "A lot has happened, both good and bad. The first thing I'll tell you, for the tourists and snowbirds who aren't connected to the local gossip that's been lighting up the phone lines all night, is that as of this morning, all four of the Finney siblings are in official police custody."

A cheer went up in the room. Leigh sucked in a breath and looked at Warren. "So fast?" she mouthed. No wonder the investigator had looked so happy last night. The Rangers must already have been in the process of getting the warrants. But for what, exactly?

The noise level in the room rose as multiple people called out similar questions.

Bev shushed everyone with a gesture. "There are a million rumors flying around, but I'll tell you what we're pretty sure of. Neighbors over at the Finney mansion — where Bruce lives — say the Rangers showed up en masse over there in the middle of the night. They seemed to be searching all over, but apparently they concentrated a lot of attention on the boathouse, and they ended up hauling one boat away altogether."

"They dumped that body in the ocean!" someone shouted. "The one that washed up on the beach!"

Bev nodded. "Seems like a darn good possibility, doesn't it? At about the same time, two Rangers showed up over at the Silver King and left with Sharonna Finney in the back seat. Russell was staying in a condo not far from the mansion, and they picked him up there. And we have it on good authority that Janelle was arrested at her place in Corpus Christi."

Another cheer broke out. "They were the ones that murdered Stanley too, then!"

"I bet they were all guilty, one way or another!"

"And we got 'em!"

"We did it!"

"That'll teach people not to mess with a birder!"

Bev waited a moment before reining in the levity. "I happen to know that our 'random observations' were helpful to the Rangers on several key points," she said with a sly smile. "So yes, y'all deserve a lot of credit. There are a whole lot of questions still to be answered about exactly who did what to whom, but I think we can all rest easy knowing that Stanley's killer is behind bars now. And hopefully, he and/or she will be staying there a good, long while!"

The next round of applause, Bev cut off short. "But I'm afraid our job isn't quite done," she announced, her face turning grim. "Because I haven't got to the bad news yet."

Leigh turned to Warren, her face a question mark. He responded to her in kind. She was not the slightest bit interested in hearing any bad news. If the Finneys were in custody and the Rangers were on the case, what else was there to say? It was more than she could have hoped for! As far as she was concerned, the Harmons could now be officially excused. They still had their Saturday play day left, and she intended to make the most of it. After all, she was on vacation.

"Now, this gets a little complicated, so bear with me," Bev began.

Leigh looked around like a caged animal, but neither of the exits were close to her chair, and she didn't fancy being tackled by Sue, much less Bonnie, if she attempted a premature escape.

"We believe that the reason behind all this mayhem is the Finney Enterprises fortune," Bev continued. "As some of you know, Cortland Finney was a dear friend of mine and Hap's, but there's no love lost between us and those no-good kids of his, and we're not going to pretend otherwise. A lot of evidence out there is pointing to the same picture, and it's this: after Cort died, the kids got into some illegal shenanigans with their parents' business. And when it looked like the law was about to catch up with them, they decided to sell out, split the cash four ways, and skip town. We don't know how Ted Sullivan the CFO was mixed up in all that, but we do know he wound up dead and that the Rangers think the Finneys killed him. Next thing that happens is that a fancy diamond trader from New York City comes down to Port Mesten — and she winds up dead, too."

The crowd began to buzz with hushed murmuring. Clearly, not

everyone had heard this part of the story.

"That's right," Bev asserted. "Her name was Eva Menlin, and she came down here to make a special delivery. She came to deliver the Finney children their inheritance cashed out in diamonds, so they could escape the law and keep their money by sneaking it out of the country."

"Diamonds!" a woman in the back shouted, standing up. "That's crazy! It sounds like some corny spy movie!"

"You're telling me," Bev agreed. "But it's real, Mary Lou. Uncut diamonds are as good as cash, but they're small enough to hide in a pocket and you can take them on a plane and sell them anywhere in the world."

A few people swore under their breath, but one man called out impatiently, "So what's the bad news? What do I care about the Finneys' fortune, so long as Stanley's killers are brought to justice? We're here to make the outdoors safe for birders!"

"I second that!"

Bev's stony scowl silenced the dissenters in a heartbeat. "Keep your knickers on, Wes! I'm getting to that part!" She paused a moment. It was a pause that Leigh suspected would have been shorter had Bev been more fond of the man complaining, but he had annoyed everyone the previous day by "gripping off" about seeing a white-tailed kite no one else saw — a major birding faux pas.

"Here's the deal," Bev continued. "We don't know where the diamonds that Eva brought with her are now. The Rangers may have them. Or the Finneys may have hidden them somewhere. But there are two facts that disturb us greatly, and they should disturb anybody who cares about the birdlife of Port Mesten."

Leigh raised an eyebrow. She hadn't given much thought to where Eva's diamonds had ended up, and she didn't particularly care. But she did wonder what birds had to do with it.

"Fact number one," Bev began, ticking on her fingers. "None of the Finneys *did* skip town, and the diamond trader has been dead since at least Wednesday. If they got the diamonds from her before killing her, what have they been doing since? Why hang around town waiting to get arrested for three murders *and* their illegal business dealings?"

"That makes no sense," someone grumbled.

"Exactly," Bev agreed. "Fact number two: Somebody dropped Eva Menlin's body in the water, then made the fatal mistake of murdering an innocent birder, early Thursday morning. Thursday night, *somebody* was wandering around those same wetlands in the very area where Stanley was chased and killed. Sandy and Raymond saw the tracks at dawn on Friday, and they were fresh since the rain at midnight. That means somebody — and they say it was somebody with big feet — was snooping around in the dark that night. There was nearly a full moon, but it was cloudy. Now, I ask you. *Why?*"

The room went quiet.

A sinking, slippery feeling oozed about Leigh's insides. *Footprints.* The timing of them was odd, wasn't it? Of course, any ghoulish bystander could be curious to go and see where the murder had occurred. That explanation wasn't insane. It wasn't even all that unlikely.

But until now, Leigh hadn't realized there was another option.

"You think that somebody lost the diamonds!" a woman screeched in a high soprano. She was sitting directly behind Warren, and Leigh felt him wince.

"Shush!" Bev said sternly. "We can't let anyone overhear!"

"Oh, my God!" a man exclaimed. "It could have happened! If the murderer had the diamonds in a pocket, and then chased Stanley across the mud flats, and they struggled…"

"Indeed," Bev replied. "He or she might not have noticed the diamonds were missing until after they'd fled the scene. And once daylight broke, they could hardly go running around searching in full view of everyone — with poor Stanley's body lying right there."

"Why, I'd call the police if I saw anyone running around off the boardwalk out there, whether I knew about Stanley or not!" another woman said indignantly. "They'd be pestering the birds and damaging fragile habitat!"

"Yes," Bev said heavily. "They would."

"Well, do you think they *found* the diamonds?" someone else called out.

As Bev paused and cleared her throat, Leigh made a note of how gifted the woman was at creating anticipation. The temperature in the room started to climb dramatically.

"There's been no official word on that," Bev answered in a quiet voice.

"Oh, but they must have!"

"I certainly hope so!"

"Well, the Finneys are all in custody now, aren't they?"

"Like that matters!" a woman said frantically, popping out of her seat. "Can you imagine what would happen if they *didn't* find the diamonds? And if word got out?"

A man stood up too. "Oh, good Lord! It would be a free-for-all!"

The room exploded into anxious chatter, which Bev let flow for a while before reining in her audience again. "As far as Hap and I know, no one else has put all these facts together but us," she emphasized. "Because no one but our group here and the Rangers know about those footprints — and we were the ones who alerted the Rangers. But that doesn't mean it won't get out. By now everyone in Port Mesten knows Eva was a diamond trader, and today it'll spread all over creation that the Finneys have been arrested. As famous as the family is, reporters all over the country are going to be asking why, and soon. So I'm afraid that it's not a matter of *if* this is all going to come out, my friends. It's only a matter of when. We don't know for a fact that no one else saw those footprints. We can't even be sure the police themselves won't leak something. God knows the locals have leaked enough already!"

"Oh, but the *herons!*" Sue said miserably. "If people are tromping around all over the wetlands, the birds will leave and not come back!"

"It'll be a disaster area!" Bonnie wailed. "People'll be jumping in their pickups all the way to Dallas and driving down with buckets and shovels and the forks off their kitchen tables! And never mind where the murder actually happened, either. Folks'll be tearing up every inch of that preserve as sure as if it was bulldozed!"

"Oh, but they can't!"

"The birds! The preserve will be ruined *forever!*"

"We can't let that happen!"

"What can we do?"

Bev shushed the crowd with a dramatic waving motion. "What *can* we do?" she asked. "That's why we're here right now! We have to think, and we have to think fast. Because once a mania like this starts, no one is going to be able to stop it. Let's not fool ourselves! No fence, certainly no yellow tape... the lure of millions in diamonds will sure as shootin' turn our bird-watching mecca into Texas' next gold rush!"

"NO!"

"That's terrible!"

"Criminal!"

"We have to stop it before it starts!"

"Wait, did you say *'millions?'*"

"Shut up, Wes!"

"Now just hold on a minute here," a relatively calm voice demanded. Leigh recognized Walter, the pathologist, standing up two rows behind her. "For all we know, the murderer found the diamonds already. Maybe he's got them stashed somewhere. Or maybe the Rangers have already recovered them. Before we go into a full-out panic, it seems like we should make sure there's something to panic about."

"I agree with you," Bev said quickly. "But let me finish, because there's more. It makes sense that if the diamonds were easy to find, like just lying in a bag or an envelope right out on top of the sand somewhere, then the murderer would have found them Thursday night, right?"

"We still don't know that he didn't," Walter persisted.

"Yes, we do," Bev retorted. "Because our dawn patrol this morning reported a boatload of fresh footprints in the very same spot — made just *last night.*"

Leigh drew in a sharp breath. Warren looked over at her with an equally surprised expression.

"Sandy and Raymond have been out again themselves, and they've verified it," Bev continued. "The prints are the same big ol' boots as before, there's just more than twice as many of them. So whoever was out searching Thursday night almost certainly was back at it again on Friday."

"The sky was clear last night," a woman remarked hopefully. "There was a nice moon. Maybe they did find what they were looking for."

"But if they found the diamonds, why didn't they skip town before they could get arrested?" another woman argued.

"Yeah, why did they go back home and go to bed?"

"If the Rangers had the diamonds, would they tell us?"

"The Rangers won't confirm or deny whether anybody has any

diamonds," Bev answered. "But you have to figure that if they did recover them, there'd be no reason they wouldn't want to crow about it. No, Hap and I have given this a lot of thought."

She paused for effect, then continued methodically. "It seems to us like if you lose something, and then you go back and retrace your steps and you can't find it, that means one of two things. Number one: somebody else took it. Or number two: it's dropped out of sight. And our money's on number two. Think about it. Whatever little pouch or envelope those stones might have been in would have gotten waterlogged right quick. Whether it was dropped in the water or not, the way it rained afterward, it could have gotten washed into a gulley or settled down into the silt. And God forbid, if whatever the diamonds were in got opened up and they spilled out, nobody'd ever find all of them."

The room broke out in groans and sighs.

"So as much as we'd like to hope otherwise," Bev concluded, "we believe that those diamonds *are* lost somewhere in the preserve. And the story *will* get out, folks, sooner or later. You and I can't control either of those things. The question for us is: how can we protect the birds?"

Leigh startled a little. That particular question had hardly been uppermost on her mind. Nor had it been what she'd expected to hear. Maybe Bev and Hap were honest enough to have no interest in hunting for the diamonds themselves, but what made them think that an entire roomful of people, many of whom they barely knew, would feel the same? She looked at Warren and saw his brow furrowed with thought. Hap was sitting in a corner of the room behind Bev, looking equally thoughtful.

"Maybe we could get some kind of legal protection on the preserve?" a women suggested. "So the local police could throw people out?"

"We should contact the Audubon society. I bet they could help us."

"And the Sierra Club! They have a legal team."

"There has to be a way!"

Leigh cocked an eyebrow, amazed. She would have been less surprised by a stampede on the door. But evidently, Bev was right about the primary concern of at least some of her fellow birders. Leigh's mind wandered as the calm, intense discussion continued.

Big footprints. She tried to picture Bruce, or Russell, splashing around in the sand and the mud in the wee hours of the morning. The murderer would have to carry some kind of flashlight. He would be angry at his own clumsiness in losing the diamonds. And terribly worried about being seen. *Again.* Had he not already murdered one person who had accidentally witnessed something he shouldn't have? He would not want to do it again.

But hadn't Bruce and Russell both approached her just yesterday — talking about *her* having something they both wanted — after the first set of footprints were made?

They had.

Leigh regrouped. She tried to overcome her own sexist assumptions. There was nothing stopping Sharonna or Janelle from tromping around in oversized rain boots, was there? And how did she know that one or the other wasn't trained in jiu jitsu or something? Perhaps Janelle's performance at the laundromat had been some carefully calculated act. Or maybe harmlessly nutty Sharonna was actually criminally insane Sharonna?

Leigh dropped her face in her hands and found both slick with sweat. The room was a sauna again. She was sympathetic to Bev and the others; really, she was. But at this particular moment, she could muster only so much concern for a hypothetically endangered bird habitat. All she wanted was to get the hell out of here and take her husband for a walk on the beach.

The Finneys had all been arrested. Nothing else mattered.

"You okay?" Warren whispered, pulling one hand away from her face.

Leigh nodded and smiled at him, but felt like both were a lie. Something was still bothering her. Something she almost remembered, but not quite. Something about the footprints. And possibly... the airport. Something that made her nervous.

She told herself to cut it out. The Finneys were *in jail*. She should be celebrating and forgetting, not looking for unsettling vagaries to dwell on.

"Let's skip out as soon as there's a lull," she whispered back. "We have a date today. *All day* today."

He smiled and caressed her shoulder.

I am on vacation, she told herself firmly, determined to revive her earlier optimism. *And I am no longer involved!*

Chapter 24

Leigh was thoroughly enjoying herself. She and Warren had walked out on the pier, watched the surfers and the fishermen do their thing, had coffee and donuts for a mid-morning snack (the cranberry bread had been so terribly long ago, after all), and were now wading barefoot in the waves as they made their way slowly back down the beach, walking hand in hand like teenagers. "Business Warren" of days past had exchanged his stuffy professional attire for a pair of shorts and a lightweight button-down shirt, and Leigh could admire the good looks of "Vacation Warren" all day. They'd made reservations on a dolphin cruise in the afternoon and the only major decisions left to be made were where to eat lunch and dinner.

Yet still, every once in a while, a niggling feeling intruded on her happiness. The feeling that she had forgotten something, that she should be worrying about something, that she should stop what she was doing and try to figure it all out before something really bad happened.

She quashed that feeling mercilessly.

"This is interesting," Warren said, stooping down to pick up a fragment of shell with funky spots like a giraffe's.

"That's a broken piece of a crab carapace," Leigh said knowledgably.

"Oh." He tossed it back in the ocean. A very large bird cruised along the waterline, not too far above their heads. "And I suppose you know what that was, too?"

Leigh smirked. "Brown pelican," she answered. "Not to be confused with the white pelican."

Warren raised an eyebrow. "They've done it, haven't they? They've made a birder out of you."

Leigh laughed. "Well, um… some of the names are easier to remember than others."

His gaze focused over her shoulder across the road, and Leigh turned to glimpse the roof of the pavilion. They had reached the north entrance to the preserve.

When Leigh turned back to him, he looked away toward the Gulf. "So, you want to keep walking this way, or are you ready to head back?" he asked cheerfully.

Leigh smiled. They had been married entirely too long for him to fool her. "If you want to see the preserve, it's okay," she offered gamely. The prospect of returning didn't thrill her, but nor did it wield the same creepiness factor it had when the Finneys were still on the loose. Besides which, it was too important a part of Port Mesten's mystique for Warren to miss out on because of her. "It's a big place. I can avoid the areas I want to avoid, no problem," she assured.

"Are you sure?" he questioned. "The last thing I want to do is ruin your mood. But I have to admit, I'd like to at least get a glimpse of these mythical wetlands before we leave. I've heard so much about the boardwalk and the alligators and the herons and the quicksand..."

Leigh started walking toward the road and pulled him with her. "The alligators are only at the other entrance. I *think*. But you'll love the herons. They are seriously cool looking. And yet they seem rather sinister, somehow..."

She fought back against the pang of trepidation that taunted her as they crossed the road and entered the nature preserve. It was a beautiful morning, and the parking lot was nearly full. The trails and boardwalk were humming with visitors, and the mood was lively, but respectful. Leigh's cynical side wondered if half the crowd were gawkers who were only here because of the murders. On the flip side, however, the whole "serial-killer" thing had probably scared some people away, so maybe the crowd was average for a Saturday. A good percentage of the people were older adults, as usual, and many had binoculars and cameras with zoom lenses, identifying them as legitimate nature lovers. Leigh and Warren merged with the crowd, and she began to feel more comfortable. She was perfectly safe here, and not needing her disguise anymore was heavenly. How she loved letting her unfettered hair fly in the breeze! If she was lucky, she might even return to Pittsburgh with her face tanned.

They walked through the pavilion and along one of the far trails, and Leigh amused herself by pretending to identify birds (with ridiculous names she made up on the spot) until Warren caught her out by finding an educational sign with pictures on it. They circled back to the main boardwalk, and Leigh accompanied him partway down. But when they reached the first resting platform, well short of the location where Stanley had died, she seated herself on a bench. "You go on to the observation tower," she instructed, pointing ahead. "I'll wait here. My feet can use the rest."

Warren studied her critically. "Are you sure?"

Leigh smiled. He loved observation towers. "Go," she repeated.

He went.

Leigh's feet were enjoying the rest very much. But Warren hadn't been gone thirty seconds when an elderly couple approached the platform moving at a snail's pace, assisted by one younger woman and two metal walkers. "There's a bench just ahead," the younger woman said to them encouragingly.

Leigh got back up. She walked to the edge of the platform and leaned her elbows over the railing. *Footprints.* She didn't want to look for them. But of course, she couldn't help it.

Her eyes scanned the sandy plains with their tufts of grass, pools of shallow water, and maze of streams. Wherever there wasn't high ground, water, or grass, the earth was topped with a smooth flat of muddy sand. She could make out no footprints from where she stood. But she knew they must be out there. No one could walk on the flats without leaving some trace. Not even a bird.

She could go a little closer and look.

But she *shouldn't.*

Why did she even care?

Because something was still wrong, that's why.

No! Leigh forced herself to look in the opposite direction, out over the remainder of the preserve. She wasn't sure, but she thought she saw a spot of pink along a distant pond that could be a roseate spoonbill. Gulls and pelicans soared and swooped overhead, along with some kind of hawk. Herons stalked among the grasses, and coots squabbled with each other as they glided about in the reeds. Schools of tiny fish laid claim to wide, shimmering swaths of shallow water that to them must seem vast as the ocean. An amazing abundance of wildlife called this marshland home. And when word got out that millions of dollars' worth of diamonds had been lost somewhere within it, it would never be the same again.

Leigh exhaled with a sigh. The birders would try everything they could. But she doubted it would make any difference. The preserve already forbade visitors from leaving the trails. It could close entirely, even attempt some sort of fence, but people would breach it. The only way to keep out the fortune hunters would be to staff the entire place with paid, muscled security 24/7, and who could possibly foot the bill for that? Indefinitely?

There was no hope.

She lowered her eyes. A little brown spotted bird with long legs, one of those sandpiper/plover/yellowlegs things that the birders were always arguing about, was strutting around near the base of the platform looking for insects at the water's edge. She watched as it darted after a bug, having to dodge around a discarded juice box to reach it.

Leigh frowned. As soon as the bird had moved away, she stepped carefully around the edge of the railing and off the boardwalk. She walked the few steps over the ground, retrieved the crumpled juice box, and returned to drop it in the trashcan that was conveniently available right there on the platform. *People!* She returned to her place and looked out again. But now, all she could see in front of her were her own footprints in the mud.

She was bothered again.

Why?

She didn't know. It was only that her tracks were so incredibly obvious... The birders could not have been mistaken about the footprints they had seen the last two nights. *Two nights.* What had happened last night, anyway? If all the Finneys were arrested elsewhere, the one who was here searching must either have found the diamonds or given up and gone home sometime before dawn. If the police had recovered the diamonds during the arrests, they would almost certainly have said so. The fact that they didn't meant that the murderer either found the loot and immediately got rid of it again or never found it at all. And if even the person who dropped the diamonds had given up searching for them... those diamonds were never going to be found. Not unless the water was drained and every cup of sandy mud here was poured through a flour sifter. In the meantime, the whole preserve would be overrun with greedy, noisy, disrespectful, trash-dumping, nature-wrecking fortune hunt—

Leigh stopped in mid-thought as an image popped into her head. It was an image of something she had seen — seen and dismissed as unimportant. It could still be unimportant.

Or it could be the answer to everything.

She started walking toward the observation tower. Then she began to jog. It was an incredible long shot, and she was probably crazy. But what could it hurt? The worst that could happen was that someone would yell at her. And most likely she would ruin her shoes.

It was worth it.

For the birds, of course.

She had to slow down for two groups of people who were walking abreast and blocking the whole boardwalk, but otherwise she kept up a brisk pace. By the time she reached the spot where she had first encountered Barb on the path and Walter stuck out in the muck, she was breathing heavily and sweating again. She stopped and looked out. The tracks left by her and Walter and all the police officers were gone now, washed away by Thursday night's rain. But she did see one new set of tracks in the distance. Boot tracks, and big ones, just as Sandy and Raymond had reported. And wait — there was another set over that way. And over there…

Leigh turned and jogged to the spot where she had left the boardwalk to go fetch Walter. She looked at the line of tall marsh grass facing her and smiled. The trail she had beaten through the brush was still identifiable. She doubted the same was true of the paths she and Walter had followed when they discovered Stanley's body, since a whole crime scene team had examined that area. But this place hadn't been a part of that process.

A couple with children approached, and Leigh pretended to be tying her shoe. As soon as they had passed by, she looked up and down the visible length of the boardwalk. There were several other visitors within sight, but none appeared to be paying any attention to her. Even the people visible up on the observation tower were looking the other way.

She darted into the grass and moved swiftly out of view. The brush was tall enough here to swallow her up entirely, so she doubted her misdemeanor would get her into trouble. It was possible that someone up on the tower could see the grass moving, but once she got where she was going, she was pretty sure that risk would be eliminated. The area where Stanley died was difficult to see from the tower; the view was blocked by a line of scrubby trees and bushes in addition to the tall grass. She wasn't sure, but she thought that same natural screen would hide her destination as well. But if it didn't... Well, let somebody yell at her. She was doing this for a good cause.

She continued to follow her previous trail until the grass thinned out and she neared the water's edge. Straight ahead she could see the line of grass that had tricked her into thinking she could take a shortcut to Walter. Instead, she had plunged ankle deep into the water. This time she didn't step out into the open, but stayed hidden in the brush. Then she began moving in a parallel track to where she had sloshed along in the water before. She looked up toward the tower and was pleased to see nothing but grass tips and distant branches. *Perfect.* She could conduct her analysis in private.

A crackling sound somewhere to her right made her stop a moment. She stood still and listened, but heard nothing else. She chastised herself for panicking and started moving again. Of course there were other creatures around and about! Any bird could make such a sound. There were no alligators, at least. They liked deeper water.

Relax, Koslow.

She refocused on her mission. Where had she jumped back out of the water before? She studied the mud on the bank.

Boot tracks.

Her heart began to pound. So, the murderer had been here, too.

A shiver began to rock her shoulders, but she stilled them with determination. It was at least seventy-five degrees out here, the sun was shining, and she was hot. Besides which, all the murderers were in jail now. It was over.

But...

Shut up!

She looked further along the water line. Where was her scraping? When she had jumped back up on this bank before, she'd made a huge gouge with her right foot. Would the rain have completely filled it in?

Probably.

She turned and doubled back. She was approaching this wrong. She needed to look at the bank from the opposite direction, the direction she had seen it from last time. She said a fond farewell to her eighteen-dollar discount sneakers and splashed out into the water. As the cool liquid soaked its way through to her toes, she turned around and tried to remember exactly how everything had unfolded two days earlier.

She had been moving along the bank, looking at the clumps of grass. She had wanted to find something halfway solid-looking to step on. Something that would hold her weight for a second, at least. And then she had seen something right over…

She stopped. A grin spread over her face. It had been right here.

A piece of trash.

She'd seen the bit of wet cloth lying half submerged at the base of the tangled clump of grass. She hadn't looked at it closely. Why would she? It could have been anything. A piece of a reusable shopping bag. A baby's sock. A torn shred of landscaping fabric.

She would never know unless she found it again. But that was a big "if." Because whatever she had seen here before, it was no longer visible.

"But this is where it was," she whispered to herself. "I'm sure of it." She didn't know why she was sure. The clump of grass in question didn't look like it used to. The weight of her body had almost completely smooshed it down into the mud. But some of the blades were still sticking up, and if she used her imagination, she could almost see a shallow dent in the bank where her other foot had landed and dug a trench.

She squatted down, careful to keep her butt out of the water. "No other way to know!" she whispered encouragingly to herself as she stretched out a hand. Her fingers traced the grass blades down to their source and hit slimy mud, sending a cloud of brown up into the water. She could see nothing now; she would just have to feel. She pushed her fingers blindly into the sandy silt and wiggled, trying not to think about pinching crayfish and sucking leaches. In a matter of seconds, she felt something solid. It was fabric.

Her fingers closed around the material. She jerked it up with a rush of excitement and instantly lost her balance. Her prize came up out of the water just as her rear end went down in it, and as oozing cold seeped rapidly through her underwear, she pretended to herself that she had intended to sit down all along.

Hey… it worked for Mao Tse.

Leigh remained sitting in the mud as she stared at the dripping material in her fingers. It was navy blue. It was made of an unassuming canvas-like material. But it was more than just a scrap. Now that she could see the whole thing, she could tell that it was a small change purse. She shifted her fingers to feel of its middle, and her heart skipped.

There was something hard and gritty inside.

Many, many small somethings.

The diamonds!

A distinctive click sounded from somewhere behind her right ear. It was followed by a calm, low voice she'd never heard before.

"Hand that to me. Or my next bullet goes straight through your brain."

Chapter 25

Leigh didn't move. Birds overhead were still squawking. She could hear children shouting and squealing, people chatting. The sunshine was warm and the water around her butt and ankles was cold. The rest of this scene could not possibly be real.

"Excuse me?" she said lamely, not moving.

"You heard me," the deep voice growled. In her peripheral vision she could see a massive, beefy hand stretching out, palm open. "Hand it over. *Now.* You make noise, I shoot."

More happy, chatting voices. The people on the boardwalk were so ridiculously close by — yet none of them could see her. Leigh swallowed hard and tried to think.

Who the hell was this? Did it even matter?

No. All that mattered was getting through the next few seconds alive. And as scared as Leigh was, she knew better than to think that following his directions, however simply they were put, was necessarily her wisest course of action. What did he want? He wanted the diamonds, obviously. Once he had them, he would want to get out of here without being followed. Both could be accomplished far more easily if Leigh ceased to breathe. What were three bodies as opposed to two? Or was it four as opposed to three?

He could wrest the purse from her at any moment; he could shoot her dead and take it at any moment. But so far he had opted for neither, and she thought she understood why. *Noise.* There were people all around them. To engage her in any kind of struggle risked her screaming, and if he shot her, everyone would hear. Either way, 911 got called. His best chance to get the diamonds and get away unseen would be to threaten her into cooperating. Then he could gag her and strangle her quietly.

Pass.

Leigh tried very hard to concentrate. She really didn't think he would shoot the gun. Dozens of witnesses would see him running away, the police would be called within seconds, and they were on a friggin' *island*. There was only one road out southbound and a ferry to the north, so unless he had a boat he'd have to swim his way out of town. Of course, if the rest of him was as big as his hand, he wouldn't need to fire the gun to shut her up, either temporarily or permanently. But that was a chance she'd have to take, because as far as she could figure, one chance was all she had.

She was in a terribly awkward position, sitting in the mud with her face turned away from him. But the pose did offer her one advantage: if he couldn't see her expression, he couldn't anticipate her actions.

Leigh looked at the hand that was stretched out to her left side and began, very slowly, to feint as if she was passing over the purse that was in her right hand. Then, with a flash of wiggling movement she prayed was difficult to follow, she pitched her body forward and to the left while revving up her right arm and throwing the purse as high and as hard as she could in the opposite direction.

Simultaneously, she screamed her head off.

She felt the canvas purse leave her fingers just as her face hit the muddy water with a bracing splat. Every muscle in her body tightened as she awaited the crackling sound of a shot, a piercing pain... but all she felt was the cold and all she heard were the fluent curses of her assailant. She lifted her head from the water.

He had moved away from her by several feet. He was pacing frantically, swatting at the tall grass, his gaze alternating between scanning the ground at its base and peering over the top of it toward the boardwalk. Leigh's screaming had stirred up a commotion of chatter — as well as a few additional screams and yells — from the unseen visitors beyond. Feet pounded on the wooden boards from all directions.

Leigh's first sight of the man scrambled her brain. She didn't know him... but she did. He was quite tall, quite large... but he looked so silly now. Everything he wore was cheap-quality tourist stuff and appeared newly purchased, even though it was spattered with mud. But nothing fit him well. His fisherman's cap was way too small and sat perched uncomfortably high on his head, and his khaki slacks were so short they revealed several inches of his surprisingly hip-looking black leather boots.

Gucci shoes?

That was it!

She had seen him at the airport in Corpus Christi... standing next to Eva Menlin! He must have come with her... they were working together... But he couldn't be her husband, could he? Her husband had been at their home in New York City when he'd reported her missing.

Leigh stared at the man's heavily muscled shoulders and tree-trunk thighs as he slashed viciously through the grass with a forearm. She imagined him chasing Stanley, tackling him, strangling him with his bare hands...

No, this behemoth was no ordinary traveling companion. He was a goon. *Eva's* goon. She must have brought him along for her own security, which wasn't a bad idea when delivering millions of dollars' worth of diamonds to a bunch of crazy people. But he had found out more than he needed to know, perhaps, and he had turned on her. Maybe Eva's professional reputation and family's good name prevented her from ripping off her clients, but a hired hand would have no such compunction. He had seen a chance to end his days as a working man, and he had taken it. Then some nerdy old birdwatching retiree had gotten in his way...

Now Leigh was doing the same.

She scrambled desperately to get up, but the damned muck was difficult to maneuver out of, particularly when she was trembling. All she needed was a couple more seconds of confusion, just the slightest additional delay before he found the purse again, and she should be able to escape. Surely he would just run, then. Chasing her down and killing her, after all, would cost him valuable time.

Her flailing around wasn't pretty, but eventually she got to her feet. She shot a glance in the man's direction and was happy to see him bending over and searching wildly through the grass, cursing fluently as he did so. He must not have seen where the purse landed, either. *Perfect.*

She whirled and started off in the opposite direction. She knew better than to scream now – the man was angry enough that he could shoot her in the back out of spite. She leapt into the cover of the grass and started on a detour that would get her back to the boardwalk without getting any closer to him, but she hadn't gone six feet before she screamed again, this time unintentionally.

Another man had planted himself directly in her path. This one's long legs assumed a wide-based stance, and his lean, sinewy arms held a gun at eye level, pointed at the center of her chest.

Are you freakin' kidding me?

Who the hell was this?!

This man wore jeans, short boots, a tee shirt, and a light jacket. His brown hair was short and nondescript and his eyes were an expressionless, steely gray. Leigh had never seen him before. "Be quiet and put your hands up!" he ordered in a firm, yet hushed tone.

"Freeze!" another male voice boomed in the distance.

Somewhere, a woman screamed.

"I said freeze!" the unseen male voice repeated.

Leigh stayed frozen. She didn't know whether the man in front of her would shoot her or not, but she knew for certain that the goon behind her would. God only knew what the third man wanted, but shocked inertia kept her hands at her sides.

A vicious angry growl sounded close by in the brush, followed by the pounding *whoomp* of bodies colliding and a series of inarticulate grunts.

"Don't move!" Leigh's captor yelled at her, swinging his firearm to the side. He stepped away from her toward the melee. "Freeze! Police!"

Leigh exhaled with a rush and an expletive. *NOW you tell me?*

Heedless of his instructions, law officer or not, she started moving. Leigh Koslow Harmon was getting the hell out of here.

She had moved only another three feet when a shot crackled through the air.

The sound was so loud it battered her eardrums and rattled her skull, and she fell to her knees, wondering if her head was all there. Panicked hands felt her face and her hair for blood just as the sound of a man groaning and screaming overcame the buzzing in her ears enough to register.

"Hands behind your back! Hands behind your back!"

Now people were screaming all over the place.

"Leigh!"

Warren's call carried over the general clamor, and Leigh lifted her chin. *Oh, right.* Her husband had been here too, hadn't he? He must be worried about her…

She tried to get up, but her legs felt like jelly. She looked down at her hands. No blood. That was encouraging. The rest of her body looked intact, too. It was the goon over there groaning… he must be the one who'd been shot.

"Leigh!" Warren called again.

"I'm okay!" she yelled back, finding her voice. She put her hands down on the sandy soil for balance, then pushed herself slowly back upright on gimpy legs. "I'm coming!"

"No, you're not," the steely-eyed gunman argued, appearing out of nowhere to level his gun at her again. "I told you to hold still."

Leigh almost laughed at him. A person could only have a gun pointed at them so many times before thinking she must actually be asleep.

"You said you were the police," she rasped instead.

"Texas Rangers, Company D," he replied coolly. "Put your hands up."

Leigh stared back at him with disbelief. "Me? What did I do? I'm on your side!"

"Don't make me tell you again."

Leigh put her hands up.

The officer stepped around her and briefly patted the pockets of her shorts. There was no place else she could hide a weapon, seeing as how her cleavage couldn't conceal a cough drop.

"All right," he said, no less coolly. "You can relax, but stand still for now." He kept his gun out.

Leigh said nothing sarcastic. But she thought plenty.

She looked over her shoulder where the Ranger was looking and could see Eva's erstwhile bodyguard thrashing around on the ground. His hands were cuffed behind his back, but still he kicked wildly at the officers who surrounded him. One of his shoulders had a fist-sized spot of blood on it, and he was simultaneously groaning like a baby and swearing like a sailor. The officers were shouting commands at him as they gradually closed back in.

Leigh tried to slow her breathing, then caught her captor's eye. "My husband is worried about me. Can't I go out now and show him I'm okay?"

"He heard you," the Ranger replied with maddening calm. His gun was still trained and ready.

Leigh's patience, such as it was, snapped. "What *is* this?" she demanded angrily. "I am the victim here! Why are you acting like I did something wrong?"

The Ranger had the gall to smirk at her. "Well, now, Ms. Harmon," he said levelly, even as the shouting next to them increased, along with the din from the unseen crowd on the boardwalk. Leigh was bothered that he knew her name. If he understood everything that had happened, why was he holding a gun on her?

"I don't suppose," he began, his lips lifting into the slightest of smirks, "you want to tell me how you, and only you, knew *exactly* where to find those diamonds?"

"I..." Leigh's mouth hung open for an unfortunately long period of time. Her face took on the hue of a tomato. *Why was it*, she thought to herself bitterly, that for her, and only her, the God's honest truth always sounded so flippin' ridiculous?

"I stepped on them," she answered finally.

The Ranger's smirk grew smirkier. "Oh you did, did you?"

"I know it sounds stupid," Leigh said defensively, shoving away the highly practical thought that she should probably shut up until she had a lawyer. She didn't and shouldn't *need* a lawyer, dammit! "But that's what happened. I was trying to get to Walter and I was looking for someplace solid to put my foot, and there was a piece of cloth stuck in a clump of grass, and I stepped on it."

She paused, allowing him to digest the concept. A swarm of activity continued behind her; the goon was still groaning and cursing.

"So why come back now?" the Ranger asked.

"Because I only just this morning found out that whoever killed Stanley must have dropped the diamonds!" Leigh insisted. "Even then, I didn't remember seeing the cloth until I came across another piece of trash over by the bench. I'm only here today because my husband wanted to see the preserve... but then I remembered seeing the blue—"

Without warning the Ranger stepped up, grabbed her by the wrist, and jerked her forward. Leigh shrieked in surprise as she stumbled, wondering if she were about to get her first taste of police brutality. But she understood the Ranger's actions when the ground on which she'd been standing was taken over by the writhing body of the oversized maniac who, even though he was cuffed and bleeding from one shoulder, had somehow managed to pull a knife. For such a large man, he was amazingly agile. He twisted his body and kicked out in the air toward his captors, holding the knife behind him. He was surrounded by three men, all with guns drawn, any of whom could have finished him off at any time. But no gunshot came. The officers seemed content to stay back and wait out their quarry.

Leigh offered no resistance as the Ranger pulled her farther away, out into the shallow water. She looked toward the boardwalk and could see that the crowd had been pushed back and was being held at bay by a local policeman. Warren was there, standing right behind the patrolman, and Leigh could see his shoulders slump with relief at the sight of her. But in the next second all hell broke loose again.

The goon, who had yet to give any sign of either tiring or giving up his pointless battle of resistance, had noticed her. At least she assumed he had, because the vile string of insults now foaming out of his mouth were distinctly targeted towards the female of the species. "You *blah blah*... you ruined everything you *blah blah*... how did you even know where to look, you *blah blah*... I'll *blah blah* your *blah blah blah*..."

He wriggled and bounced on the bank like some demented inchworm, moving rapidly closer to Leigh. But again, his struggle was pointless. He couldn't move anywhere near as fast as she could, even if there were not now four Texas Rangers ready to shoot him, *again*, if he managed to get to her. At least, that's what she was hoping they would do.

But perhaps that wouldn't be necessary. "Excuse me?" Leigh yelled back at him, even as she continued to move away. The Ranger told her to be quiet, but she didn't care. Her whole body flamed with fury. This man had wanted those diamonds so badly he had killed the woman who hired him to protect her. He'd killed a perfectly innocent birdwatcher who just happened to be in the wrong place at the wrong time, and he would certainly kill anyone and everyone who tried to prevent his escaping now, including her. "Are you talking to *me*?" she taunted.

The Ranger yelled at her again.

"You little *blah blah bl*—" The goon's last insults were unfortunately garbled. Squirming with rage in his single-minded pursuit, his prone form had wiggled out of the grass and off the bank, and his last kick had propelled him neatly out over several inches of water. The man remained oblivious to his situation even as his body splashed down and his still-moving mouth disappeared below the water line, and Leigh watched with grim satisfaction as he sucked in a lungful of muck, then roared back up two seconds later, gasping, sputtering, and coughing — but no longer kicking.

"Move in!" one of the Rangers shouted, and the discombobulated goon was swiftly tackled, disarmed, and shackled.

A cheer rose up from the boardwalk.

"Can I go now?" Leigh asked when the crisis was over, trying her best to appear a good citizen. Her previous captor had been an active participant in the melee; she could have crept off.

The cool-eyed Ranger studied her with a look that was both annoyed and admiring. "For now," he answered. He pointed toward the people on the boardwalk. "Stay with the local officer until we have a chance for some more questions."

"Can't wait," Leigh quipped, already walking. She was prepared to hear more insults from the bodyguard, but he seemed to be preoccupied with coughing. She held her head high as she sloshed across the mud. As horribly embarrassing as it would be to get stuck right now in front of everybody, fear of quicksand wasn't enough to make her take anything but the most direct route to Warren. She could feel her husband's frustration at being restrained by the police officer, and when she came close enough he broke away and met her halfway.

Leigh's knees went wobbly as she collapsed against him.

He enfolded her in a warm, crushing hug. "Five minutes," he whispered in her ear, his voice husky with emotion. "I left you alone for *five minutes*..."

Chapter 26

"I can't tell you how much I appreciate this," Leigh said, watching with glee as the fins of yet another group of bottlenose dolphins appeared beside the boat. She, Warren, Bev, and Hap were cruising around the ship channels, taking in the local sights and enjoying the warm Texas air in the hour before sunset.

"Oh, now, Carl was happy to do it," Hap insisted, leaning out over the railing next to her. "We all felt bad that you two missed your cruise earlier, and Carl doesn't need an excuse to take this old girl out on the water on a day like today."

"At least let us reimburse him for the gas," Warren offered.

"Not a chance," Hap declined. "We'd already collected a little money to get a defense fund set up for the preserve. Thanks to you, that unsolvable problem was solved before we'd spent a dime! Seems the least we could do is treat the two of you to a charter dolphin watch and a nice, romantic dinner out on your last night here. The rest will go to the preserve's regular foundation, don't you worry."

One of the dolphins leaped partway out of the water, and Leigh smiled as she heard its happy clicking sound. "The kids would love this."

Warren smiled in agreement. "We'll have to bring them here sometime."

"Absolutely!" Bev insisted. "Can't promise you we'll still be working at the Silver King or the Grande, of course. Their future's pretty much up in the air. But wherever we end up, you and those twins of yours are always welcome! What kind of cookies do the young'uns like?"

Leigh turned to her hostess with both a laugh and a groan. "Do you have any idea how long I am going to have to starve myself to recover from what was supposed to be a week of fresh air, exercise, and caloric moderation?"

Bev chuckled without remorse. "I just make the treats, darlin'. The consequences aren't my problem."

"Now you see what I've got to live with," Hap laughed, patting his protruding belly.

"So *that's* why I married you!" Warren exclaimed to Leigh, putting a hand to his own trim waist.

She punched him. "And I thought it was because you enjoyed spending quality time with law enforcement."

Bev and Hap both laughed, albeit a little nervously.

"We really are sorry this week hasn't been more… relaxing for you," Bev said sadly. "We'd hoped to show you a better time."

"Oh, please," Leigh said quickly, "none of what happened was your fault! And you've been fabulous in helping us out."

"Absolutely," Warren agreed. "I would never have been able to finish my work here if it weren't for you and your birder friends keeping an eye on… things. We owe you so much."

Bev smiled. "Well, we birders stick together," she said smugly.

Hap made a snorting sound. "I still say you can't be so sure about that."

"Now, Hap!" Bev protested. "I never did disagree with you! You know I took the risk of renegades into account."

"Do you mean," Warren asked, "you thought that some of the birders might go rogue and start hunting for the diamonds themselves? I have to admit, I was wondering about that myself."

Bev shrugged. "Well, sure. People are people, after all. But that didn't make forming the group a bad idea. The cause needed an army to have a fighting chance. Besides, I figured having a little peer pressure could help keep folks on the straight and narrow. If any of the regulars suddenly started wintering in the south of France, someone was gonna know the reason why!"

Leigh chuckled. "I thought the birders showed amazing devotion to the cause."

"So did I," Warren agreed. "Just remind me never to get on their bad side."

"And how," added Hap. "Some of those people are wicked scary, I'm telling you."

"Oh, they are not!" Leigh found herself defending, even before Bev could say a word.

Hap's blue eyes danced as he teased her. "You telling me you'd be up for meeting the likes of Bonnie in a dark alley? That woman nearly took my head off last week. Said I smeared her binocular lenses when all I did was pass the blame things across the table."

"You had rib sauce all over your fingers and you made her miss the pipit!" Bev chided.

Hap sighed dramatically.

"You won't find me criticizing them," Warren stage-whispered to Hap as he gave Leigh a hug around the shoulders. "They're the only people I know who've ever been able to keep an eye on the missus."

Leigh grumbled, albeit good-naturedly. Unbeknownst to her at the time, the Rangers had been keeping a pretty good eye on her, too, especially this morning. Eva Menlin's hired bodyguard, who was known to Eva's husband, had been located and interviewed at a local motel shortly after her body was identified. But he claimed that Eva had dismissed him from the job as soon as their business was concluded on Wednesday, and that it was a last-minute decision on his part to stay another few days and "soak up some sun." He insisted he had no idea that Eva had failed to get on her plane, nor did he have any explanation for why her rental car had been found abandoned twenty miles from the airport.

The Rangers didn't believe him, of course, and after receiving multiple reports of overnight footprints at the preserve, the real scenario had not been difficult to surmise. Still, they lacked direct evidence to tie him to Eva's and Stanley's murders, and thus had spent all of last night and this morning lying in wait at the wetlands, hoping to arrest the bodyguard with the loot in his grubby paws. But in order for that to happen, he had to find the diamonds.

Leigh still wondered if he ever would have. Considering how deeply her foot had smooshed the purse down, she doubted it. Not that she got any credit for having served up the Rangers' evidence on a silver platter... Oh, no. All she got, as usual, was a dressing-down for interfering. But the bodyguard *had* taken the bait. Twice, in fact, since he'd attempted to take them from her by force, and then had retrieved them again just before the Rangers closed in. Leigh didn't care to think about how close he'd come to being shot while standing within inches of her. Nor did she care to think what might have happened if he had seen the results of her pathetic toss, which had barely moved the purse six feet. What mattered was that she had bought herself enough time to get away from him — and out of range of the Rangers' bullets. The only people who would benefit from those diamonds now were the company's creditors.

"The birders did a good job of helping get those Finneys rounded up, too," Bev said proudly. "Those kids may not be guilty of triple homicide, but single homicide is bad enough!"

"You got that right," Hap agreed. Then he exhaled loudly. "You know, I keep hoping to hear that one or the other of them was innocent. Of the murder, or the fraud, or something. But no. That's not what Bobby Jo's passing on. It sounds like they all knew about the funny business with the stock. They couldn't care less what happened to Cort's company, I guess because they didn't trust each other enough to keep a four-way partnership going. They all just wanted to get out of it as quick as they could with as much money as they could."

"Even if it meant being chased after by the law the rest of their lives?" Bev questioned.

Hap shook his head. "I expect Janelle was the only one who really understood what was legal and what wasn't, at least in the beginning. Bruce and Russell probably thought they could manage without getting caught, and Sharonna doesn't think, period. By the time they all got the whole picture, there was no turning back."

"How was the CFO involved exactly?" Warren asked. "Do they know yet?"

"Well, officially we don't know anything, of course," Hap said slyly, casting an eye toward his buddy Carl, who was driving the boat with headphones on. "But Bobby Jo hears things, and she told her daddy that the four of them have been telling four different stories ever since they were arrested. About the only thing they do agree on is that Ted Sullivan was no innocent. How things went wrong with him, though... Well, their stories are all so tangled up, Bobby Jo says she doesn't think anybody may ever know what really happened out at the house that night."

"He died at the Finney mansion?" Leigh asked.

Hap nodded. He threw a sober look at Bev. "They were all together that night. Did you know that? Cort always used to say he never even tried to get the four of them in the same room. Not after their mother died. I guess that first Christmas without her was a real doozy. Cops called out and everything. He used to joke with me — and it was only half a joke — that he was glad he was going to be dead at his funeral. Because the next time those four got together, something truly terrible was going to happen."

"Good Lord almighty," Bev muttered. "And to think I bad-mouthed Sharonna for staying in Fiji instead of flying back for her daddy's funeral!"

"It was a good thing, I guess," Hap continued. "Why they all got together that particular night to meet with the CFO, I don't know. But something terrible sure enough did happen."

"Which one of them killed Ted Sullivan?" Bev asked.

"Janelle says Sharonna crushed his skull by hitting him over the head with some kind of planter," Hap answered. Then he paused.

"Do you believe that?" Bev pressed.

"Well, no," Hap replied. "Because the other three all say Janelle did it."

Nobody said anything for a moment. Leigh thought about asking who had disposed of the body, but the truth was, she didn't care. The family owned a boat, and they were all guilty. Still, it would be easier to stomach, somehow, if one were guiltier than the others. "So, was Janelle the mastermind, then?"

"'Mastermind' is giving her too much credit," Warren protested. "What she did required some accounting savvy, but it was still short-sighted and just plain dumb."

"Yep," Hap agreed sadly. "That's what Cort always said about her. No common sense."

"Poor Cort," Bev said loudly, putting her arm around her husband's waist. "He was a good old soul, and so was his wife, from everything I've heard. I suppose we can at least be grateful they died without realizing what a lousy pack of brats they'd raised."

"That's one way of looking at it," Hap said skeptically.

"It's just as well there were never any grandkids," Bev mused.

"Only one spouse left behind, for that matter," Hap added.

Bev let out a snort. "Misti? Please, that girl will divorce Bruce in a heartbeat once his money dries up. Sad to say it, but I don't see anybody pining from loneliness over those four."

Leigh felt a sudden pang. "Bev, that reminds me, have you decided—"

The shorter woman turned to Leigh with a chuckle. "Are you still on about that? Jiminy crickets, child, you're as bad as Joyce!"

"What's this?" Hap asked.

Bev laughed again. "Your cousin here's done everything but get down on her knees and beg me to spend Sunday night over at Joyce's motorhome, babysitting that crazy cat!"

Hap stared at Leigh. "But they'll be back on Monday, won't they?"

"Yes," Leigh replied, her mind tortured once again with the image of a pitiful, mourning set of aquamarine eyes. "But we're flying out early tomorrow, so Snowbell will be by herself all day, too. And I just hate the thought of her being alone all night, not having any idea when or if anyone is ever coming back. I just keep imagining her sitting up in that front window, staring out, with little kitty tears streaming down her — "

"Oh, good Lord almighty!" Bev conceded with a groan. "Fine! I'll sleep with Snowbell. Maybe I can even get Hap to join us."

"Say what now?" her husband interjected.

"Will that make you happy?" Bev asked Leigh.

Leigh grinned from ear to ear, then leaned down to give her cousin-in-law a hug. "Perfectly."

Another dolphin made a leap, this time nearly clearing the water's surface before splashing back into the chop of the boat's wake.

The foursome cheered. Then, almost as if it were jealous of the attention, a brown pelican swooped down and began to glide along beside the boat.

Leigh laughed and gave the bird some applause as well.

"So, are you having a good vacation?" Warren asked, smiling down at her. "Despite all?"

She reached up and kissed him. "I am having a fabulous vacation," she replied. And it was true. Despite everything unpleasant that had happened, in sum total for the week, she'd still had a darned good time.

Why shouldn't she?

She was not involved.

About the Author

USA-Today bestselling author Edie Claire enjoys writing in a variety of genres including romantic fiction, mystery, women's fiction, ghostly YA romance, humor, and stage plays. She is a happily married mother of three who has worked as a veterinarian, a childbirth educator, and a medical/technical writer. When not writing she enjoys travel and wildlife-watching, and she dreams of becoming a snowbird.

"Port Mesten" is a fictional town, but for those wishing to recreate Leigh's experience (at least the good part!) Port Aransas, Texas comes highly recommended. Its nature preserve is truly a birdwatcher's paradise!

Edie plans to add a new installment to the Leigh Koslow mystery series each year. If you'd like to be notified when new books are released, you can sign up for the New Book Alert on her website: **www.edieclaire.com**. You may also visit her Facebook page at **www.Facebook.com/EdieClaire**. Edie always enjoys hearing from readers via email: **edieclaire@juno.com**.

Books & Plays by Edie Claire

Leigh Koslow Mysteries

Never Buried
Never Sorry
Never Preach Past Noon
Never Kissed Goodnight
Never Tease a Siamese
Never Con a Corgi
Never Haunt a Historian
Never Thwart a Thespian
Never Steal a Cockatiel
Never Mess with Mistletoe
Never Murder a Birder

Romantic Fiction

Pacific Horizons

Alaskan Dawn
Leaving Lana'i
Maui Winds

Fated Loves

Long Time Coming
Meant To Be
Borrowed Time

Hawaiian Shadows

Wraith
Empath
Lokahi
The Warning

Women's Fiction

The Mud Sisters

Humor

Work, Blondes. Work!

Comedic Stage Plays

Scary Drama I
See You in Bells

21911543R00120

Printed in Poland
by Amazon Fulfillment
Poland Sp. z o.o., Wrocław